Maoshan isn't like other traditions. We are ghost hunters, spirit mediums, and exorcists. When creatures out of nightmare trouble Chinatown, people come to the Maoshan for protection. With paper talismans we drive away the spirits, with magic gourds we imprison them, with peachwood swords we destroy them. People fear those who live at the border of the spirit world. They say a haunt of death taints us. They might be right. The decades Father spent hunting devils might be the reason I became what I am.

PRAISE FOR M. H. BOROSON AND
THE GIRL WITH GHOST EYES

"*The Girl with Ghost Eyes* is a fun, fun read. Martial arts and Asian magic set in Old San Francisco make for a fresh take on urban fantasy, a wonderful story that kept me up late to finish."
—#1 *New York Times* bestselling author Patricia Briggs

"Lyrical and captivating . . . a thrilling adventure through historical Chinatown, and an exquisite blend of history and myth set in a spirit-world you'll never forget."
—Rob Thurman, *New York Times* bestselling author

"An impressive first novel set in a beautifully realized world of Daoism and martial arts . . . One of those books you can't wait to get back to."
—Lian Hearn, author of the international bestselling Tales of the Otori series

"A brilliant tale of magic, monsters, and kung fu in the San Francisco Chinatown of 1898 . . . This fantastic tale smoothly mixes Hong Kong cinema with urban fantasy, and Li-lin is a splendid protagonist whose cleverness and bravura will leave readers eager for her future adventures."
—*Publishers Weekly*, starred review

"Packed with evocative imagery of the multitudes of spirits lurking just out of sight. Li-lin is a strong, determined character."
—*Library Journal*, starred review, Debut of the Month

"[A] dazzling fantasy novel full of Chinese folklore and ancient monsters and magic."
—Goodreads, Best Books of the Month selection

"A thrilling world of kung fu, sorcery, and spirits . . . a compelling page-turner . . . nicely channels Hayao Miyazaki's powerful visual imagination . . . a bright new voice in fantasy."

—The A.V. Club

"A joy to read . . . blends fluid, kinetic martial arts sequences with grotesque creatures and enough dramatic tension and pathos to hook readers and keep them."

—Barnes & Noble Sci-Fi & Fantasy Blog

"A well-researched look into Chinese folklore, as well as commentary on how Asian immigrants were treated during the 19th century."

—Bustle.com, 15 Diverse Magical Fantasy Novels to Read ASAP

"*The Girl with Ghost Eyes* delivers a compelling heroine torn between talent and tradition in a fascinating Chinatown full of monsters, magic, and kung fu. A must-read for fans of historical fantasy and Chinese lore."

—Betsy Dornbusch, author of *Exile*

"Filled with wonderful detail from Chinese folklore and mythology, and plenty of action as two tongs battle to control Chinatown. The very best fantasy employs strong characters who are real people with real problems. I enjoyed every page."

—LibraryReads, Top Ten Books of the Month selection

"Li-lin is one of my all-time favorite female characters after reading this book; I simply fell in love with her . . . I expect to see *The Girl with Ghost Eyes* on lots of 'Best of' lists this year. It's certainly going to be on mine. Highly recommended."

—The Speculative Herald, 10/10 rating

"Masterful writing . . . Boroson has done his research quite extensively, and he's approached every aspect of the book with thoughtfulness and respect . . . I am absolutely ravenous for more of Li-Lin's story."

—Christina Ladd, Geekly Inc.

"This debut just wowed me through and through. I can't mention enough how enthralling this story is."
—Fantasy Book Critic, #1 Debut of the Year

"An unforgettable heroine must battle to save her father and her town from supernatural forces—despite the obstacles her own immigrant community sets against her because she's only a woman. In this page-turner of a novel, M. H. Boroson transplants Chinese folklore, magic and mysticism to 19th century Chinatown and succeeds spectacularly."
—Janie Chang, author of *Three Souls* and *Dragon Springs Road*

"A delightful blend of fantasy, horror, mystery, and suspense, with a heavy dose of Chinese mythology and a touch of Bruce Lee . . . a real palate-cleanser if you've grown used to medieval fantasy and Christian-based horror and unspeculative historical fiction."
—Top New Fantasy

"Boroson's meticulously researched novel is a beautiful blend of ancient Chinese myths and hard historical realisms."
—*High Voltage*

"[A] suspenseful, tightly plotted story about magic outside the European tradition."
—*The Globe and Mail*

"A magical tale steeped in Chinese folklore and history, with memorable characters, exciting action, and one very special eyeball spirit."
—Books, Bones, and Buffy, Best Surprise of 2015

THE GIRL WITH GHOST EYES

M. H. BOROSON

New York

Talos Press books may be purchased in bulk at special discounts for sales promotion, corporate gifts, fund-raising, or educational purposes. Special editions can also be created to specifications. For details, contact the Special Sales Department, Talos Press, 307 West 36th Street, 11th Floor, New York, NY 10018 or info@skyhorsepublishing.com.

Talos Press® is a registered trademark of Skyhorse Publishing, Inc. ®, a Delaware corporation.

Visit our website at www.talospress.com.

10 9 8 7 6 5 4 3 2 1

Library of Congress Control Number: 2015937874

Print ISBN: 978-1-940456-66-9
Ebook ISBN: 978-1-940456-45-4

Cover illustration by Jeff Chapman
Cover design by Claudia Noble

Printed in Canada

For Sally Elizabeth Wright
My best friend, my partner in crime, and
a brilliant photographer in her own right.
Wild horses will always surround us.

And also
For Lam Ching-Ying.

How could ghosts gain a foothold in American cities? People move about like the tide, unable to form permanent ties with places, still less with other people . . .

—Fei Xiaotong

ONE

I placed a paper shirt into the furnace. The shirt was painted to resemble dark linen, broad at the shoulders, with buttons down the front. It was a fine shirt, but not too fine, the kind of shirt a hardworking immigrant would wear to dinner. Nothing about it would catch a devil's eye.

The paper shirt warped and blackened. The embers glowed brighter, and the paper shirt caught fire, sending out a surge of heat that pressed against my skin and made me shuffle back. Flames lanced up from the burning paper, smoke rose and ashes fell, and I knew the fire was doing its work. The crackling flame turned the paper into spirit. What had been merely paper among the living became real among the dead. I could imagine my husband's face, his flattered, generous smile. He would look so handsome, wearing his new linen shirt in the city of the dead.

Tonight I came to my father's temple with a sack of paper offerings: shoes, trousers, shirts, horses, pots and pans, a table and three chairs. My husband would want for nothing in the dim lands. I was dedicated to that, as his wife, and as a priestess of the Maoshan lineage.

Maoshan isn't like other traditions. We are ghost hunters, spirit mediums, and exorcists. When creatures out of nightmare trouble Chinatown, people come to the Maoshan for protection. With paper talismans we drive away the spirits, with magic gourds we imprison them, with peachwood swords we destroy them. People fear those who live at the border of the spirit world. They say a haunt of death taints us. They might be right. The decades Father spent hunting devils might be the reason I became what I am.

How bitter it must be for the great sorcerer of Maoshan, to have a daughter like me. Xian Li-lin, the girl with yin eyes, oppressed by visions of the spirit world, doomed to live a brief, painful life. Even the upward tilt of my eyebrows gives me the look of a murderess. And everyone knows a widow brings bad luck. Especially a young widow.

Yet despite our temple's unsavory reputation, a man sat in the Hall of Ancestors, burning a red candle. His forehead was shaved and his hair was braided into a queue down his back, like most Chinese men. People come to the Hall of Ancestors to burn candles and paper offerings for their families. The debt we owe our parents and grandparents does not end simply because they die. By lighting the way for his ancestors, the man was paying homage to his history, to those who came before him. It was a profound practice.

The temple's front door swung open, disturbing me from my reverie. A gust of evening air swept through the temple, making the candles flicker, distorting the smoke from the thick sticks of incense and the furnace. I turned to face the entryway. The door hung open for a moment, and then two men entered.

The first man had white in his hair, which he wore in a plump queue. One of his sleeves dangled, empty, where he was missing an arm. Something about him gave me an impression of weakness, as if the young man at his side were grown and he only a child. But he wasn't young. He was perhaps forty-five years old, Father's age. A bristly white mustache sat on his face and he chewed on his lips. He had a lurching stride—as though he'd known how to move once, but allowed his training to lapse once his arm was lost, and now his balance was upset at every step or turn. It was an awkward, ungainly gait that embarrassed me to watch. The man's eyes had a narrowness that made me think of snakes.

But he had to be somebody important. The young man walking at his side was Tom Wong, son of the most powerful man in Chinatown. I glanced at Tom. With his soft lips and bright eyes, Tom was almost too pretty to be handsome. Seeing him brought back memories. He had been my husband's friend. Tom met my eyes with his own. He touched the brim of his black hat and gave me a warm smile.

Gathering my long hair behind me, I stood to greet the visitors. The sleeves of my yellow robe dangled below my wrists, and I tightened the belt at my waist.

The man in the Hall of Ancestors looked up at Tom Wong and the man with one arm, and a worried look crossed his face. He stood, bowed, and hurried out into the night. His candle stayed lit behind him. The air from the door made it flicker a little.

The one-armed man reached out his hand and lit a cigar at the man's ancestral candle.

I stared at him, my mouth open. The words dried out on my tongue. Such an act of disrespect left me speechless.

Taking quick, nervous puffs from his cigar, he lurched into the central chamber of Father's temple. The temple is open to everyone, but there was something intrusive about this man's presence here. He behaved less like a visitor, more like an invader. His eyes darted around the room, taking in the scrolls and lanterns, the conical red candles, the idols, the names of dead men on the wall.

"You are the Daoshi's daughter?" he asked, his voice weak in his throat.

It was a familiar question. I was also a Daoshi, but my father was a renowned exorcist. I nodded. "My name is Xian Li-lin," I said, "and I am a Maoshan Nu Daoshi of the Second Ordination."

"No higher than the Second?" he asked, and his voice was spiced with contempt.

I lowered my eyes, shamed. Pointing out my inadequacy was unnecessary, cruel, and it stung like a slap across

my face. I didn't like the one-armed man. He reminded me
of a teenage boy I knew in China, who always sought the
company of younger boys. They were the only ones who
would treat him with respect.

"Yes," I said, "only the Second. But Father will return
some time tonight, and he holds the Seventh Ordination.
He will be able to do what you need done."

"Actually," he said, "I am looking for a Sangu."

My eyes widened. The word Sangu means Third
Aunt—the unmarried woman, half-crazy, who shrieks at
spirits in the night, drinks too much rice wine, and weeps
all day. The woman haunted by ghosts and visions, vulnerable to spirit possession. It was a polite term. Supposedly.

Having yin eyes is a curse. It was my secret. How
could this man know that I see the spirit world? I went pale
at the thought. Not even my father realized. Only my husband, and—

I turned to Tom Wong. "You told him?"

Tom's eyes twinkled, playful and knowing. "It was
necessary, Li-lin. This is important."

"What is important?"

"Mr. Liu needs something," he said.

I looked at Tom for a moment, considering his words.
Mr. Liu, he said. Tom was of higher station than anyone
I knew, and yet he had addressed the man respectfully,
which meant I needed to treat him with great respect. No
matter how I felt about him.

I took a breath and faced the man with one arm. "Is
there something I can do for you, Mr. Liu?"

He focused his snake eyes on my face. "I have been
dreaming of my drowned friend, Shi Jin. He comes to me
in dreams. He says he needs someone to bring him a soul
passport."

My mouth opened, but I said nothing. The thought
sent me reeling. If the dead man needed a passport, it
meant that the guards at the gates of Fengdu, the city of the
dead, had refused to admit him. Locked out, Shi Jin would

be forced to wander forever, a spirit lost without home. No burnt offerings would be able to reach him.

"His corpse?" I asked.

"Lost at sea."

I shook my head. My father could speak a few words over a corpse and the guards would open the gates for its higher soul. But without a corpse, there was only one chance for Shi Jin.

Someone needed to travel to the world of spirits and bring the dead man a passport. But not just anyone could do it. It had to be a woman, and the woman needed to be cursed with yin eyes. It had to be a woman who couldn't shut out the horrors of the spirit world, no matter how hard she tried.

A woman like me.

My yin eyes were my secret, and my shame. And now this man, Mr. Liu, was giving me a chance to use my curse for something positive. And still I hesitated.

"My father," I said. "I should wait for him. He will return some time tonight."

Mr. Liu shook his head. "There can be no waiting," he said. "It has been forty-eight days since Shi Jin died."

I caught my breath. After death, a man has forty-nine days to make it through the gates. Forty-nine days for his family to burn offerings and grieve. If he still has not crossed the Helpless Bridge when forty-nine days have passed, there is no hope for him.

And still I said nothing. I knew how to dance the Steps of Yu and travel the realms, but I couldn't do such a thing without my father's permission.

Tom Wong broke the silence. "Li-lin," he said, his voice gentle on my name, "Mr. Liu is a close friend of my father's, from China."

I glanced at Tom, thinking about his words. A friend of Mr. Wong. Tom's father ran the Ansheng tong. Some would call him a gangster, but the Ansheng tong was so much more than that. It was a benevolent organization that

gave support to immigrants and outsiders, people with no
family of their own. The Ansheng tong was my father's family, and so it was mine. Mr. Wong was a great man, and he
did so much for so many people. Including us. Every good
thing in our lives—the temple, Father's job, our home, my
immigration—was thanks to Mr. Wong. Father and I owed
everything to him.

"If I do this," I said, looking Tom in the eye, "my
father will gain face with Mr. Wong?"

Tom answered me with a radiant smile. And with that
the decision was made.

I turned to Mr. Liu and saw his eyes on me. He was
sizing me up. "Aren't you young for a Sangu?" he asked.

"I am only in my twenty-third year, Mr. Liu," I
said, "but I have more training and discipline than most
madwomen."

"Li-lin is the right madwoman for the job, Mr.
Liu," Tom Wong said with a warm laugh.

Mr. Liu's eyes were focused on me, and they were
shrewd, petty, and intense. "Is this an auspicious night for
spiritual travel?"

I nodded. "I consulted the almanac this morning,
Mr. Liu. The Tong Sheng says that tomorrow is the Night
Parade of a Hundred Devils, but tonight there are no
adverse influences in the spirit world."

"Well then," said Mr. Liu, and his eyes took on a mean
look. "Are peach trees blossoming in your garden?"

Shock rushed through my entire body. He was asking
if I was menstruating. The question left me speechless, and
I must have turned bright red. Tom's eyes widened in surprise and discomfort. Mr. Liu's question was so rude, the
answer so private. I tried to calm myself.

There were legitimate reasons he might ask such
a question of me. Menstruating would make it easier for
me to cross over to the spirit world, and harder to return.
The question was relevant, but I was horrified that he even
mentioned it. These were matters I would choose not to

discuss. And yet I needed to show respect to my elders, and Mr. Liu was an important man.

I looked down so the men could not see my face, and then I answered him. "No, Mr. Liu, this is not the time of blossoms. Now I shall gather what I need to make the passport."

I came back with the supplies. Father's altar dominated the heart of the large chamber. Colorful silk lanterns hung above it, red, yellow, and blue-green, and the altar was surrounded by bright brocades, candles, idols, and incense—a clutter of magnificence. Five different kinds of fresh fruit were displayed nearby, on copper plates. A painting on the wall showed Guan Gong, god of war and literature, holding his bladed polearm in his right hand. Statues of the Five Ghosts hulked nearby. In warlike postures, they glared from behind black beards.

I crossed to the corner, to the plain wooden crate I used as my altar. I laid my peachwood sword down beside it. Tom Wong and Mr. Liu stood quietly while I lit the lotus-shaped oil lamp on the altar, refreshed the tea and rice in the offering cups, and swirled the water in the dragon bowl.

To make the passport I took a reed brush and wrote Shi Jin's name in black ink on a sheet of yellow rice paper, distorting the Chinese characters into ghostscript. To the left of the name I drew seven small circles in vermilion ink and connected the circles with lines; the circles represented the seven stars of the Northern Bushel. I wrote the four yin trigrams of the Yi Jing along the bottom, the names of Hell King Yanluo and the Grandfathers at the top. At the lower right corner I stamped my chop, printing the passport with my name and lineage.

I lit a match and burned the paper. Fire blackened the passport. Transmuted it into spirit. As the ashes crumbled, the passport took shape in the world of spirits and drifted to the floor.

"Is that all?" Tom Wong asked.

"Not yet," I said, turning to him. I tied a red string to my wrist, feeling the silken cord tighten against my skin. "The soul passport has been sent to the spirit world, but there are no messengers in the lands between. I need to enter a trance and deliver it to Shi Jin by hand."

"Is that dangerous?"

"The spirit world is full of dangers," I said. "But my peachwood sword will protect me, and a red string will guide me back to myself. You'll keep my body safe while I'm in the spirit world, Tom?"

He nodded, and his eyes were filled with encouragement.

Ghosts and goblins prowl the spirit world, and I would not be foolish enough to travel there defenseless. I took a grease pencil and wrote a spell on my peachwood sword, then replaced the sword at my belt. It would cross with me when I entered the world of spirit.

Then I began. Clicking my teeth, I closed my eyes and thought of the sun and the moon. I felt sunlight stream in through the place between my eyebrows, and moonlight through the soles of my feet. I let them radiate within me. Once my skin was filled with shining, I began to dance.

The Pace of Yu would allow me to wander the three realms. I stamped the floor hard with one foot, and dragged the other. I danced the broken, halting steps of Yu the Great, who beat back the floods. Singing, stamping, and dragging, I danced as Yu, who could transform himself into a bear, yet walked with a limp. Yu the king, the sorcerer, nearly a god, who slew the beast with nine heads. His power cascading through me, I danced the same series of limping steps over and over, making intricate magical gestures with my hands.

There was no way to tell when I stopped dancing in my body and began, instead, a dance of spirit, but there it was. I crossed over without knowing it. I stood outside myself, a spirit in the spirit world, inches from my body yet unfathomably far away. The red string was secure around my wrist; it extended through unnatural fog, through impossible angles, back to where my living body stood, swaying, entranced. I had no other anchor.

In spirit I had the same form I had in flesh, my hair long and unbound, wearing the yellow cloth robe of a Daoshi. I had the same skills, abilities, limitations, in spirit as in body. Even my peachwood sword was at my belt, thanks to the spell written on the side. I crossed the room and picked up the spirit passport. It would guide me to Shi Jin. He'd been sending dreams to Mr. Liu, so he couldn't be far. Probably within half a mile.

I let the passport lead me. It pulsed in my right hand, drawing me toward the man whose name was written on it. I went out through the temple door and peered into the night, where the passport drew me. Wind was blowing from the lands of the dead.

I stopped for a moment, taking in the transformed world ahead of me. The sky of the spirit world had never seen the light of the sun, and the drifting clouds glowed a burnished orange in the light of the moon. There was an uncanny beauty to the spirit side of Chinatown, lit by perpetual moonlight, but brighter and more golden than the moon looks from the world of the living.

Beautiful and eerie, the world of spirits would be a terrible place to spend eternity; unable to enter the cycle of birth and death and birth again, and yet unable to establish a home in the lands of the dead.

I stepped outside, crossing the string of protective cloth talismans over the door. I felt the protective spell give way for me as I walked through it, easy as walking through a spider's web, and stepped out into a ghostly mirror of Chinatown. On Dupont Street, immigrants were walking home for the night, or walking to work. They all wore the same nondescript dark clothing, and their braids swished with each step. They had the indistinct look of ghosts, half-there and half-gone, but I knew I was the ghost among them. No one could see me.

From Telegraph Hill, there was the sound of a train chuffing down its tracks. Its steam whistle called and faded into distance. A vegetable seller strolled past, oblivious of me. Baskets of carrots, yams, and leafy greens were balanced on a bamboo pole across his shoulders. This was Chinatown, and it was my world. Such a small world, twelve square blocks in all, yet I seldom ventured outside the six or seven blocks my father protected.

"Aah!" a seagull cried from a lamppost. The sound of its caw was like laughter and mourning intermingled. "Aah! Aah!" It cocked its head in my direction, opening its third eye. "Xian Li-lin!"

I took a deep breath. "Jiujiu," I said. Of all the ghosts and goblins that inhabit the world of spirits, Jiujiu was the one I'd known the longest. She was one of the Haiou Shen, the spirit-gulls. Her flock had been slaughtered long ago. She had come to Chinatown somehow and found a new flock to join.

Many spirits are invisible to ordinary people, but the Haiou Shen are visible. They simply look and sound like normal seagulls. Regular people don't see the third eye in a spirit gull's forehead, beady and black in a vertical slit. Regular people hear their human speech as the inarticulate cry of gulls. It is the blessing of regular people; they do not witness the monstrous, and thus they can live normal lives.

"There will be pain, Xian Li-lin!" the seagull cried. "There will be loss!"

I sighed. "Life as usual, in other words," I said, but the warning made me tense. Spirit gulls sense each change in weather. Over the years Jiujiu has warned me about many hazards, but she never gave me enough information to avoid them.

It worried me that Jiujiu was paying me a visit now, when I was out of body, vulnerable.

Something bad was going to happen, and I had no way to know where it was coming from. Girding myself, I checked the red cord on my wrist. It was secure. A line of red string stretched back to my body.

The passport tugged me toward a bulky man standing in the shadows at the end of the street, where Dupont met Jackson. He must have been a big man in life, and his spirit body was no different. Strong shoulders filled out his threadbare robes. His face looked hard behind an unkempt black beard. His eyes had the half-mad look of someone who has spent many years alone.

I hesitated. This might not be as simple as Mr. Liu had led me to believe. Was this rabid-looking ghost what the spirit gull just warned me about? I bit my lip in frustration. Trying to sidestep Jiujiu's warning could cause the suffering she'd foretold.

But a man needed my help, and it didn't matter if he was dead, or if death had driven him mad. I had sworn my oath a long time ago. I would never hide from monsters. Never again.

For reassurance I let my fingers stray to the hilt of my peachwood sword, and I walked up to the ghost's place in the shadows.

His hair was wild. Dark and tangled into knots, it sprawled over a forehead that had not been shaved in a long time. Wandering through death, he had neglected his queue. I winced. The braided hair was a symbol of a man's service to the Emperor; it comprised one third of a man's higher soul. It was no wonder Shi Jin was lost. He had abandoned one of his strongest connections to the world of the living.

There was an odd feeling in my spirit body. It took a moment to identify it. My stomach was itching. I found it odd that even here, between the lands of the living and the dead, travelling far from my body, I felt an itch, as though insects were crawling along my stomach.

The man turned to face me as I approached him. His eyes were bloodshot, and under his beard a long scar ran from his cheek to his neck.

"Shi Jin?" I said. "Here is your passport to the lands of the dead." I reached out both hands to offer him the passport, as young people are supposed to do. One uses both hands to show undivided attention.

Shi Jin grabbed my elbow and yanked me down to the ground. I toppled, off-balance and disoriented. Then he stepped behind me and snapped my red string.

TWO

Falling is a chaotic feeling. A coordinated body turns into a mess of arms, legs, and hips moving in their own directions when it falls. I sprawled forward. My knees and hands took the brunt of the impact, and then my chest thudded down against the cobblestone, and my chin landed on my forearm.

The burly ghost grabbed my red string. My eyes widened. This was a trap, that much was clear, but I needed a chance to think. Then Shi Jin attacked with a bellowing war-cry, leading with a spinning kick that had enough force behind it to collapse a ribcage.

Fifteen years of training took over. Father's voice, telling me to repeat that move *again, again, again, again. Two hundred more times, Li-lin. Someday your life might depend on this.* Rolling up into a crouch, I slammed my elbow into the ghost's ankle. It hit with a sharp sound, interrupting the momentum of his kick.

Pain and surprise registered on the ghost's scarred face. He looked at me, saw I had taken a warrior stance, and hesitated. I took that moment and leaped for my red string.

He stepped back and away, holding onto the string, appraising me. There was a stark, tense moment as we each sized up our opponent. The itching on my stomach grew worse, and a sick feeling rose from my gut. I knew what the itch was.

Someone was cutting my flesh. Carving a talisman into the soft skin on my belly. Probably Mr. Liu. He was engraving some kind of spell in my skin. I felt exposed, powerless. Violated.

The ghost spoke, and his voice creaked as though it hadn't shaped words in a generation. "Give me the passport," he said.

My pulses raced, and I felt all control slipping away. My body was defenseless. I felt small and afraid. And I didn't understand why any of this was happening.

"The string will lead you back to my body," I said. "But you won't be able to do anything to me. Not without—"

He snorted. "Give me the passport."

So that was it. I had made the passport myself, sealed it with my name and lineage. It could grant him passage to the city of the dead, but it would also grant him control over my body. Permanent control.

"You're going to possess me," I said.

We faced each other, our stances closed, defensive. He was bigger than me, much bigger, but I could draw my peachwood sword before he reached me. I could chop him to pieces.

I was angry. Like a fool, I walked right into their trap. I was powerless to stop Mr. Liu from carving a talisman into my skin. The talisman could make Shi Jin undetectable inside me.

I felt heat rush up to my head. I was seething with anger. I wanted to cut this ghost to ribbons. And he wasn't even my biggest problem. My body was unconscious and vulnerable, and if the one-armed man was carving talismans into me, it meant he had power. If he was ordained past the Second, I couldn't hope to defeat him with magic.

Their plan was solid. If I hadn't dodged Shi Jin's kick, I would have been trapped in the spirit world already, and a ghost would be walking in my skin. Their plan only missed one thing. They had underestimated my martial arts training.

Shi Jin advanced a half-step. I took a half-step back.

Anger, fear, and shame tried to take hold of me, but I resisted. I needed to resist. I couldn't let myself be impaired by emotion, not now, with men attacking me in two worlds. I needed clarity of mind. First I needed to defeat Shi Jin and recover the red string. Once I'd done that, I'd return to my body, find Mr. Liu, and make him pay. He had cut my skin. It was a violation, and he was going to suffer for it.

I drew my peachwood sword.

Shi Jin snorted, a wet sound moving out through his beard. "A practice sword? You brought a child's wooden toy, girl."

I flicked the sword forward, a quick stroke— Dragonfly Skims the Water—and left a clean slice on his arm. His eyes bulged in surprise and a red stain began to spread from his cut.

"This wood came from a peach tree that grew at Mount Longhu," I said, "in the shadow of the Hanging Coffins. My husband cut the wood himself. He was a Daoshi of the Seventh Ordination. Do you understand? He carved the Seven Stars into its blade, and danced their power. The simple fact that it is made from peachwood means it will be enough to harm a dead man like you. But endowed with the power of the Seven Stars? My sword can slice you apart as easily as steel cuts flesh, you dead ghost."

I aimed the sword and shot into motion.

Shi Jin stumbled away in panic. I lunged at him, striking out with a forward thrust of the sword that left a deep red gash along his shoulder. Blood sprang from his wound. He cried out and I saw victory close by. In a thrill I pushed my advantage, driving forward. It was time to finish this. I dropped into a side-bow and swung my peachwood sword in a horizontal chop.

The sword turned to smoke.

I blinked. My sword had vanished. That should have been a finishing blow. It should have disemboweled him. But my hand was empty.

Shi Jin's beefy fist caught me in the sternum with a thud. I staggered back, dizzy and confused, then stumbled and fell to my back, landing with a thud on the cobbled street.

The ghost laughed. "Where's your magic sword, girl? Without it you're just a slab of meat ready to be hung in the butcher shop."

Amid the pain, the dizziness, and the disorientation, it was reflex and reflex alone that started me rolling away before the big ghost was on me again. Rolling on cobblestones took its toll on my hips, but I managed to stay just outside the range of the kicks and stomps he aimed at me. Then I sprang up to my feet and faced him in a horse stance, fists ready.

The ghost was twice my size but fury contorted my face so much that he looked into my eyes and hesitated. I must have looked like a mad dog, nostrils flaring, teeth gnashing. I wanted to rip the ghost to shreds, and Mr. Liu after him.

Shi Jin came down on me like thunder, like a rainstorm. He weighed at least twice as much as I did. His fists hailed down and found only wind. I stepped to the side and hammered a kick into his knee. He gulped in surprise and took a step back.

"A slab of meat, am I, you dead ghost?" I said.

The big man's face registered determination, and something else. Was it regret? He said, "Yes, meat. I'm a ghost and you're still alive, but which of us is being carved like roast pork?"

The thought of Mr. Liu cutting my stomach was sobering. In the world of the living, Mr. Liu must have broken the spell on my sword. That would explain why it vanished. And if he broke my spell, it meant he had power. At least the Third Ordination.

I cursed. I was unarmed in the spirit world, facing a dangerous opponent, and if I defeated him I'd still have to face a man whose magic was stronger than mine.

It made no sense. No one would bring so much force to defeat me. I had some skill with kung fu and magic, but the ghost was big and well trained, and Mr. Liu had more powerful magic than I did. Either of them could have beaten me on his own, yet they still felt the need to ambush and disarm me. I wasn't being underestimated. I was being overestimated.

"You aren't after me," I said. "You want to possess me and murder my father when he isn't expecting it."

An affirmative snort moved the ghost's black beard.

"Why?" I asked. "Father protects Chinatown from evil."

The ghost circled, saying nothing. If I lost this fight, Father would die in shame, murdered by his own child's hand.

My hand.

Cutting my stomach and possessing me were violation enough, but they were going to use me as a weapon against my father, and I would never let that happen.

A quiet anger found me. I wanted to punch the ghost until his spirit blood dripped from my knuckles. I wanted to pin him face down on the street and bash his brains out on the cobblestones. With the right strategy, I could even do it. But if I lost, Shi Jin would take the passport and murder my father. There was only one proper way to act.

I turned and ran.

Behind me I heard a startled huff of breath. Shi Jin ran too, giving chase. He pursued, relentless, angry, huge. His heavy steps smashed down on the cobblestones. But I ran faster, and every second put him farther behind me.

Through streets of Chinatown lit smoky and golden by the moon of the spirit world, I ran.

In blurs of dreaming light, Chinatown's spirit world shifted around me. I had never spent so long out of body before. How long had it been—hours? Days? No, not days, not yet.

The passage of time was my friend now. If I kept the soul passport out of Shi Jin's hands long enough, Father would come home. He would go to the temple and find me unconscious, out of body. He wouldn't be able to wake me, so he would examine me to find out what was wrong. He would find the one-armed man's talisman carved into my skin.

If I could do that, if I could just keep the passport away from Shi Jin for enough time, then Mr. Liu's plan would be thwarted. With enough time, Father wouldn't be taken by surprise, even if the ghost managed to possess me. He'd have talismans and weapons ready for the ghost. There would be no stabbing him in the back or poisoning his tea.

I just needed to stall long enough and I would save my father.

Saving myself was another matter. Somehow I needed to get back. Back to my body, back to Father. He might need my help. Mr. Liu was trying to kill him. And he would be alone without me. No one would braise his pork, fry his vegetables, or prepare his tea.

I thought about the passport. I could destroy it, and then Shi Jin would never be able to possess me. But then he might smear my red string with his spirit blood, destroying it. So long as he thought he might be able to succeed, I would still have a chance. So long as I held the passport, he would continue hunting me. I needed to delay that for a while, but he would find me eventually. And then there would be a reckoning.

I found my way to Dupont, to Father's temple. We lived in a small apartment in the basement. I approached the temple, and something like a slight wind began to blow. A force pushed me away. It felt like an ocean current. Looking up, I saw Father's cloth talismans. They hung over the door, shifting in a slight wind. Father's talismans barred all spirits from entry, with all the authority of a Maoshan Daoshi of the Seventh Ordination. Nothing short of a deity could force its way past the talismans. My red string would have granted me entry. Without the string, I couldn't cross the threshold and enter my home.

My father's talismans, his power and his magic, forced me out. Staring at my home, I felt helpless. I had no home, no place of safety anywhere. It was nearly enough to make me give up. Frustration and despair took over, and I felt tears begin. I forced the tears down. I refused to cry.

To be so near and yet so far. My body was inside, but even if I stood next to it, it would be impossibly far away. My body and I were worlds apart. Without the red string, I would never be able to retrace the passage across the fields of life and death. I could stand next to myself and still be lost.

If I manifested myself to Father, would he save me? Or would he exorcise me? I couldn't truly say.

I curled up in the shadows of the painted balconies along Tian Hou Temple Street and slept.

Dreams have never been my friend. A feverish mixture of images swirled in my mind, and there was never a way to distinguish memory from prophecy. In dreams I ran down an endless road. I did not know what I was running from, but I knew I needed to keep running. I ran for hours, until my throat was dry and my feet were raw and bloody.

"Aah!" a gull cried, sad and laughing. "Aah! Aah! Xian Li-lin!"

That was no dream. Waking, I shot to my feet. Across the street, Shi Jin hulked, staring at the gull, open-mouthed. He must have been hunting me in my sleep when he heard it say my name.

I smiled. For once Jiujiu's warning had been helpful. I wondered what offering I could burn for the spirit gull, if I made it back to my body.

Shi Jin turned his attention back to me. He'd lost the element of surprise, but he still held too many advantages. I was faster, but his long arms and legs still made it unlikely for me to defeat him. There's a reason I prefer to fight with a weapon in my hand.

I turned and ran again.

In the afternoon I strolled down to Fish Alley. The smell of the fish was strong and rank, but somehow it came to me from a distance, almost more a memory than a smell. Eternal moonlight was shining in the world of the spirits, but I could tell the time of day by watching the men haggling for better prices at the stalls. "That's been sitting out here all day," a buyer would say, and the fishmonger would reply, "Only the freshest fish, morning and afternoon." Like actors in an opera, everyone knew their lines, their cues, and they knew how the story would end.

Dead fish hung along every stall, their scales glistening. Fish bones littered the alleyway.

I turned to see Shi Jin walking toward me. Bones crunched under his heavy footsteps. His posture was aggressive, arrogant, perhaps a bit mad.

I stood my ground, facing the ghost. "Give up," I said.

His beard puffed out as he snorted. "Surrender?" he said. "To you?"

"You're trying to possess my body, Shi Jin. It was supposed to happen last night. My father was supposed to come home and find his daughter waiting for him. He wouldn't be on guard. And you were supposed to be in control of my body, planning to kill him. But that's not what happened, is it?"

Shi Jin's eyes were sharp and thorough, not missing anything. "I am listening," he said.

"My father came home and found me unconscious. Next he checked to see what was wrong with me, and he found a talisman carved into my stomach. From there he figured out your plan. So now, even if you possess me, you won't be able to take him by surprise. Your plan has failed," I said, "so you might as well return my string."

A slow smile spread behind the ghost's black beard. "That was their plan," he told me. "My plan hasn't failed."

There was too much in his words for me to respond. Whose plan was it? *Their* plan, he said. But even that wasn't my immediate concern. I began inching away. "So what is your plan?"

"To leave here. To get out of the land of spirits."

"In my body."

"Yes."

"Give me back the red string," I said. "You don't want to be a woman, do you, Shi Jin?"

He looked away for a moment, ashamed. "Even that would be better than this. This place is wrong, girl. There is no daylight. There are things here out of the nightmares of men."

"I know," I told him. "There are fox-spirits, walls that move to block your path, and eel-women who lurk beneath bridges. Hungry things drool in the shadows. And tonight is the Bai Gui Yexing, the Night Parade of a Hundred Devils."

"Tonight?" he asked. His face registered fear.

"Yes, dead man, the most freakish of spirits walk tonight. You know we cannot kill each other in the spirit world, but if we fight, we can harm each others' spirit bodies. You would not want to face the Night Parade with a broken arm, Shi Jin. Give me my red string and I will give you your passport, so you may cross the gates and enter the city of the dead."

He snorted again, but this time, I thought, it was an expression of loss, not contempt. "My forty-nine days are long past, girl. The only way for me to get out of here is to possess you."

I had run before because losing would have meant more than just my end. At that time, losing would have killed my father. But Father would be safe by now.

"I'm sorry," I said, and launched a flying kick at the ghost. I gave him no time to block or dodge. My heel

connected with his massive chest, and he stumbled backward, trying to regain his balance.

I took slow, deliberate steps, relaxing as I approached
him. I brought forth in myself the experience of liuhe, the
Six Integrations, so spirit could guide my skills and energy.
I was an army now, hands and feet and knees and elbows
working together. To beat him I would need relaxation,
smoothness of movement, nimbleness, stability, and emp-
tiness, but more than anything I needed strategy.

Shi Jin lunged at me. I brushed aside the jab from
his right arm, but the reverse punch he followed it with
was quick and powerful. I weaved to the side and his fist
swung by me, close and fast enough that I felt the wind of
his swing in my hair.

I chambered a leg and shot a kick into his ribcage. My
foot thumped against his chest. Grunting, he sprang away.
The kick probably hadn't broken any of his ribs, but I was
wearing him down. He brought his spirit body back into
alignment, finding his centerline.

Pedestrians stepped around him without seeing him,
without knowing he was there. He stamped a foot, leaned
into the opposite leg, and extended his right arm, with the
palm facing inward. I recognized the form. It was bawang
dou jia, King of Kings Shaking His Armor. A posture
designed for powerful strikes. From there he could launch
any number of large movements capable of shattering my
bones.

But any of those movements would leave him unpro-
tected for a moment. And that was precisely what I needed.
I needed him to swing hard and miss.

I stepped rapidly forward and faked a lunging kick at
the knee with his weight on it. He shifted back and lifted
the leg, stepping forward into a kick of his own that likely
would have broken me if it landed.

The beauty of a fakeout is that I was nowhere near
where he expected me to be. Instead of kicking, I dropped
my foot to the cobblestones and leaped, twisting my
hips and lifting up into the air. All the momentum of his

forward kick added to the momentum I had built with my running steps, my lunge, and my leap. I raised my knee in a hard half-kick and drove it against the side of his head with a cracking noise. He fell backward and I was falling with him, but I wasn't finished. I swung a foot at his neck and hooked his throat.

We hit the street, hard, but he hit harder. I jammed my shin against his throat. He made a wheezing sound, struggling for air. I scrambled to my hands and knees but Shi Jin grasped my ankle in one huge hand. He yanked on my leg with unbelievable strength. To keep my knee from dislocating, I spun in the direction of his force, and brought the heel of my other foot down against his face.

His nose broke with a wet crunch, and I felt his grip go limp around my ankle. I yanked it away and crawled out of his reach. Blood poured down over Shi Jin's mouth and beard. The side of his head was a bleeding mess where my knee had torn off a chunk of his ear. Clutching his face in pain, he struggled to focus his eyes on me as I got to my feet.

"Now," I said, trying to conceal my weariness, "I will have my red string."

The ghost looked at me, his eyes raging over his smashed nose. "Cao ni zuzong shi badai," he cursed—fuck your ancestors to the eighteenth generation. He dabbed two fingers into his blood, and before I realized what he was doing, he smeared blood along the red string.

I stood in silent horror. The string wasn't mine anymore. With Shi Jin's blood on it, the string was ruined. It would no longer lead back to my body.

I was trapped in the spirit world, the country of monsters, and I had no way to get out.

THREE

I stared at the frayed end of the string, smeared with the dead man's spirit blood, and I wanted to scream. It would be a powerless scream, and once I began screaming, I would never stop. There was an ache growing inside me, despair, loss, and failure. There had been so much I still wanted to accomplish.

I felt tears begin to form. I suppressed them.

Shi Jin curled on the cobblestones, pressing thick fingers against his nose to stop the flowing blood. I stepped back and away from him, weary to the bones of my spirit. The red string had lost its connection to my body. It was useless now. Neither of us was getting out. There was no longer any need to fight.

I looked up at the moon, shining its gray and gold light over the afternoon. I would never see the sun again, and I mourned that loss. I would never have a chance to avenge myself on Mr. Liu, prove my worth to my father, or reach a higher Ordination. The knowledge left a taste like bitter ashes in my mouth.

I smoothed my long hair, thinking. Mr. Liu had come to Father's temple with Tom Wong. And I had been led into an ambush. Did Tom know?

No, not Tom. No friend of my husband would do such a thing to me. Tom might steal and he might lie, and he might kill a man in a fight, but I was his best friend's widow. There was no way he would allow a man to cut a magic talisman into my skin.

At that thought, my eyes cleared. There would be no tears. Mr. Liu had cut me. He had carved my skin while I lay helpless. He must have pushed back my clothes to reveal my stomach. No man had seen my stomach since my husband died, and now this man had seen me, touched me, and cut me.

And it wasn't even personal. He didn't see me as an enemy, or even as an obstacle to whatever he was planning. He didn't see me as a threat at all; all he saw in me was a useful tool. He wanted to aim me and shoot me like an arrow at my father's heart.

Where tears and hopelessness had threatened to overwhelm me, I was now overcome with rage. Mr. Liu had cut me. It was a violation, and I would make him suffer for it. I would make that snake-eyed, one-armed weakling pay for what he'd done to me.

But how? Mr. Liu was a man of power. He'd broken the spell on my peachwood sword. I could haunt him from the spirit world—move objects around, possess people— but he was a Daoshi, of the Third Ordination or higher. If I approached him in spirit form, he could drive me away with an octagonal mirror, trap me in a bottleneck gourd, or burn a paper talisman and incinerate me.

It wasn't enough to wait and hope for the best. It wasn't enough to rely on Father's power and ingenuity to rescue me. I had to create my own opportunity. I needed help, that was clear, but I didn't know where I could find it.

Was there anyone else in Chinatown who could help, I wondered. If there was any other woman around with yin eyes, I didn't know her.

That left me with few options. Father could burn a talisman of spirit sight, but the spell would only last as long as the paper kept burning—a matter of seconds. I had slim chance of catching him during one of those brief spans of time. Neither youzi leaves nor the tears of a dying dog would be available. And if he sent his orthodox spirit servants, the Five Ghosts, for me, they wouldn't help me re-attain my body. The Five Ghosts do not rescue; they annihilate.

I couldn't remain here, not if I wanted to warn Father about Mr. Liu. And I felt a need, after so many years of being forced to the margins, I felt a need to face the man who tricked me, the man who violated me. I needed to prove that Xian Li-lin is her father's daughter, her husband's wife, and no one's victim.

I needed to find a way out of this land of ghosts and monsters. It was evening. I could tell by the last stragglers at Fish Alley, the smell of stale fish. It was evening, and tonight, I knew, was the Bai Gui Yexing—the Night Parade of a Hundred Devils. The most outlandish among the monsters were going to walk tonight. These creatures were Yao, meaning they had no relation to the human world. They were grotesqueries, the nightmares of childhood. The breath at your shoulder when no one's there? You might find polite, modern ways to explain the feeling, but you know in your heart that it's one of the ghosts and goblins we call yaoguai.

City lights had left them few shadows to inhabit. There was no place for them in a land of street lamps, telegraphs, and cable cars. They retreated to forests, fields, streams, hills, and mountains, or they lurked in the shadows. But tonight the world belonged to them. They were gathering in throngs, to romp through our cities. Ordinary people might even catch a glimpse of them, but no one would believe them. "You're drunk," they might say, or "you're mad," and jokes might be made about smoking too much opium.

Such is the nature of the Yao. A man takes a wrong turn down a street he has traveled every day and finds himself somewhere unfamiliar. Shadows lean oddly, buildings look different, and something is moving at the edge of what you can see. Yao presses at the edge of the ordinary, making even your home feel strange. A shadow flits across the wall when no light source is moving. An old umbrella shifts strangely in the closet. Maybe for a moment you see human features in the window, watching you. And why is the dog barking at a dark corner? Nothing is ever as simple as it seems. At the edge of perception, weird things dance and howl.

Would one of those weird things be able to help me? It was possible. I could strike an arrangement with one, draw up a contract, burn offerings, maybe even enshrine its image with the small deities of our temple. A contract with me would give it a relationship with the human world, ending its outsider status—if it restored my relationship with the human world.

Of course, it was far more likely that one of them would eat me. Or gouge out my eyes and play with them like marbles. Or peel the skin off my spirit and wear me like a coat.

I looked at the shining fish scales along the ground of the alley, and I shuddered.

The thought of approaching the Night Parade filled me with dread. All the old childhood fears rushed through my mind, and I felt small and weak. I was defenseless. I had no peachwood sword, no paper talismans, no bagua mirror or magic gourd. If a single one of the freak spirits attacked me, I'd have no choice but to run, and I was thinking of approaching them when their power was at its height, the strength of numbers behind them.

I shook my head. It was foolish, I knew. Pigs go willingly to the slaughterhouse, knowing no better. I knew better. I could look for the hundred horrors of the Night Parade, to face possible torment and possible salvation, or I could remain out of body forever, in a world without sun, without family, knowing I had chosen to hide from monsters.

It was dark, and somewhere in the San Francisco night, they were out there. The freaks of the spirit world would be dancing, reveling in their obscene freedom, and I was going to find them.

I was going to find the Bai Gui Yexing—the Night Parade of a Hundred Devils.

FOUR

I have heard people say that anyone who watches the Night Parade will go mad. The monsters that populate the Night Parade are among the strangest of the ghouls and devils that trouble the human world.

I had never witnessed a Night Parade. For many years, I had seen signs of the monsters' passage through Chinatown. Occasionally, at night, I heard unearthly sounds of music, of festivities, coming from the street. I always heard it between eleven and one, the hour of the First Earthly Branch, when the forces of yin and shadow are at their peak; between eleven and one, when Father always insisted I remain indoors.

Tonight I ventured out to the forbidden spectacle, looking for help in the unlikeliest of places.

After Mother died, I swore I would never hide from monsters. But now I was actively searching them out, and not just one monster, or two; tonight I was going to find the Bai Gui Yexing. Among the horde of monsters, there had to be something that could help me find my way back to my body.

I decided to wait for the monsters at the intersection of California and Dupont. It was here, in the evenings, where Father often stood with an iron basket, burning paper offerings for the dead. It was here where Father performed his public rituals. These red brick walls were grimed with soot from Father's festival rites. Here I would feel at least a little comfortable facing a horde of spirits.

A street lamp flickered at the corner. A pedestrian walked near me, his shoulders hunched as though it were cold out. But it wasn't cold. On some level, he could tell tonight was different. He didn't slow down or stop to read the bulletins posted on the walls. I watched him go, hoping he would make his way to shelter.

Ding-ding-ding, went the cable car as it slowed to a stop. *Ding-ding. Ding.* The men climbed down, their queues swaying behind them. They were heading home or going out to gamble, and though none of them could see or sense me, they swerved around me as they walked, as a stream shifts around a stone. I marveled once more at the ways the living accommodate the things they cannot see.

"Pungent tofu?" asked a boy. He was wearing a straw hat, and he held out a plate of tofu. He was pale-skinned, and his eyes had the glazed look of someone who has spent far too many hours working.

"Pungent tofu?" he offered again.

"You can see me?" I asked.

There was no sign of comprehension on his face. "Pungent tofu?"

I looked in his eyes and saw infinite sadness, infinite loss. There was a hollowness behind his eyes that seemed to go on forever. That was when I realized the boy was dead.

"Pungent tofu?" asked the ghost again, extending his plate of fermented soy cake.

"Not right now, but I thank you," I said to him.

Ding, went the cable car as it started to move again. Its driver had clamped it back on the fast-moving cable. *Ding-ding*, it picked up speed, *ding-ding-ding*, and there was another sound under it. The sound came dimly over the din of a Chinatown night, but it was clear, and it was music. The plucking of a pipa strummed through the air. It sounded like water on stones, like wind brushing through trees, and behind it, they came walking.

It was the Bai Gui Yexing, and they came hopping, crawling, flapping, creeping, scraping, prancing, and floating, the devils in their multitudes. The shapes of the advancing creatures made me dizzy. So many were things I'd never seen, or never believed in, or had never heard of. The Daolu Registers list eighty thousand demons, but not even that could give name to the shapes in front of me.

In the unearthly crowd I observed the familiar monstrosities before I could make out the incomprehensible and foreign. A red crowd of huli jing, fox spirits, followed the patriarch fox. He was a proud old beast boasting five bushy tails and a laughing cleverness behind his eyes. I had seen huli jing before, but they'd been younger than the master of this skulk.

In the air near the five-tailed fox, ghost fires glimmered. When a fox walks through a graveyard, the last breaths of the recently dead climb out of men's throats and follow the fox. They burn for weeks, a dim, blue, floating flame.

Watching the foxes, I swallowed. The mischief of the huli jing may be innocent and it may also be cruel. Stories assailed my memory. The huli jing could be seductive vixens, harmless pranksters, or malevolent forces. I had no way to tell how dangerous these were. There were fox spirits who lived among people as wives and friends. Others engaged in mischief, turning a miser's gold into moths, and there were some of a more malicious bent, who would push a blind child down a well.

A pair of old shoes clattered near the foxes. The shoes were empty, but they proceeded with a man's careful stride, following the rhythm of the music. A snake with two heads slithered past, singing to itself; colors of peach and sand mottled its sea-green scales. Nearby floated a paper lantern in whose glow I could see oversized features, eyes and a mouth and a protruding tongue, all crude and much too large, like a child's drawing of a face.

Next I saw a woman's head. The head was no different from any Chinese woman, with her hair long and braided, but her body was far from the head. An elongated neck stretched out under the head, dozens of yards long. Her body traipsed behind, in a white, two-piece outfit, with broad sleeves and dark patterns along the blouse. Her neck curled around itself, writhing like a snake.

My mouth was open, my eyes wide. It felt like I was witnessing the dreams of opium smokers. I did not blink.

Shuffling along the ground was something like a centipede, only it was about three feet long, and it had a duck egg for a head. Someone had drawn a face on the egg in grease pencil. The head turned this way and that, looking about.

My mind felt hazy, as though I were dreaming. I watched the Night Parade progress. There was a puff of black smoke that moved as though it were being carried along by a wind, but there was no wind, and the smoke did not disperse as smoke does. Within the little cloud I could make out the features of a human face, made of smoke.

A man came walking. His skin was of a dark blue and he was taller than a human man standing upon the shoulders of another. He was barefoot, and his feet were reversed, heels in front and toes in back. His lips were long, an arm's length from the rest of his face, and swung about as a dog shakes its tail. Gray birds flew around him, and he spoke to them in their language.

"Pungent tofu?" asked the boy again. He swayed on his feet and stared at me with hollow eyes and an uncomprehending face.

I couldn't respond, too caught up was I in the ghastly figures of the Night Parade. The corner of Dupont and California would never be the same to me. If I managed to get back to my body, the streets would feel transformed.

A three-legged toad came hopping. It was the size of a cat, and I heard a clinking behind it, as of coins. It moved in an irregular gait, leaping and lurching down the road, bulbous eyes glancing in all directions.

A head was walking down the street. A human head, except it was waist height, and turned upside down. Hair moved beneath it like the legs of a caterpillar, brushing the road with innumerable tiny follicles. The inverted head continued down the way.

Up in the air, floating like a bat above the rest of the monsters, there was a white woman. Or segments of a white woman. Her head was flying there, and she wore a wide-brimmed hat over dark blond hair. She had a beautiful face, a young face. Men would fall in love, go mad, or write poems, if they saw her face, but her innards dangled under her throat. Her heart throbbed, her lungs pulsed, and coils of intestine bobbed as she flew through the night. She was a horror and an affliction. She radiated malevolence. I saw her silhouette pass in front of the moon, and I shuddered.

There was a blue-skinned man in Buddhist robes, with one huge eye in the middle of his forehead. He carried a goosewood staff, like Father's. I'd heard of the blue monk, Lan Heshang. Travelers had encountered him in the mountains and in the woods. When the travelers spoke to him, he said nothing. But still, he had my attention. His goosewood staff suggested he knew how to work spells, and he might follow a Buddhist moral code. The blue monk might be able to help me.

My attention turned again to the woman's flying head with its trail of organs. During the day she must steal men's breath with her beauty, and at night she tore free of her body and flew to prey on their spirits. She was as deadly and soulless a predator as any in the spirit world. I thought I needed to tell Father about her. But if he killed her, it would look to the rest of the world as though a Chinese immigrant had murdered a young white woman and cut out her guts. The backlash from such an event would be horrific beyond belief.

The crowd of monstrosities continued, surging like a waterfall. I felt exhausted simply from watching the freaks. My eyes glazed over, my mind barely able to catalogue the glut of horrors before me. Things that were unnatural or supernatural, things that had no place among men, found

their own place among the Night Parade. The Bai Gui Yexing was a dance of nightmares, a community of the fearsome, freakish, and unwelcome.

Perhaps, I thought, that is how the white folk see
Chinatown. We live together in a community of outsiders,
united only by being different from those around us.

And with that I made up my mind. I was going to
talk to the least foreign of these ghosts and goblins. I chose
the blue-skinned monk, who carried a goosewood staff,
whose Buddhist robes and shaved head marked him as a
soul-searcher.

I stood from my perch and began walking toward
him. "Pungent tofu?" the boy ghost asked again.

"Maybe later," I said, to be polite. I knew better than
to trust the food and drink of spirits. He looked despond-
ent, holding out his tofu, and I walked toward the blue
monk.

Something whinnied, and I was nearly trampled by
a kind of creature that had the shape of a couch. A hairy
couch. It clopped past on its wooden legs, snorting at me
in derision.

"Blue monk!" I called out as I approached him. "I
need your help."

He turned to face me, and I saw that mud had dried
upon his orange robes. His hands were blue as corpses and
twice the size of a man's hands. There was old dirt lodged
beneath his fingernails. He held his staff in one hand, and
with the other he idly rubbed his chest, regarding me with
the eye in the center of his forehead. The eye was as big as a
man's fist, and it looked bored.

I bowed to him. I started to speak, and then I stopped,
unfamiliar with Buddhist forms of address. "Shifu," I
guessed, addressing him as a teacher, "I am trapped in the
spirit world. I need help to return to the world of the living."

He blinked his big slow eye and said nothing.

"Will you help me?" I asked.

Saying nothing, he looked up at the sky, and around
at the revelry of monsters. He blinked his enormous eye.

Then he lifted his staff and turned away, rejoining the procession.

I stamped my foot in anger. If the blue monk wouldn't help me, which among the monsters might? There were so many of them, and so strange. They might not comprehend any language I knew. They might kill me as soon as I drew their attention. None seemed half so human as the Buddhist, nor so approachable. I saw none who might help. I cursed—and then I heard a soft snigger.

A big orange cat was trotting toward me. It looked like it had been in many scraps, but still it carried itself with the pride of a tomcat. One of its eyes was larger than the other, and it had two tails. I blinked. "Mao'er?"

The cat spirit stopped trotting and bowed its neck. "Miao, Dao girl," he said.

"Mao'er, can you help me?" I blurted.

A lazy look swam from his smaller eye to the bigger one. "Help you, Dao girl? Why should Mao'er help?"

"I helped you once, long ago."

The cat spirit gazed at me, shrewd and aware. "Mao'er be a cat, remember," he said. "And never was a cat born that honored its debts."

I sighed. I'd been a little girl, maybe nine years old, when my father caught Mao'er stealing fish oil from the lamps. Unable to capture the cat itself, Father bound Mao'er's power in a bottleneck gourd.

When I first saw Mao'er, a group of boys had him cornered. To them he looked like a mangy orange cat, with a forked tail. They poked him with sticks, yanked on his tails, scorched his fur with matches.

I looked at him and saw what he was. A spirit cat, a strange and changing thing, a creature of mischief and reckless appetite.

On that day long ago, the boys tormented him for what felt like hours, and I could not interfere. It would cost Father too much face if his daughter was seen fighting with boys. So I turned and went into the temple. Father paid me no attention. I walked into the back room. I found the gourd where Mao'er's power was held, and I broke the seal.

Three boys had gone to the infirmary that day, suffering from animal scratches. And that night, late, a cat yowled outside our basement door, and I went to speak with it.

Years had gone by and now I was trapped in the spirit world, in need of an ally. Mao'er sat back on his haunches, watching me through uneven eyes. "It's true a cat spirit honors no debts," I said.

"And has no friends!" he added.

"A cat spirit honors no debts and has no friends," I said. "But you like me."

His eyes narrowed, and he looked away. "No like anyone," he said.

"Except for me."

He looked back, scowling, then licked his paw and said, "Need help nownow?"

"Yes, Mao'er," I breathed. "I need your help now."

The shift was too fast for me to see. One moment I was looking at an orange cat, and a moment later I was looking at a girl of maybe fifteen years, wearing a faded orange qipao dress, its sleeves long and embroidered. She squatted on the ground and licked the back of her hand. "Need catch mouses?" she asked.

I stared. I had never seen Mao'er change shape before. The transformation was unnerving. The girl had Mao'er's eyes; the whites of her eyes were forest green flecked with earthy brown, and her eyes held the same mischief and brightness.

"No," I said to her, "I'm not looking to catch mouses. Mice, I mean."

Something hot swooped over me. I turned and saw a man's bald head flying past, mounted on a kind of wagon wheel. The wheel was on fire, and yet the flames did not seem to be consuming it. I blinked and the burning wheel had flown off.

The Night Parade had passed. I saw the tofu boy hurrying to catch up, heard the strumming pipa recede into the distance.

The girl yawned, and the inside of her mouth was a cat's mouth, lined with a cat's teeth around a cat's sandpapery tongue. "Need fighty?" she asked.

"No," I said, "no fighting."

The cat-girl pouted. "No fighty?" she asked, disappointed.

"Can you help me back to the world of the living, Mao'er?" I asked her.

She looked away and stretched. Slowly, carefully, she stretched her spine one way and then the other. She was a slender, tattered thing, and oddly beautiful. "No," she said, "nono. But can catch mouses. Miao."

FIVE

That night we traveled Chinatown together in the spirit world. Mao'er had returned to his feline form. Skulking along on padded paws, he showed me his favorite places to hide, under shadowy staircases in dim alleys. We roamed my town, taking unfamiliar paths along familiar roads.

"Mao'er sneak in there, steal dry fish," he said, indicating a warehouse on California with a flick of his whiskers.

"But that's an Ansheng warehouse," I sputtered.

"Yesyes?" he said.

"Father has warded it."

The cat sniffed in disdain. "Mao'er know back door."

I stared at him. "Mao'er," I said, "is there a . . . back door . . . to my father's temple? Or to our quarters?"

He shifted again, but this time he took on the shape of a hefty little boy, with buckteeth and one protruding eye. "Mao'er try," he said. "Lamp oil yum, miao. No way in. Mean, miao, mean."

I sighed. Of course Father had warded our home and his temple. Every floorboard, every corner was protected by talismans, shielded by bagua mirrors, with painted images of door gods mounted at the entryways and wood blocks beneath the thresholds. Of course it was.

Mao'er showed me a narrow passage between two brick buildings off Fat Boy Alley. The passageway opened to a slightly larger niche. It was almost morning, and I curled up and slept.

My dreams were troubled by monsters. No one could witness the Bai Gui Yexing and come away from the experience undisturbed. All night I saw them, the distorted faces, the freakish apparitions. The sadness of the tofu boy, the malice of the flying head, the indifference of the blue monk, all of it drifted through my dreams in a chop suey of horrors.

I woke, disturbed, hungry, and worried. "Great Boqi," I prayed, "eat these evil dreams." I could not afford to allow my vital energy to be sapped by nightmare, not here, not now, when so much was at stake. If Mr. Liu wanted to kill my father, it probably meant the one-armed man had something planned, something big and ugly, and he saw Father as a threat to his plans.

Once I was back in my body, I could warn my father, and he would know what to do. So my path was clear. Stay intact in the spirit world, and find a way to return to my own skin. I stood and stretched under the tarnished brassy light of the moon.

If I stayed trapped here long enough, it would eventually start to seem normal, the days lit by moonlight. But I had not been here long enough for that. I found the spirit moon disturbing.

Near me was a pile of dried fish. It was a gift from Mao'er, no doubt. But the cat was nowhere to be seen.

I took the dried fish and chewed on it. It was better than I expected; there was dried salmon, dried tuna, dried squid, dried cuttlefish sliced into salty strips, and some fish I could not give a name to. All of it was salty, oily, and chewy. In my mouth, the flavors tasted lovely but felt somehow hollow, as though I were eating shadows. Which, I supposed, I was.

I stood, stretched, and went to find Mao'er. He wasn't in the alley, so I started walking toward Jackson, chewing the fish.

It had been two days. For two days I'd been away from my body, cut off from the workings of the human world. For two days, Mr. Liu had been gloating over what he'd done to me. How he'd played me for a fool. How he'd out-witted me, cut me, and trapped me.

Or maybe he hadn't been gloating. He might see it as no greater a victory than drinking a cup of tea. That he had defeated me might be inconsequential in his eyes, no greater an achievement than killing a moth.

I walked along, and the thought of Mr. Liu made my spirit body stiffen with outrage.

I swallowed the last of the dried fish. Mao'er was crouched and quiet on Dupont south of Jackson when I found him, intent on hunting. He had a cat's shape once more. His two tails were flat to the cobblestones behind him. I approached him and he half-cocked his head in my direction.

"Mao'er hunt. Hushy hushy now, Dao girl?"

I looked toward the street, where the cat had been hunting moments earlier. A tiny spirit was walking slowly across the cobblestones. It was milky white and small enough to fit in the palm of my hand. It had tiny white human arms and tiny white human legs, but where a man has a torso and a head, the spirit had an eyeball.

A full-sized, human eyeball.

An eye was walking across the street. And it was looking straight at me.

"Yaoguai," I said. The eyeball spirit was clearly one of the ghosts and goblins, freakish creatures that have no rela-tion to the human world. It was the kind of thing my father would destroy without hesitation.

Even after all my years of seeing monsters, even after witnessing the Bai Gui Yexing, I continued to be both fasci-nated and repelled by the outlandishness of spirits.

I watched the creature proceed. Its legs took short, determined strides. It was a human eye with tiny arms and legs attached, and it was watching me. It made its way across the street and never took its eye off of me. It was creepy, but there was something familiar in its gaze, some-thing that evoked a feeling of having known it all my life. I couldn't identify what was familiar about the eye.

"Don't hurt it," I told the cat spirit.

He hissed. "Dao girl starve Mao'er?" He shifted into the shape of a hefty little boy with a mouth full of sharp teeth, swishing two tails behind him.

I turned toward him, still keeping an eye on the eyeball spirit. "I will bring you spirit mice, Mao'er, and saucers of fish oil. Leave this spirit alone."

He gave a soft hiss. "Mouses good. Oil yumyum. Dao girl better deliver. Or Mao'er piss on your shoes, Dao girl. Miao."

We both turned our attention back to the eye. Mao'er shifted back into the shape of an orange cat and scampered into the shadows. I knew I'd see him soon enough. He wouldn't forget the food I owed him.

I crouched down and faced the little spirit. Some of the yaoguai can change shape and size, and many have unexpected strengths. Yes, the eyeball spirit looked harmless, but in the land of monsters, it is always best to be prepared—and feared.

I tried to make my voice sound impressive, like my father's. "My name is Xian Li-lin. I am a Maoshan Daoshi and a killer of monsters. What kind of monster are you?"

Tilting its eyeball up to look at me, the spirit huffed. "Hardly polite to call someone a monster when you've only just met."

I blinked and stared. "A yaoguai is lecturing me in manners?"

"Harrumph," he said, crossing his arms. His gaze somehow seemed harsh, disapproving. Familiar. "I will lecture you in manners, young lady," he said, "and you will listen."

I smiled, leaning back. "What will you do to me if I don't listen?" I asked. And then I said, under my breath, "Little monster."

The spirit had no face other than its eye, but in that moment I could have sworn he was scowling. "If you continue to be rude to me," he said, "why would I guide you back to your body?"

SIX

"You know how to lead me back to my body?"

"You heard me," the eyeball said, uncrossing his arms and crossing them again behind his back. He looked . . . smug.

It's strange to crouch on a street corner talking to an eye. It's hard to look into an eye and talk to it. But this yaoguai had just offered me hope. He claimed he could lead me back to my body, back to my life.

"What will it cost me?"

"Not a thing," he said. "But I expect you to be polite."

"All right," I said, though I did not relish the thought of having to be polite to one of the yaoguai. "What shall I call you?"

He looked surprised. "I . . ." he said. "I don't think I have a name."

I raised an eyebrow at that. "I can't address you respectfully if you don't have a name," I said. I thought for a moment. "How about Mr. Yanqiu?"

He hesitated. "Mr. Yanqiu," he said, thinking. "Mr. Eyeball. Yes, I think I like that."

"Mr. Yanqiu, please will you lead me back to my body?"

He gave me a scornful look. "Maybe later."

"Later? I need to get back as soon as I can."

"You called me a monster, young lady. And I will not lead you anywhere until you apologize for it."

My mouth dropped open. I had agreed to be polite to him, but the little monster wasn't going to make it easy for me.

"Mr. Yanqiu, Shifu," I said, addressing him as a teacher, "I lose much face for insulting you. Shall I knock my head to the earth nine times?"

"That will do nicely," he said.

"What did you say?"

"You offered to knock your head to the earth nine times, and I accepted."

I looked at him, startled. "But . . ." I said. One only knocks one's head to the earth before the truly great, like Empress Dowager Cixi or the Emperor, yet manners dictate making the offer.

"You made an offer," he said, "and I'm accepting it. Do you want to find your way back to your body or not?"

Frustration made me clench my fists. I was angry, resenting it. I felt shame, both for my behavior and for my powerlessness. Could the spirit really guide me back to my body? He claimed he could, and he made that claim without me telling him anything. Somehow he'd known that was what I wanted.

I had little choice. I could humble myself before this monster and maybe make it back to my body, or I could save face and stay trapped in the spirit world. Holding back anger, I positioned myself on my hands and knees. I closed my eyes and prepared to smack my forehead to the ground.

And then the eyeball laughed.

His laugh wasn't grumpy and cruel as I expected. It was a light laugh, playful, warm, and welcoming.

"I'm only teasing you, young lady," the eye said. "Come on. Get up and follow me."

Eyes wide, I stood and brushed myself off. "Little monster," I said under my breath.

"I heard that," he replied.

Mr. Yanqiu's tiny legs made him walk slowly, so I lifted him to my shoulder and let him ride. I turned where he said I needed to turn, followed where he told me to go. Lefts and rights, we walked through a fog between life and death, tracing mystic steps along the spirit side of Chinatown.

"We're getting closer," I said. "I can feel it."

"Of course we are," he said.

Through a thin sheet of mist I saw Father's temple. Its wood and brick were almost the same vivid colors I remembered, hardly dampened by any of the spirit world's ash-and-gold moonlight. I started walking toward the temple.

"Not there," Mr. Yanqiu said. "That isn't where we are going."

I turned to him, puzzled. "But that's where I left myself. My body."

"Turn right," he said. "Two blocks down, on Dupont."

I did as he said, stepping through the afternoon crowds, until we arrived outside Dr. Wei's infirmary. Dr. Wei was Father's friend; they often smoked cigars and played fantan together, all the while arguing. Dr. Wei incorporated American medicine into his practice, and supported the young Emperor's reforms. Father argued that the old ways are best, that the Empress Dowager knew best, and that China should remain as it had always been.

Outside the infirmary door was a string of talismans painted on cloth. They were Father's talismans, as strong as they come, to keep out spirits and diseases, but a new talisman had been added. A talisman I'd never seen before.

My name was written on it, in ghostscript, surrounded by a drawing of a door. I gazed at it, amazed.

My father had posted a talisman that granted me passage through his magical barriers.

Father had always been so distant, so powerful. I was stunned that he'd gone to such an effort for me.

I was so grateful that tears almost came to my eyes. Father had made a talisman for me, just for me, so I could come find him here. It was unlike him to be so considerate. A rush of emotion swept through me, all of it confused. And yet I still didn't understand why my father wanted me to enter here, the infirmary, and not our home.

I turned my head to face the eyeball spirit. "Is he injured?"

The eye looked away, saying nothing. It felt to me as though he was protecting me from knowledge that might cause me pain. His gesture reminded me somehow of the look on my father's face when he's hiding something. When Father looks away, blinking too fast, I can always tell that he's lying.

I stopped and thought for a moment about the eyeball on my shoulder. It was a strange monster, one of the yaoguai, and it had no relation to the social order. Something was wrong. My father would never summon a yaoguai into Chinatown. And how was it that Mr. Yanqiu was able to navigate the passage between the world of spirits and the world of men? He had no kind of red string to guide him.

There was something I was missing. Without something like a red string, the spirit on my shoulder shouldn't have been able to find his way across the realms. Not unless he was anchored somehow, tethered, as though he was part of a living body.

I thought for a moment about the human body, the amazing dynamism of it all: the way vital energy flows along meridians, rising from the Bubbling Springs on the soles to the Upper Cinnabar Field in the skull, giving life to the spirit of each organ, the spirit of each limb, the spirit of each . . .

And then I had a sinking feeling. It felt like a piece of glass had fallen from the top of a building, fallen slowly and in infinite quiet, and shattered to a hundred pieces at the bottom.

"You," I said to the eyeball spirit riding on my shoulder. "I know what you are."

He looked at me, curious. "What am I, Li-lin?"

I couldn't speak. I felt words choke in my throat. "You're his eye," I managed to squeeze out. "You're the spirit of my father's eye."

Mr. Yanqiu leaned back quietly.

"But it makes no sense," I continued. "In order to send you to me in the spirit world, Father would need to . . . he would need to . . ."

I couldn't bring myself to say the words out loud. *He would need to gouge out one of his own eyes.*

The eyeball nodded. "He's recovering in the infirmary now. You're unconscious in the cot next to his."

"Why would he do something like that?"

"He could tell your red string had been broken. You needed a guide to bring you back to the lands of the living. He sent me."

"No," I said, "no. It makes no sense. He wouldn't. He wouldn't do that. Not for me."

The spirit of his eye looked at me sharply. "But he did."

Mr. Yanqiu was the spirit of my father's eye, but he had been without conscious thought until Father's spell. He didn't know Father as I did. My father wouldn't do this for me. There must have been some other reason, something I didn't grasp yet.

I lowered my head and walked to the infirmary's front door. The string of cloth talismans formed a barrier, and I felt it push against me, a sensation like a gathering wind. There was no going forward against the force of the barrier. But then the talisman with my name on it opened a path for me. It felt like a tree had been interposed between me and the wind; I heard the roar of it go on to each side of me.

I moved past the barrier, and Mr. Yanqiu dropped off my shoulder with a yelp. I turned to see him flopped face-first on the ground behind me, pushing himself up. "How undignified," he said.

"You can't make it past the talismans."

"Obviously not," he said, brushing off dust from the street with his tiny hands. He had the injured look of a man whose pride had been wounded. My father's spell had locked him out, excluded him. Treated him like any other strange monster.

I looked at the eyeball spirit, concerned. "Listen, Mr. Yanqiu. I'm going inside to join spirit with body. I'll probably be in there for a few hours, to talk with Father and Dr. Wei. Do you think you'll be safe out here until I can come back?"

The eye gave me a shrewd look. "You won't come back," he said. "Once you're back in your body you won't even be able to see me."

I blinked at that. "You don't know," I said. "You don't know that I have yin eyes, do you?"

"Yin eyes? That means you can see spirits?"

"Yes."

With a tiny white hand he scratched his chin, or, where his chin would be if he had a face. "Am I a yin eye?"

"Hm," I said, stalling. "You are . . . that is, Father does not have yin eyes. But now you are a spirit, and maybe it depends which eye you were. I do not know whether you are yin."

"Harrumph," he said.

"Do you think you will be safe?" I repeated.

"I can take care of myself," he said, with a scowl in his voice.

I walked to the door. My body would be resting inside the infirmary, unconscious, and my father would be there too. Missing an eye, recuperating under his friend's care.

The door opened, and one of Dr. Wei's apprentices rushed out, his braided queue shaking behind him. I saw the door closing behind him, and darted through while it was still open.

The infirmary was active. Dr. Wei, his wife, and three other apprentices were there, tending the needs of a few sick people. Like so many other good things, the infirmary was paid for by Mr. Wong; it was open to anyone who paid dues to the Ansheng tong. The English-language papers liked to portray the tongs as crime syndicates. But were it not for Mr. Wong's philanthropy, sick people would go untreated, corpses would go unburied, immigrants would find no place to work or live, and ghosts would go unexorcised.

I found my body resting in a cot on the second floor of Dr. Wei's infirmary. I approached my body as if it were a different person entirely. Her lips were parted, and I could hear her breath dragging in and out. Without hun, the higher soul, the body's breath would be shallow; it would generate less and less qi, or lifeforce.

I had gone out of body before, but never for so long. My body looked so young. So innocent. The face I saw was almost a child's, untouched by evil, and not the face of the brokenhearted widow. My mouth seemed limp, my cheeks sallow in the infirmary's lamplight. Bare of my usual expressions, silly or caustic, my moon-shaped face looked bland as tofu. Stretched out on the cot, my body seemed small and fragile.

However, the best weapons often seem small and fragile. And I hadn't forgotten about Mr. Liu. I knew my skin would be marked where he had cut me, and I was going to use every weapon at my disposal to make him suffer. I was going to teach him that Rocket's wife is no one to be trifled with. He would pay for cutting my skin. He would pay for costing Father his eye.

I glanced to the next cot over, where Father was sleeping. The entire right side of his face was wrapped in bandages, and bandages covered much of his scalp. Graying hair poked out from between the bandages. Under a trimmed, gray-white mustache, the edges of his mouth were turned down, as if in a disapproving frown. Father was so sleekly built that he seemed to leave almost no impression at all on the cot.

He had never struck me as small before, and yet here he was, resting, wounded. He gave a soft whimper in his sleep. He was in pain. If I knew my father, he had refused to take opium for his pain.

He was in pain, and I hated it. He was suffering for me, because I had fallen into a trap. If I had waited for him, asked permission like an obedient daughter, he would not be suffering now. But I had thought I could make my own decision, and now my father would pay the price for my transgression. My father was half-blind, and it was my fault.

Why had he done it? Why had he sacrificed his eye for me? Conflicting emotions surged through me. I was tempted to feel cherished, but that couldn't be right. There had to be more to it. I was missing something. And I would have no way to learn what it was until he awoke.

The loss of my father's eye was one more debt I owed him, one more debt I could never repay. But there was something I could do.

I was going to find the man responsible for this, and I was going to crush him.

SEVEN

I took it slow. Moving back into my body, the twelve pulses would grow quicker, the breath would grow deeper. I relaxed into myself again, feeling the cords of my spirit realign with muscles and sinews.

It was a wonderful feeling, a homecoming. My senses woke up and nearly overwhelmed me. The smell of plywood and straw came to me, the smell of fish oil burning in the lamps, and the aromas were so strong, so full.

I came back into my body. I felt heavy. The weight of my body felt insurmountable, like a mountain pressing me down. But then I felt stronger than I realized, strong enough to move my body's weight. My pulses throbbed inside me, and I felt qi circulating along my meridians. The world came in through my closed eyelids like the slow warmth of sunlight. I hadn't realized how much I loved being alive. It was wonderful to breathe air again, rather than echoes.

I opened my eyes, blinked a few times as I adjusted to the light of the lamps in the room. Dr. Wei's infirmary was a series of square rooms full of cots. Everything was bright, everything stood out with a depth I had begun to forget. My eyes felt dry, and the smoke from the burning lamps made the sensation worse, but I was glad to be back. So glad.

Glad, and hungry. While I was unconscious at the infirmary, they probably poured medicinal broth down my throat, but now I was starving. I wanted food. A meal began to form in my mind. Pork and fish and spinach. Maybe fried in peanut oil, with a five-fragrance powder.

The thought of food made my mouth begin to water, and I sat up in the cot.

Someone gasped. Mrs. Wei was standing in the doorway, covering her mouth with one hand. Before I could say anything, she turned and ran out, probably to get her husband, the doctor. Her large bamboo earrings shook beneath the tight knots of her hair as I watched her speed away from the room.

Mrs. Wei was a strange one. When I was a little girl, growing up without a mother in a town where just about everyone was a man, I had always wanted a chance to know Mrs. Wei better. Father had kept me apart from her, and I never knew why.

Dr. Wei came into the room, wearing a white jacket as if he were an American doctor, his spectacles high on his nose. He was a man of two worlds; his medical kit carried syringes, stethoscopes, and respirators alongside acupuncture needles, moxa sticks, and fire cups. "Li-lin," he said, taking a seat on a stool at the edge of my cot, "are you all right?"

I nodded and spoke. "Yes," I said. Or tried to say. My throat was so dry that the word came out as some kind of inhuman hiss. I cleared my throat before speaking again. "And Father? How is he?"

Dr. Wei pursed his lips. He took off his spectacles. He wiped the lenses clean on a piece of cloth, and said, "He's lost an eye, Li-lin. He'll be half-blind for the rest of his life." The doctor gave me a moment to let that sink in. "He carried you here, then he went outside. One of my apprentices found him a few minutes later. He was sprawled out on my front step, holding a knife. Apparently he burned a paper talisman and then he cut out his eye."

I listened to him and let the words register. Father burned a talisman first, I should have realized that. The talisman would have specific instructions written on it, commanding his eye's spirit to follow those specific duties. I needed to ask Mr. Yanqiu what those duties were.

"Why would he do such a thing, Li-lin? Why would he cut out his eye?"

I shook my head. "He sent the spirit of his eye to help me," I said.

Dr. Wei laughed, a dry chuckle I had heard often when he thought Father was making a silly argument. He saw my expression and went quiet. "You can't be serious."

I lifted my chin and said nothing. Dr. Wei stared at me. "But Zhengying wouldn't do such a thing, Li-lin, not for you."

"I know," I said, looking down. Dr. Wei was one of a half dozen people who called my father by his personal name. He knew my father well.

"When he brought you to the infirmary," Dr. Wei said, shifting on the stool, "someone had cut you. I applied phenol to your wounds. But those wounds were some sort of spell. Someone carved a spell into you. Who would do such a hideous thing? And why?"

"A man named Mr. Liu," I said. "I think Tom Wong may have helped him."

Dr. Wei gave a short, disbelieving chuckle. "Mr. Wong's son is a sworn brother of the Ansheng tong, Li-lin. He would never lift a hand to strike at your father's family. Who is this Mr. Liu?"

"I am not certain, Dr. Wei. I think he's a Daoshi. Mr. Liu is about Father's age, and he's missing his right arm. Does he sound familiar to you?"

The doctor tsked. "Too many men in Chinatown missing an arm or a leg," he said.

I sighed and looked away. He was right. Some men lost limbs working the gold mines during the rush, others building the railroads. I looked back at the doctor. "I think Mr. Liu is somebody new, Dr. Wei. I think he came to San Francisco recently."

He looked thoughtful for a moment. "The American officials wouldn't admit a laborer who was missing an arm, not after the Chinese Exclusion Act."

I followed his line of thought. "So if Mr. Liu came here recently, he'd have to be classified as a merchant."

Dr. Wei gave me a meaningful look over his spectacles. There could only be two ways a man with one arm had gotten classified as a merchant: either he already owned a successful business in San Francisco before he even arrived, or someone had bribed the immigration officials on his behalf.

That was how I got in, after all. The Exclusion Act made it so that Chinese females could only come to America if they were the family of a merchant. Mr. Wong had found American officials who were willing to classify my father as a merchant, in exchange for a large fee.

"But the only people in Chinatown who have that kind of influence," I thought aloud, "are the Six Companies and the Ansheng tong."

"You're forgetting the Xie Liang tong, Li-lin."

I blinked at him. "The Xie Liang tong? They're nothing but a joke. They're ruffians and clowns."

Dr. Wei shook his head. "Is that what your father has been telling you? The Xie Liang tong has been gaining in power every week."

This was news to me. Mr. Wong's group, the Ansheng tong—Mr. Wong's group, that Father and I worked for—was the only power worth reckoning with among the criminals. Father always told me that the Xie Liang tong was a group of arrogant upstarts. Their leader was a prancing fool who wore American clothes and chose a ridiculous name for himself.

I looked over at my father, asleep on the cot. He looked small, and weak, and alone. I thought about Mr. Wong and the Ansheng tong. Their power was old, and perhaps it was fading; perhaps the old ways, the ways of the Triads, could not thrive in this new world. Maybe it took a dangerous idiot in an American suit to prosper in a world where telegraphs send messages across the world and cable cars speed through town, propelled by steam so intense it was as powerful as hundreds of horses.

"Dr. Wei, did my father talk to you about anyone else? Was there anyone else he was frightened of, or suspicious about?"

He pursed his lips, in a moment of quiet thought. "I'm not sure he'd like me telling you this, Li-lin," he said, pushing his spectacles higher on his nose, "but yes. It happened few months ago. At the Laba Festival, there was a man there. He was a Buddhist monk, but for some reason, Zhengying seemed horrified to see him. I have never seen him so afraid, Li-lin. He was shaking, and he wouldn't tell me why."

"A Buddhist monk? Why would Father be afraid of a baldie?"

He gave a half-laugh. "I really don't know. What's stranger is, I met this man later, on my own. He seemed almost dainty, the way he went out of his way not to hurt anything."

"Do you know his name?" I asked.

"Yes," he said. "He goes by the name Shuai Hu."

"This man, Shuai Hu, he stays with the baldies at the monastery on Washington?"

"Most likely."

That made me feel nervous as well as excited. The baldies at the monastery were practitioners of a different kind of kung fu. Father had trained me in the martial arts of Wudang Mountain, which emphasize the building of one's internal energies, and round, smooth motions, but the baldies at the monastery trained in Shaolin, a warrior art focused on strict, rigid motions. I had always wanted a chance to test my skills against theirs. If any of them was involved in the attack on Father and me, I would soon get my chance.

"How much longer will Father be asleep, Dr. Wei?"

The doctor glanced over to the cot where my father lay sleeping. "It's hard to say, really. He stirs every few hours. For all I know, he could wake up in the next few minutes, but he could also sleep another day."

I brushed back the sheet on my cot and started to stand. "Li-lin," the doctor said, "you can't just rush out of

here. You suffered an attack and a coma. It will take time
for you to recuperate."

I stuck out my arm. He gave me a skeptical look,
then took my pulse. I waited while he counted the pulses,
moving his grip to different points along my forearm. "All
right," he said, with some reluctance. "Your twelve pulses
are healthy." He took his stethoscope and checked my
heartbeat. I waited once more, breathing as he instructed.
Shaking his head, he said, "Your cuts were superficial and
you're strong as a horse. I'd still advise you to give yourself
time to recuperate. Go home, drink plenty of liquids, make
some herbal soup. Don't go out and rush into something
dangerous."

"Of course not," I lied.

I had bled on my Daoshi robes, so Dr. Wei had burned
them. Now I wore the infirmary's long linen nightshirt
as I descended the stairs, trying not to scratch at the cuts
on my stomach. I passed Dr. Wei's wife on my way to the
front door. She gave me a look that seemed to be both suspicious and hostile. I tried to ignore her glare. Maybe she
thought I was making a play to be her husband's concu-
bine. I brushed past her and walked out the door.

It was late afternoon by now, and Chinatown was
bustling. A vendor had set up his stall nearby and was
shouting, "Cabbage bean pear potato! Cabbage bean pear
potato!" There was the smell and sound of laundry being
washed by hand. Water splashed, clothing splunked, and
steam poured through the air, warm and fresh.

I had left the spirit of my father's eye waiting in the
street, promising I'd come back for him, but now he was
nowhere in sight. "Mr. Yanqiu?" I called. "Where have you
gone, Mr. Yanqiu?"

A few moments later he came stumbling out of a
cloud of steam on the ground. "Marvelous," he said. "Simply marvelous. What do they call that?"

"That's steam," I told him. "It comes out of hot water. There are people inside that basement, and they use the water to wash laundry. The water gives off steam, and the steam rises through that vent you found."

"Steam," said the eyeball spirit. "I'll have to remember that. But what is this 'hot water' you mentioned?"

"Come on, Mr. Yanqiu," I said with a smile. "Let's go back to Father's apartment, and I'll heat you a cup of tea."

EIGHT

The spirit of my father's eye waited outside while I changed my clothes in the cellar room where Father and I lived. I took off the long infirmary gown and examined the cuts in my skin. They weren't deep, but they were ugly, and they stung.

I studied the cuts. They were extensive, elaborate. And, I realized, it was more than just one spell.

At the center of my stomach, starting just below my ribcage and extending below my waist, there was a spell that would open me to spirit possession. As I deciphered the ghostscript, I realized how grotesque it was. It not only opened my body to Shi Jin but to any other unnatural thing that wanted to take me. It was an invitation. Spirits of disease could have taken up residence inside me. The spell wasn't merely intended to use me as a weapon against my father; the spell was also intended to violate me, pollute my body and spirit. It was designed to cut me open and shit inside.

The first spell was signed, Liu Qiang, Maoshan Daoshi, Fifth Ordination.

"Fifth," I said, and spat a string of curses. Even a Daoshi of the Third was out of my league. Liu Qiang's spells could brush mine aside like cobwebs. I wanted to cry out in frustration.

Next to that pattern of cuts, on my side, was a different spell. My father had also cut a spell into my skin. It countered Liu Qiang's, closed my body to invasion, sealed me up and protected me. Nothing could enter my body except for something with my name.

The air in the room felt suddenly tight. I stopped breathing. I hadn't realized how close I'd come to failing. The power of my father's spell was beyond my comprehension, the precision breathtaking, but none of that would have mattered. His spell left a door open for my name.

My soul passport would have been enough. Father's spell wouldn't have protected my body from possession. The ghost could still have gotten into my skin and murdered my father.

The second spell was signed, Xian Zhengying, Maoshan Daoshi, Seventh Ordination.

I breathed deeply, taking it all in. "You idiot," I sputtered.

Father and Liu Qiang had carved me up like a piece of meat. They took their knives and used my body as their magic battleground. Liu Qiang was far more powerful than me, but Father was far more powerful than Liu Qiang—and yet Father would have lost this battle for my body.

Liu Qiang was clever, I'd give him that. Apparently he'd been ordained into the Maoshan lineage. He must have known Father was stronger in the Dao. He made his spell so broad and monstrous so that Father wouldn't know what he was really planning.

Father's spell, the second series of cuts, wouldn't have kept him safe. If I had lost the fight in the spirit world, Shi Jin would have robbed me of the soul passport. He would have risen up in my body. Father was probably so confident in the power of his magic that he wouldn't have seen it coming when the ghost drove a knife into his heart.

My own father had cut a spell into my flesh, and it wasn't even the right spell.

Every part of this deepened my sense of violation, of humiliation, and that drove my rage. I felt my face start to turn purple. My teeth clenched. I found my hands clutched into fists, and my fists were turning hard as iron. They say a good woman is a quiet woman, but I found myself shouting. No words came from my mouth, just incoherent sounds. I punched the air, knowing my fists swung with enough force to break boards if I struck them.

I forced myself to begin my breathing practices, to envision light radiating from the Golden Stove point behind my navel. I needed to harness this. Control my anger. Shape it, as a talisman gives shape to a Daoshi's will. There was something here I could learn from.

Liu Qiang, of the Fifth Ordination, had outwitted a Daoshi of the Seventh Ordination. A weaker sorcerer could trick a stronger sorcerer into casting the wrong spell.

I smiled at that, and my grin was hard and sharp as a steel blade.

A Daoshi of the Second might be able to find a way to overcome a Daoshi of the Fifth.

I might be able to destroy Liu Qiang, even without Father's help.

I changed out of the infirmary clothes and put on an atonement robe. The robe was made from linen the color of sand, with black trigrams embroidered on its wide sleeves. The robe flowed around me, and I moved through a sequence of martial arts postures to make sure it would accommodate my motions.

Upstairs, the temple was dark. I was unaccustomed to finding darkness in the large chamber, since Father lights candles and lanterns for the ancestors day and night. I lit a single candle to see. My peachwood sword lay on the floor, two spells written on it in grease pencil—my spell to bring it with me to the spirit world, Liu Qiang's spell to cancel mine.

Rage began to flow inside me once more. The peachwood sword had belonged to my husband, and to my mind it still did. I used his sword to fulfill his ambitions. And that one-armed weakling, that filth Liu Qiang, had written a spell on Rocket's sword.

I wiped both spells off the wood and gathered some matches, a bagua mirror, and my rope dart. I like the rope dart. Half a pound of iron shaped like a dart, tied to a rope. The rope dart can slice an enemy like a knife or stab into him like a spear. When the weight gets spinning fast enough, it can shatter stone.

Jiujiu the spirit gull had warned me when the ghost Shi Jin was approaching me in my sleep. For the gull I burned a talisman of protection. Whatever predators might hunt her in the world of spirits would find her slippery, evasive. For a day, the gull spirit would glide untouched out of the jaws of monsters. She had protected me, and I was protecting her in turn.

I took a flask of lamp oil for Mao'er. We use fish oil in our lamps, and cats love to lick it up. Later I would make mice out of paper and burn them for him. Mao'er would be rewarded for helping me and sparing the spirit of my father's eye.

I needed to eat. In order for my spells to work at their strongest, there were purifications I needed to undertake. I could eat no grains or meats. On the wood stove I fried greens and herbs in peanut oil, seasoning them with bean paste and spice powder.

I hadn't forgotten my promise to Mr. Yanqiu. I heated a cup of water and brought it outside. He was shivering when I found him, and his tiny body was curled up for warmth.

"It's not that cold out," I said, surprised.

"It is if you're a naked eyeball," he replied, and I thought that if he had teeth, they would have been chattering.

"Here, then, Mr. Yanqiu," I said, pushing the cup of warm water toward him. "Climb on in."

He eyed me suspiciously, reaching out a tiny white hand to test the water temperature. "Oh," he said, "oh, that's nice." Without any further hesitation, he lifted himself up over the teacup's rim and splashed down into the warm cup of water.

"How is that, Mr. Yanqiu?"

The gurgling sounds he made could only be described as blissful, so I went inside and came back out with my meal and a pair of chopsticks. Sitting on the rickety wooden steps, I ate my food. It was pungent and salty and I loved every bite.

I told my father's eye about the last few days: Liu Qiang and the soul passport, Shi Jin and the ambush, Father sacrificing his eye. Father casting the wrong spell. The rise of the Xie Liang tong. Shuai Hu, the Buddhist monk who frightened my father.

The cuts on my stomach were itchy, and I put down my plate. "I'm going to kill Liu Qiang," I said to myself.

Mr. Yanqiu heard me. He treaded water in the teacup. "You said he's stronger than you, Li-lin. How does that work?"

"A Daoshi of the First Ordination is a novice. Barely any power at all. I hold the Second Ordination, so I have twice as much power as a novice. A Daoshi of the Third would have twice as much power as me. A Daoshi of the Fourth has double that. Liu Qiang is a Daoshi of the Fifth Ordination."

"So he has eight times your power?"

"That's right. A Daoshi of the Fifth is considered a senior student, not a fully ordained priest."

"And your father has four times as much power as he does?"

"No," I said. "Daoshi of the Sixth and Seventh are considered fully Ordained priests. A Daoshi of the Sixth has twice as much power as a Daoshi of the Fifth, but Daoshi of the Sixth and Seventh can also call upon the power of their lineages."

"What does that mean, Li-lin?"

"Eighty generations," I said. "My father holds the Seventh Ordination. In himself, Father is four times as strong as Liu Qiang, but he also draws upon the power of the eighty generations who came before him."

"So that's . . ."

"The power of eighty generations of men of the Seventh," I said. "Hundreds of Daoshi like Liu Qiang could work together and still fail to match my father's power."

"You should wait for your father to recover," said the eyeball. "You can't hope to stand against a Daoshi of the Fifth Ordination."

I shook my head. "I will find a way. Whatever he's up to, I will stop it, and I will end him. His magic may be a great deal stronger than mine, but he's still human. I can break his bones. I can slit his throat. He carved me up like a fish, Mr. Yanqiu. He cost Father an eye. I'm going to make him pay for everything he's done."

The eyeball grunted in the water. He knew there was no changing my mind. "So what are you going to do, Li-lin?"

"Well, someone must have helped Liu Qiang through immigration. It had to be someone who has wealth and connections. That just leaves the Six Companies, Mr. Wong, and the Xie Liang tong."

My father's eye stirred in the water. He leaned back, listening. "Which do you think it is?"

"Well, the Six Companies run legitimate businesses. They don't break American laws if they can help it. I can't see them hiring a sorcerer to kill anybody, and I can't think of any reason they'd want to go after my father.

"We know Mr. Wong has the money and the connections. He bribed officials to get them to allow me in, after all. And his son Tom was with Liu Qiang. But there has to be more to it than that, Mr. Yanqiu," I said. "Father is one of Mr. Wong's sworn brothers. Mr. Wong would never take action against him, and Tom wouldn't hurt me.

"That just leaves the Xie Liang tong. I always thought they were ridiculous, like children wearing clothes made for adults. But Dr. Wei says they've grown powerful."

"And you think they helped Liu Qiang come into the country?"

"I think it's likely."

"So, first stop, the Xie Liang headquarters?"

"It isn't time for that yet," I said, shaking my head. "The Xie Liangs wouldn't have dreamed this up on their own. If they're involved, it's because someone recruited them."

"Who?"

"I don't know yet, Mr. Yanqiu. I don't know why anyone would try to harm my father."

"Does he have enemies, Li-lin?"

I responded slowly. "No. Not in America, anyway. And we left China a long time ago."

"So why was he afraid of that monk?"

"I don't know, Mr. Yanqiu. That might be the most baffling piece of information. I've never known Father to be afraid of a living human."

"Do you think the monk could be behind the attack?"

I thought for a moment. "It doesn't seem likely," I said. "I can't see a Buddhist recruiting gangsters and sorcerers to do his bidding. But there's something very odd about my father being afraid of this Buddhist monk. I think I need to find out more about this man Shuai Hu."

The eye leaned back in the teacup, watching me. "He might be dangerous, Li-lin," he said.

"I know. I won't confront him. I just want to ask around, see what I can learn about him."

"That's not the whole reason," Mr. Yanqiu said.

"Oh?"

"No, Li-lin. You've lost face. Liu Qiang tricked you, and it cost your father his eye to get you out of Liu Qiang's trap."

I hung my head. "What does this have to do with the monk?"

"You want to investigate Shuai Hu because you're trying to prove something, Li-lin. You know your father is afraid of him. You want to gain face. You want your father to see how brave you are."

"You're right," I said. "Investigating the monk could get me hurt, or worse. The martial arts of Shaolin are legendary. Shuai Hu is a mystery to me. Even my father finds him intimidating. It would be foolish for me to try to learn more about him."

"I'm glad we agree," Mr. Yanqiu said.

"But it would be more foolish to sit and wait," I said. "When Father wakes up, he's going to fix everything. The best I can do is give him all the information he needs."

"Li-lin, please don't take foolish risks," the eyeball said, splashing in the teacup.

"I need to learn everything I can, no matter the risk," I said. "This monk terrifies my father. I need to find out why."

NINE

Chinatown's Buddhist monastery was on the third floor of an apartment building on Washington, between Dupont and the Flower Lane. I could see white and yellow blossoms in the Flower Square. Hills rose to the north. The Sub-Treasury Building towered to my east. I walked toward the monastery with Mr. Yanqiu riding on my shoulder.

On the street outside I caught sight of a boy, maybe ten years old. He was playing with a balloon made from a pig's bladder, tossing it up and catching it.

"Child," I said, "I would like to speak with you. What do you know of the monks who live here?"

"The baldies?" he asked. I laughed and nodded.

He held his balloon in one hand and sized me up with his eyes. "What will you give me to tell you about them?"

I had no money or sweets to bribe him. All I had were empty threats. "Child, I am called Xian Li-lin. Does that name mean anything to you?"

"Xian," he said, thinking. "Like the Daoshi? You're the exorcist's daughter?" The boy took a few steps back.

I smiled grimly. For once there was an advantage in being feared.

"Now," I said. "You will tell me how many baldies live in that room."

"Twenty-six," a voice said from behind me.

I swung around and faced a tall man in orange Buddhist robes. His head was clean-shaven. He may have been the tallest man I'd ever known except for Rocket, but where Rocket's face had been sincere and youthful, this man's face seemed jovial and somehow ageless. His mouth was open in a lopsided grin. Sizing him up, I saw that his shoulders were broad, and his arms were thick with muscle. If he had even a moderate amount of training, he'd be a good fight.

I glanced him over, looking for weapons. Belted at the waist of his orange robe, he carried a wooden drum shaped like a fish. Aside from the drum and its striker, he was unadorned. He wasn't even wearing the peachwood beads monks usually strung into bracelets and necklaces.

"Don't you have better things to do than frighten innocent children?" he asked. The boy turned and ran away.

"I have come to the monastery to speak with Shuai Hu," I said, mustering as much authority as I could into my voice and bearing. "I am Xian Li-lin, the Daoshi's daughter."

He leaned back, crossing strong arms in front of his chest. "You're a Daoshi too, aren't you?"

I blinked. No one ever seemed to realize that. Long ago I had given up on reminding them. "Yes," I admitted, "I am a Daoshi too. How did you know?"

"I have known many dangerous females in my time. It is never wise to underestimate an enemy."

My eyes narrowed. I snapped a glance at Mr. Yanqiu. He understood me, and started to climb down from my shoulder. Then I turned back to the muscle-bound monk. "Are we enemies, then?"

The bald man shrugged and then looked away. "I honestly hope not, Daonu Xian," he said, addressing me respectfully. "I have no wish to harm you."

His statement irritated me. It reminded me of all the men who thought I was merely a girl, that I posed no threat. "You think you could harm me, Shuai Hu?"

His lopsided grin grew broader, acknowledging that he was, indeed, Shuai Hu. "I try to do no harm."

"You haven't answered my question. Do you think you could hurt me?"

"You know, Daonu Xian, I expected a visit from your father, weeks ago. I thought he would come to me with flaming talismans and a goosewood staff. I would have fled and never come back. But the days went by, with no sign of the great Daoshi. Until today. Why has he sent you now?"

My mouth opened to shoot a sharp retort, but then I stopped. Shuai Hu didn't know why I was here. He thought Father had sent me. He didn't know Father and I had been attacked. He wasn't a conspirator.

It was a relief to hear. There was something unnerving about this man, immense and strong, with his lopsided smile and his happy cheeks, and I couldn't figure out what it was. Looking right at him with my yin eyes, I saw nothing more than a human man. Yet there was also something feral about him, something dangerous and uncontrollable. He reminded me of a bird in a cage with an open door, trying to decide whether to remain on its perch or fly through the opening.

Mr. Yanqiu finished climbing down my robe. He ran to take shelter in the shadows.

"My father would only come to you with talismans burning if you were a monster," I said. "You aren't a monster, are you, Shuai Hu?"

It was his turn for a surprised blink. "I try not to be."

"What does that mean?"

"Why did your father send you, Daonu Xian? Why now?"

"No one sent me," I said.

This was going nowhere. The monk wasn't going to tell me anything.

I unstrapped the bagua mirror from my back. It was a nine-inch octagon made of bronze, with a small round mirror in the center. The eight trigrams were engraved in the bronze frame. Every possible three-line combination of yin and yang, standing for all the energies of the universe, met along the frame of my bagua mirror. Focused by the laws of nature, the mirror would unmask any illusion.

"What are you doing?" Shuai Hu asked, but he was too slow.

I swung the bagua mirror out to face him and gave a triumphant "Ha!" I waited for the illusion to crumble, for the true face of the monster to be revealed.

The monk looked at the mirror, unimpressed. His face gazed from the mirror. His big jovial cheeks and expression of annoyance looked entirely human. He tapped his foot on the street.

"Daonu Xian," he said. "I ask with patience and respect. Why have you come here looking for me?"

I tried to think of a clever response, but nothing occurred to me. And then everything went mad.

Mr. Yanqiu shouted, "I've got him, I've got him!" I turned toward him. The eye-spirit had grabbed hold of a tiny blue man. I tilted my head and blinked to make sure I was seeing it right. Yes, Mr. Yanqiu was struggling to hold onto a small blue man. The blue man yelped as he struggled. Shuai Hu turned toward the sound of the two little spirits grappling. He took a half-step toward them. It was enough for me. The monk shouldn't have been aware of the spirits at all.

I launched a hammer-kick at his shoulder while he was turned to the side. It hit hard and square, knocking him off balance. He staggered to the side to recover his center, but by then I had drawn my rope dart. I started it spinning, building speed and momentum.

Shuai Hu looked at me, keeping an eye on the little spirits tussling on the street. A few moments more and my rope dart would be spinning fast enough to shatter stone.

Then Mr. Yanqiu shouted. "His shadow! Li-lin, *there's something wrong with his shadow!*"

I glanced at the monk's shadow. The eye was right. It wasn't a man's shadow. It was the shadow of a beast, huge and inhuman. Its dark outline began to ripple and pulse. Power throbbed from the shadow into the man. The shadow began to look more and more like a man's shadow, and the man began to look more and more like a monster.

Shuai Hu had grown. He'd been big before, and now he was taller and broader, and somehow more solid, as though he'd been built from bricks. And there was a second shape around him, beastly and burning, a shape of spirit threatening to burst out through every inch of the man's skin. The second shape was larger than he was, larger and longer. Shuai Hu snarled, and so did the spirit beast around him. I saw it in its primal glory. I saw its jaws, its teeth, its fur, and its wild eyes. I whispered, "That's impossible."

My mind was reeling. It couldn't be real, not here, and yet it was. Father was right to fear him.

"Let. Him. Go," Shuai Hu said, with both mouths—the man's mouth and the mouth of the monster. Three tails lashed behind him.

"Do it," I said to my father's eye. My mouth felt dry. My eyes were wide with disbelief.

Mr. Yanqiu released the little blue man. I scooped up the spirit of my father's eye. Together we backed away from the man who was born a tiger.

TEN

A few minutes later, we were on our way back to the infirmary to see if my father had woken up yet. I still couldn't believe what I'd seen. "A tiger spirit," I marveled.

"With three tails," the eyeball added.

"How do I fight something like that?" I asked. "How do I kill it?"

Mr. Yanqiu was slow to reply. "Why do you want to kill it, Li-lin?"

"Because it's a monster," I said. "That's what I do. I kill monsters."

"You used to call me a monster," he said softly.

I raised an eyebrow at that. "You aren't a tiger, Mr. Yanqiu. Tigers eat people."

"How many people has Shuai Hu eaten?"

"I don't know."

"Has he eaten any people?

"Not as far as I know," I admitted.

"I think you would have heard the news, Li-lin. Tiger attack in San Francisco!"

I ignored the jibe, and he continued. "I suggest you concentrate on Liu Qiang."

I nodded. My father's eye was right. There would be time later to deal with the tiger. "It's good to have your advice, Mr. Yanqiu. It's like having another pair of—" I stopped and corrected myself. "It's like having another eye."

Father still lay in his cot at the infirmary, but he was awake now. The right side of his head was swaddled in bandages, but his left eye shone with a harsh clarity, focused on me. It hurt to see him like this. My father had always been the most powerful of men, the most fearsome exorcist. He was the man who walked alone into a house where fox spirits were flying and left them all dead. He was the spiritual warrior whose name alone would send an army of angry ghosts into disorganized retreat.

And now he lay wounded, half-blind and suffering. Because of me.

His remaining eye blazed in his face. If anything, the bandages made his gaze seem more pointed, more intense. Anger solidified the sharp features of his face, the carefully trimmed graying mustache, the severe eyebrows.

I sat on a wooden stool by the cot. There were so many questions I needed to ask him, but he held me with the gaze of his remaining eye. "Liu Qiang," he thundered, his voice intense but hoarse. "Tell me how that weakling overpowered you."

I looked down. Apparently my father knew Liu Qiang and held him in low regard. I flushed with shame. I wanted to cry, to tear at my hair for my foolishness. Father was going to think less of me when he understood. "Liu Qiang didn't overpower me, Father. He came to the temple with Tom Wong. They asked me to deliver a soul passport."

He eyed me with a shrewd look. "And you believed this?"

"Yes, Father," I said. "Tom Wong was with him. I thought Mr. Wong wanted me to do this."

Father nodded slowly and looked away. "Tom Wong would never take action against a sworn brother of the Ansheng tong," he said. "He must have been deceived."

"But why didn't he stop Liu Qiang when he started to cut into me?"

Father looked back at me, with his forehead knitted into a severe expression. "There must be an explanation."

"Father, why did this happen? Who is Liu Qiang?"

He adjusted his position on the cot. When he answered, his voice seethed with disgust. "Liu Qiang," he said. "Liu Qiang is a small man. Weak and bitter.

"He was one of Shifu Li's apprentices, at my side. All of Shifu's students were strong and capable young men. All except Liu Qiang. Qiang was a weakling. He was a fool. The other boys and I would trip him when he was carrying tea. Once," he said, and a smile teased the edges of his mouth as he remembered, "the other boys held him down and I pissed in his face."

I could not conceal the disgusted expression on my face. The words came from my mouth before I had a chance to think. "What had he done to deserve such a cruel humiliation?"

"He wasn't one of us." My father casually sipped from a wooden cup. "Even Shifu knew he was less. He refused to ordain Qiang past the Fifth."

Hearing this made something ache inside me. My father's teacher had shown his contempt by giving Liu Qiang only the Fifth Ordination. Father raised me no higher than the Second. It burned to hear Father call Liu Qiang a weakling and a fool. It burned to know a fool had tricked me. A weakling had pushed my clothes aside and carved my skin.

My father's face had a distant look, as though he'd forgotten I was even there. "Will you tell me more, Father?" I asked.

He turned to face me. "I didn't see Qiang for years. Some time later, I was called upon to stop a soulstealer. A lifedrinker. He would hide behind a tree at night, and then he'd blow stupefying powder in the faces of men who passed by. The powder would numb their senses long enough for him to come up behind them and clip their queues."

We were quiet for a long moment. I found the notion repugnant. A queue is the symbol of a man's place in the world, connected by obedience to the Emperor. The queue is the physical embodiment of one third of the higher soul. Without it, a man would be incomplete, and, worse, he would become yao—filthy, unwanted, outside the social order. A monster.

I found myself grimacing. Any man who would do this, who would rob other men of a portion of their souls, was lower than an animal.

Father continued. "The soulstealer was cutting queues to make paper figures. These paper men were no bigger than your hand. Each time he burned a man's queue, he brought a hundred paper figures to life. The paper men had a portion of a man's spirit, yet they were not of the spirit world. They flew through the air and everyone could see them, even in daylight. Flocks of them would scream through the village at night, terrifying everyone."

He coughed a few times, and I waited for him to continue. "I tracked the soulstealer to his lair and confronted him. It turned out to be Liu Qiang. Raising a hand, he led a flight of paper men to attack me." Father's remaining eye looked distant, as if he was reliving the events of that night right in front of him.

"How did you stop them?" I asked.

"The paper figures were nothing," my father said, a sneer audible in his voice. "They were weak and flimsy, like Liu Qiang. His little paper men flew at me like a flock of birds and I cut them down with my straight steel sword. I found Liu Qiang cowering in the back of his little sorcerer's hut, and I took my sword and cut off his arm."

I blinked. That was how it happened, then. It explained Liu Qiang's missing arm, and it explained why a man would cross the ocean and hunt my father down after all these years. For vengeance. For face.

There was an eerie parity to the men now; Father cut off one of Liu Qiang's arms, and now Liu Qiang cost my father one of his eyes.

"He was going to use me to kill you, Father," I said. "He had an ally in the world of spirits. A ghost."

"The ghost was set to possess you," he said, nodding. "It was going to ambush me in your body and murder me unprepared. I know. I deciphered the plan by reading the talisman in your skin, and then I countered his spell by cutting a stronger talisman."

"Father," I said, "I brought a soul passport with me into the spirit world."

He went deadly still. The significance sank in. With the soul passport and my red string, the ghost would have been able to bypass Father's spell.

"It was a clever plan," he said slowly. "Why didn't it work?"

"I fought the ghost, Father. I defeated it."

A smug look crossed his features. "You did well," he said.

I flushed and looked down. "No better than my training," I said, and nodded. "But why did you send me the spirit of your eye?"

My father grimaced. "I had no choice. How would it look if Liu Qiang came into my own temple, trapped my daughter in the world of spirits, and I failed to retrieve her? A Daoshi of the Seventh bested by a Daoshi of the Fifth, and a weakling at that. I could not lose so much face."

Face. I should have known. For some men, face mattered more than friendship, more than money, more than love. More than an eye, and certainly more than a daughter.

The irony of maiming his face to save face probably hadn't occurred to him.

"You will destroy it, of course," he said.

I froze in place. I stared at him. My mind spun, and I felt sick. "What did you say?" I asked.

"The monster. I can't have the spirit of my eye running free around Chinatown. It would bring shame upon my ancestors. You will destroy it."

I stared at my father, saying nothing. He wanted me to exorcise Mr. Yanqiu, who rescued me when I was trapped in the world of spirits. The little monster was a friend, and the thought of killing him made me feel ill. Old wounds, old losses, came to mind, my mother's death and my husband's. I had already known too much grief, and the thought of killing Mr. Yanqiu made me want to stop living.

And yet Father was right. My feelings of friendship toward the spirit of his eye gave me no right to afflict Chinatown with one more freak of spirit, especially when the spirit was so intimately connected to Father.

Father had given his eye for me. If I left that eye alive, a walking, talking abomination, it would violate everything my father stood for.

"You will destroy it," he repeated.

I felt flimsy, as though made of paper burning slowly to ashes and smoke. There was a hollow space inside of me, and I felt distant, a ghost of myself, as I said the words. "Yes, Father. I will."

"Come," he said, and rose to a sitting position on his cot. "Let us walk to my temple."

"Father," I said. I wanted to urge him to lie back down, to rest, but I had no authority over him, and it would be disrespectful even to suggest he might be making a mistake.

He barreled down the stairs, clucking at Dr. Wei's admonitions to go back to the cot and rest. Mrs. Wei merely glared at us. I shrugged.

We left Dr. Wei's infirmary. Father had regained his customary stride, agile and proud. "It was a clever plan," he said again. "Too clever to be the work of Liu Qiang alone. He's a fool, Li-lin. Someone else must be advising him."

I nodded agreement. If what Father said about Liu Qiang was true, then someone else must have devised the plan.

Father was in charge now, as he should be, making the decisions, and yet I was worried. I needed to confront Liu Qiang and avenge myself for what he'd done. But Father was in charge. This was his battle, and he might not need my help. If he wouldn't let me help him against Liu Qiang, if he shut me out, I would never have an opportunity to avenge myself. I couldn't bear the thought of that.

Mr. Yanqiu was sitting on a step in front of a grocer's shop. "Li-lin!" he called, but I ignored him. I was going to destroy him, but I had no wish to cause him pain. It would take time to find a way to do that.

"Li-lin!" he called out. "Watch out for the dog!"

I turned to see what he was talking about. I heard a snarl before I saw it. A huge black dog was running down the brick street. Smoke rose from its nostrils, and its lips had curled back to show teeth made for ripping meat to shreds. A jaundice-yellow foam on its tongue indicated madness. It had no eyes. Behind its empty eye sockets, a white fire roared.

Raging, enormous, and on fire from within, hundreds of pounds of insane spirit dog came charging at us.

ELEVEN

I yelled, "Look out!" but it was too late. The dog struck my father's back like a giant fist. The impact knocked him toppling into me and we fell together to the bricks. My elbow hit the ground hard, and it felt like a hundred icy needles jabbed into my arm. Then Father cried out, and I heard the sound of teeth rending flesh.

Pinned under their weight, I couldn't reach my weapons. I was winded, and my elbow was bleeding from the place where it hit the bricks. Then my father's weight was lifted off of me all at once.

The hound yanked Father backward, and he half-dangled from its mouth. It shook him back and forth. It was trying to break Father's neck.

Panic shot through me. I pushed myself up from the ground and drew my peachwood sword. Father was unarmed. He flailed his arms behind him uselessly.

My first objective was to protect Father, so I took a bagua sword stance instead of my usual taiji. Bagua was designed for bodyguards. Its stepping skills emphasized moving in arcs, like a whirlwind, to divide an attacker from his target. The stepping pattern draws the attacker after you, but when he strikes you're already behind him and his attack lands in the void.

Father's good eye was wide and desperate and the dog shook him from side to side as if he were a cloth doll. It hurt to see him helpless. Fast as an arrow I stepped in and slashed at the dog's snout with my peachwood sword.

A red cut opened on its maw. That was good. It could be wounded. I spun to the monster's haunches.

It opened its jaws to snarl at me and my father slipped to the ground. He dropped like a coin in water and slumped on the street. He wasn't moving, but I couldn't see to him yet. Bagua stepping, I slipped between my father and the hound and made sure my steps drew it after me.

A foul smoke rose from the monster's snout, green and black. I could taste it in the air. The dog spirit was growling, contaminated by madness. It bared its lips and snarled, and I saw large, sharp teeth. Yellow drool slobbered from its mouth, and I was afraid. I felt frail and small and inadequate, facing the monstrous dog.

It pounced, massive and deadly. It was fast; at that speed, and with its size, it could pulverize me. I hadn't counted on it coming at me so fast.

I flowed to one side to avoid the dog, then coiled around to face it and added the momentum of my spin to a low swipe of my sword. The sword slashed the dog spirit along its hindquarters. The dog yelped in surprise but it continued plunging forward, out of my reach, before I could execute any further attacks.

The monster turned around and faced me. I wouldn't have thought it possible, but it seemed even angrier than before. A low cunning swept its features; the beast wanted to kill. I shuddered.

I glanced at my father on the ground. He was alive, but he wasn't moving. I wanted him to get up. I wanted to hand him my peachwood sword and watch him dice the monster into cubes. He didn't move.

I couldn't fight the enormous dog monster with just a sword, so I began to cast a spell. I knew my magic held little sway over the spirits, but I was fighting for my life and I was willing to hit the beast with any weapon I could find. "*Tian, De, Ziran,*" I intoned, heaven, earth, nature, "*yao, qi, yao, qi, yao, qi.*" The incantation focused my will and transmitted it into commands over the spirit world. "*Quickly quickly,*" I finished, "*as it is the Law!*"

Thin tendrils of power spread from my spell. They reached toward the dog like fingers of starlight. My spell struck the hound and crumbled into useless whispers against its black fur. I cursed.

The spell had been made of my will alone, bound into syllables and sent out into the spirit world. A single will, amplified by no more than the Second Ordination. A Daoshi of the Sixth or Seventh could draw upon the will-power of all the Maoshan Daoshi who came before him. Eighty generations add a lot of gunpowder to a chant.

But Father was prone on the ground, unconscious, and his power was with him.

That gave me an idea.

Before I could act, the dog ran at me. I jabbed my wood sword down at its face but I was too slow. It caught my left sleeve in its teeth, and my stepping pattern broke.

Panicking, I swung the sword as hard as I could, desperate to get away. The sword cut an orange gash along its muzzle. I started to swing my peachwood sword again but the dog yanked me down to the ground.

With my sleeve caught in its mouth, I scrambled to my back on the cobblestones. I was terrified. Off-balance and in the power of something so big and vicious, I felt overwhelmed. Fear filled me, and I began to tremble. I couldn't let the monster climb on top of me. If it pinned me down, I wouldn't have a chance.

My pulses pounded in my head, so loud I could barely think. The beast had two weapons, its jaws and its mass. The hound had caught me with its mouth. I'd been taken down, lost my leverage, and I couldn't strike with my left arm. But as long as the monster controlled me by the sleeve, its primary weapon was out of the fight.

The dog swung about, trying to land its weight on top of me, but I turned my legs and twisted my body away.

This was a ground fight now, and as long as I continued fighting defensively, I could never gain a position of power.

Eventually I was going to get tired. Bumping against the cob-blestones would leave me worn out, and I'd be too exhausted, too shaken, to continue fighting. I had to take the offensive.

I kicked both legs out and the momentum drove me to my feet in a kip-up. I turned to face the big black dog with the white fire behind its eyes. It still had me by my sleeve, and it dropped its forequarters to the ground and began backing away. It dragged me along, stumbling.

I wondered what would happen if I removed my robe. Allowing myself a quick glance, I saw that a crowd had gathered. Maybe twenty men stood at a safe distance, warily watching the street battle. Dr. Wei and his appren-tices were tending to Father, and Mr. Yanqiu looked ready to grab a weapon and attack the beast. In the back of my mind, I realized: everyone could see the dog monster.

There were so many people around. Removing my robe might save my life, and I knew it, but I would die before losing Father so much face. There had to be another way to get my sleeve out of the monster's jaws.

Diving forward in a front-flip, I landed rolling to my back on the cobblestones and jammed my peachwood sword in between its teeth. Still rolling, I kicked my far leg up, as hard as I could, and used the momentum to flip myself up onto the beast's back.

I touched it only for a split second, but in that moment, a horrible sensation coursed through me. It was boiling with death and fear and pain, and hunger. So much hunger. I wanted to vomit. I wanted to die. But momentum kept me going and gave me leverage on the sword in the dog's mouth. My weight and momentum pried against its jaws. I only needed half an inch, a quarter inch. . . .

Its jaws opened a little and snapped shut again, but the dog was too slow. My sleeve pulled free and I toppled off the dark beast's back and landed, rolling, back on the street.

Fast as I could, I was on my feet again. The monster turned to face me, faster than I would have thought pos-sible. But I was running toward it, and I jumped at just the right moment.

One foot landed on its back and I pushed off, and then the dog was behind me and I was running. The beast turned around again and ran after me. It was faster. I knew I couldn't outrun it. But I didn't need to.

I wasn't trying to get away. Each step brought me closer to the door of Father's temple.

And to the string of cloth talismans hanging over the door.

The dog was six steps behind me, and I began the processes of qinggong: lightness. Five steps behind, and I was transferring the weight at each step, making myself lighter. Four steps behind, and I was lifting each footstep higher, coordinating my qi with the Bubbling Spring energy centers in the soles of my feet. Three steps behind, and I placed a foot on the temple wall, then another, running two steps, three steps, up the wall. My arms stretched over my head, my hands desperately grabbing at the cloth, I felt my fingers touch it. . . .

And the monstrous black dog crashed into me. Its mass knocked me hard against the brick wall, and I began to fall, stunned and out of breath. The dog's hindquarters struck the brick and we fell together.

The hound recovered first. It turned and pounced on me while I was rolling onto my back. Its mouth opened, and I saw its sharp teeth coated with yellow saliva, smelled its foul breath.

I jammed the string of cloth talismans into its open mouth. The jaws closed, around the talismans and my arm. I felt its teeth puncture the skin on my forearm, and the pain made me cry out. Blood flowed from the wound.

I had little power over the spirit world. But my father had made those talismans. Talismans of warding, talismans of banishment, each of them amplified by the Seventh Ordination, reinforced by eighty generations of Maoshan Daoshi.

The monster's eyes went wide and bright, like little moons. Wetness filled them and the beast began to whimper. Soon, I knew, the dog spirit would break down piece by piece into bloody hunks of meat. I'd seen animal spirits die before, and it wasn't pretty. Over the course of hours, the meat would dissolve into a haze of spirit.

With my hand still caught in the dog's jaws, I pulled myself to my feet and watched the spirit shudder and convulse. "Die already, you nasty devil."

The dog monster coughed, once, and then something happened that I'd never seen before. The dog caught fire, as if from the inside. It burned like a thing of paper. Blazing bright, it was consumed in a few brief instants of flame, and then it was gone. I watched its head combust around my hand, but I felt no heat. Black ashes drifted onto the cobblestones.

A blue afterimage of the fire danced before my eyes. I looked at the ashes. They weren't in the world of spirits. They were on the street, where anyone could see them. That was strange.

I picked up the cloth talismans and examined them. A kind of spirit slime stuck to them, but their power was burning it away. They were intact. So the ashes had not come from the talismans.

Mr. Yanqiu wobbled over. "Are you all right, Li-lin?" he asked, and concern choked his voice.

"Yes," I said. Blood was trickling down my arm, and my body was sore all over. The fight with the dog had been brutal, but I was all right. "How is Father?"

"I heard Dr. Wei say he'd recover," the eyeball said.

Relief washed through me, and I nodded.

I turned to look at my father. There was blood on the street, but Dr. Wei and his apprentices were seeing to his care with focused medical attention. A memory flashed in my mind: Dr. Wei bent over my husband on the street, trying to stop the bleeding. My world ended so quickly, without warning. There could never be enough wailing for what I lost that day.

I wiped tears from my eyes. I had failed to protect my husband, but maybe I had managed to keep my father alive.

I turned my attention back to the monster's ashes. Physical ashes. That monster had nearly killed me, and I had no idea what it was. Father would, though.

TWELVE

"You Xians," Dr. Wei muttered, wiping his spectacles onto a cloth. "You will be the death of me."

Father smiled from the cot and threw an infirmary pillow at his friend. Dr. Wei managed to catch it.

"I will be fighting ghosts and goblins until my bones are smuggled back to China," Father told him, "and you will be healing my wounds."

"What was that monster?" I asked. "Was it a demon?" I knew it was rude to speak without being addressed, but I needed to know.

Father tried to shake his head, but the plaster cast immobilized his neck. "No," he said, and the word was filled with more disapproval than anyone else could have managed to pack into one word. The word told me I was a fool, I should have known better than to ask, and I shouldn't have spoken to my elders without being addressed. "That wasn't a demon, or a yaoguai, or a spirit. It was a quanshen."

Dr. Wei's face was as blank as mine. "A dog spirit?" I asked. It didn't seem right; the beast had been nothing like the fox spirits I'd learned about, or the cat spirit I knew. "But why did it burst into flames?"

Father's lips were pursed in a severe expression. "A quanshen isn't a spirit," he said. "It's a spell." He glanced at his friend. "Let me speak with my daughter alone."

Dr. Wei rose in a huff, pushing his spectacles higher on his nose. "I need to see to my other patients anyway," he said, and he strode out through the door.

"Father," I said, slowly, "was it one of Liu Qiang's paper figures?"

He tried to shake his head, but the neck brace immobilized him again, and he winced. A look of distaste crossed my father's face, and he continued. "This isn't any form of Daoist magic, or even soulstealing, Ah Li," he said, using a diminutive of my name. "It's yao shu, filthy magic. The spell comes from Japan, where they call that kind of beast an 'inugami.'" He grimaced, as if the Japanese word caused him pain. "I do not believe Liu Qiang capable of making a quanshen."

I didn't understand. "Someone made that dog?"

"Let me speak, Ah Li," my father said, looking cross. "Quanshen are a kind of spirit servant."

"Like the Five Ghosts?"

Father scowled at me. "Yes, you could say so. The Five Ghosts are my spirit servants. They will obey any Daoshi of the Seventh."

"But the Five Ghosts are orthodox warrior spirits of the Dao," I said.

"No more interruptions," my father said, giving me a harsh look. I bit my lip to keep myself from speaking again. "The Five Ghosts are upright beyond question. But there are filthy sorcerers," he went on. "Sorcerers who do not follow the Dao, and they have . . . other ways . . . of waging spirit war." That look of disgust had returned.

"To make a quanshen," Father continued, looking away, "a sorcerer begins by preparing a special blue paper for talisman-making. And then he . . . he takes a dog. Chains it up. The sorcerer puts a bowl of fresh meat just beyond where the dog can reach it. Then he . . . lets the dog starve. For days. Twice a day he puts out a fresh bowl of meat, and the dog strains at its chains, trying to get something to eat."

I understood Father's look of disgust. He continued, "Can you imagine that, Li-lin? All that hunger and desperation. Smelling the meat all day, so close. When the dog is out of its mind with rage and starvation, the sorcerer cuts off its head. He dips a reed brush into the dog's blood while it's still fresh, and he uses it like ink. He paints a victim's name on the blue paper, trapping the dog's spirit into the talisman."

"Trapping it with all its hunger and madness," I said in a soft voice. I sat in a flood of emotions. *That* had been the monster that tried to kill us? I had destroyed the spirit of a tortured animal.

Father spoke again. "A quanshen isn't a spirit, Ah Li. It's a weapon. Somewhere out there, someone is practicing bad magic. Someone took that dog's blood and wrote my name in ghostscript. I don't know how long ago that dog was killed. It could have been yesterday, and it could have been twenty years ago. Today someone burned the quanshen's talisman and unleashed the monster, with all its madness and rage. It came here today to kill me, but my talismans destroyed it."

His talismans? It seemed I would gain no face from destroying the monster, because I had used my father's talismans to do it. I sighed.

Father heard, and gave me a penetrating look. He was quiet for a few moments. "When I am well," he said, "I will perform the ritual of Third Ordination."

My eyes went wide with surprise, and my jaw may have dropped. I was so excited that I had to look down, to avoid embarrassment. "Thank you, Father," I said, "I will endeavor to honor the Maoshan lineage."

"You had better," he said.

I nodded, proud and grateful. "Father, I will find out what Liu Qiang is planning, and put a stop to his plans."

"Plans?" Father asked.

"You think a sorcerer is helping him," I said. "They must be trying to get you out of the way in order to work some powerful magic."

His gaze was stern. "Of course," he said, looking away and blinking too fast, as he always does when he's lying. "I had thought of that." I lowered my head so he would not see me smiling. "Something greater is taking place. Nothing has been right in Chinatown since I returned from the gold mine and found you out of body."

"You were coming home from a gold mine?"

"Yes," he said. "Mr. Wong is working on an auspicious project. There is an old gold mine in Sacramento. Twenty years ago the mine caved in and trapped thirty Chinese miners. They died there. Now Mr. Wong is exhuming their corpses and sending their bones to be buried in China."

"Buried with their ancestors."

He nodded. "They were exhuming the corpses when a monster attacked them in the dark."

"What sort of monster?"

"A jiangshi," he said. "Power flowing through the minerals in the ore must have touched the final breath of one of the corpses, sparking it into undeath."

"Father, you do not mean—a gan jizi?"

"No, Ah-Li, not a plague-carrier. Simply a walking corpse, mindless and blind."

I shuddered. Dead men walk stiffly, and they compensate for their blind eyes by sensing the energy in your breath. I could hardly imagine how it must have been for Father, down there in the dark, holding his breath while hunting the dead man.

"I do not imagine it was too much trouble for you, Father, a single jiangshi."

"It was not," he said.

"The corpses have been down there for decades," I said. "Did Mr. Wong tell you why he decided to undertake this now?"

Father lowered his eyes. "Mr. Wong did not tell me himself," he said. "His son gave me the assignment."

I stared. "Tom Wong sent you to Sacramento to fight a monster? On the same day that he came to the temple with Liu Qiang?"

Father tried to shrug, but the brace interfered. "Mr. Wong is doing an auspicious deed, Ah Li," he said. "Can you imagine these dead men? Their corpses have been neglected for far too long. Mr. Wong is a great man, to care for them now."

"But why now, Father?"

"It does not matter."

"Why would Tom Wong send you on a mission to help dead men, and then send me on a mission to the world of spirits?" I stopped speaking for a few moments. "What if Tom is gathering these corpses for his own purposes?"

Father's frown had deepened while I spoke. "What could it mean, Father?"

"Nothing," he said.

"Why would Liu Qiang's ambush be timed so that you wouldn't be there to protect me? What could he and Tom want with thirty corpses?"

Father huffed and grunted. "You do not understand these matters, Ah Li," he said. "No sworn brother of the Ansheng tong would point his sword in my direction."

I started to speak, but he raised a finger. "Respect your elders, Ah Li," he said, "and be silent."

I endured Mrs. Wei's glare and Dr. Wei's exasperation as I made my way out of the infirmary and onto Dupont Street, where horse-drawn carriages clopped and clattered down the wide road. My next stop would be Bai Gui Jiang Lane. I needed to speak with Mr. Wong.

THIRTEEN

"Li-lin! Are you all right? How is your father?" The eyeball spirit came after me, running on his tiny milk-white legs.

I didn't want to see him. I didn't want to hear his voice. He was sort of a friend of mine, but he was still a monstrous thing, and it was my duty to destroy him.

"What's wrong?" he called. "Can't you hear me?"

I turned to face him. "I hear you, monster," I said. "And I will exorcise or destroy you. But not today."

He took a step back, looking shocked. "Very well," he said. "I am to be destroyed. So where are we going now?"

I just stared at him, baffled. "Don't you want to live, Mr. Yanqiu?"

"Well, yes," he said, "of course. But fulfilling my duty is more important than living. I thought you would understand that."

"And what is your duty?"

"To save you."

The words struck like rain, profound and unexpected. To save me. That had been Father's command, the writing immutable on his talisman. He made this spirit from his eye, and he gave it one overwhelming drive. *Save Xian Li-lin.* Nothing else would ever be so important to the eyeball spirit as that simple command. So he saved me when I was trapped in the world of spirits, and as long as he existed he would go on trying to fulfill that duty, again and again.

Saving me was the sole purpose of Mr. Yanqiu's life.

The notion made me dizzy. In my life, no one had wanted to protect me, except my husband. After he died, there was no one who would protect me anymore. He was a man who protected everyone. It became my duty to protect them in his stead.

And here was this little monster, the spirit of my father's eyeball. He was small and prissy and ridiculous. He had no power to speak of. But it didn't matter. Because nothing mattered to him, except keeping me safe.

"Come on," I said, and held out my hand to lift Mr. Yanqiu to my shoulder.

Mr. Wong had his headquarters in the back room of a restaurant on Bai Gui Jiang Lane. The alley got its name because there was a white grocer there who could speak Chinese. The name meant White Devil Speaks.

I was walking to Bai Gui Jiang Lane when two constables approached me. The first was a young man with short hair the color of straw, and he carried himself with a pitying demeanor: he felt sorry for me. "You contract girl?" he asked in English.

Anger washed over me, a feeling cold and sharp as a dagger in the gut. He thought I was a whore. I wanted to correct him, demand respect, and make sure he never assumed such a thing about a Chinese woman again. I felt my mouth begin to contort into a snarl, but there were more important matters than my loss of face. I stopped myself from lashing out. I had no time for this.

"Velly solly," I said. "No speakee Engrish."

He gave a grim smile. "Y'unnerstood me," he said. "So? Areya or aintcha?"

"Bobby," said the other constable, in a serious tone. He was older, and he had a red-brown mustache that matched his red-brown mutton-chop sideburns. "Bobby, that's Lily Chan."

I stiffened in surprise at the name the English-language papers gave me after my husband's death. I looked at the older man, examining his features carefully. I didn't know him.

"Oh, g'day, Miss Chan," the younger constable said, tipping his round cap. His face betrayed all the predictable feelings; he looked respectful, apologetic, and very uncomfortable. "I heard. About what happened. I, um, I'm sorry. Ya know, sorry, uh, for your loss."

"Thank you," I said in English, "and good day to you, Officers." I turned and walked away.

A few minutes later I joined the line to wait outside Hung Sing Restaurant and Boarding House. Workers joined the boarders at Hung Sing to eat together at long tables. A poor substitute for having a family, but still far better than eating alone.

Mr. Wong owned Hung Sing, of course. He owned my father's temple and Dr. Wei's infirmary. He owned apartment buildings that would accept tenants without family connections. He bankrolled his philanthropy by running gambling halls, opium dens, and brothels, but the tong's good works more than made up for it. The unimportant people, the outsiders, looked to the Ansheng tong for protection, and for community. There were a lot of us, and the Ansheng's community mattered more than its illicit activities.

Father had told me that Mr. Wong spent his days in a room at the back of Hung Sing, meeting with his 438s. The 438s are the officials of the Ansheng, the men who run specialized branches of the larger organization. Father had been invited to the back room a number of times, and still boasted about it.

Delicious smells came from the restaurant. Fish fried in sesame oil. Pork and onions grilled in a plum sauce. I could almost taste the anise and cloves in the five-spice powder. The aroma of steamed rice made me hungry. I had to abstain from rice and other grains if I wanted my magic to function at its best. But the smell still made my mouth water.

"Will I be able to go in?" my father's eye asked me.

I shook my head. "Father has hung his talismans over the door of every Ansheng tong building, Mr. Yanqiu. That's part of what Father does. He keeps people safe from spirits."

"He keeps the Ansheng tong safe from spirits, you mean," the eye on my shoulder said.

I shrugged, just to watch him wobble.

A few minutes later I had advanced to the front of the line. Leaving Mr. Yanqiu behind, I entered Hung Sing.

The men in the dining area seemed so happy, gathered in crowds. They were strangers who came here from all over China. They came without families; they came without influence. If they had hailed from a respectable region, they would be eating with the Six Companies, not the Ansheng, but that's what a tong is for. It's a community of people who have no one.

I looked around the room for a moment, taking in the aromas of food. The men sat in simple wooden chairs, eating boiled alfalfa and duck soup with glassy noodles. They talked and laughed together. Hung Sing was bustling with the noise of happiness. I felt an old, sad longing. I wanted to be part of it, to participate in their family, but I couldn't. Those who were superstitious would fear me. The others would see me as an available woman, and pursue me. No one would welcome me, a friend at their table.

Even here, in Hung Sing, I was an outsider.

I strode through the restaurant and went into the hallway in back.

The hallway was not what I expected. It was dim in the hall, hot and damp. A stale smell of sweat and musk clung to the air. There were narrow doors on each side. Some of the doors were closed, and some were ajar. From the closed rooms I heard animal sounds, grunts and moans.

I looked into an open door. Inside was a narrow room, with a bamboo chair, a washbowl, and a matted bed. A woman stood at the room's wicket window, wearing a plain peasant blouse and skirt. I noticed that she was barefoot. There was an odor of staleness and salt in the air. She called out to the alley in a tired voice. "Two bits to look, four bits to feel, six bits to do," she said.

Twenty-five cents, fifty cents, or seventy-five cents toward paying off her contract with Mr. Wong.

I shuddered. I would not be able to bear that woman's life.

I raced down the hall and burst through the door at the other end.

Mr. Wong stood at the back of a large room, flanked by a pair of bodyguards. He was feeding a parrot in a cage, and the two bodyguards stepped in between him and me, drawing their weapons.

Pistols.

On the street, tong warriors carry nothing that constables could definitely identify as a weapon. A gangster caught with a hatchet will claim he cuts wood for a living, and a woodcutter will support his claim. A gangster caught with a knife will claim he's a cook, and a restaurant owner will vouch for him. None of the Chinese would carry guns in the street.

But here, in the privacy of Mr. Wong's chamber behind Hung Sing, two men pointed their guns at me.

I hate guns. Seeing them pointed at me made me afraid, the way a small child might be afraid. I wanted to mewl and beg for protection. I wanted to cower and hide under a table until the guns were gone.

Mr. Wong was wearing a bulky black shirt with a silver badge shining on the lapel. He had thin lips and a heavy face, but more than that, Mr. Wong had gravity, like a planet. Little people, people like me, like bodyguards, had a choice: we could enter Mr. Wong's orbit, or we could crash against him.

"Step aside, little brothers," said Mr. Wong. "Let me get a look at her."

Still cautious, still aiming their pistols at me, Mr. Wong's bodyguards stepped aside, and then he looked me up and down. Mr. Wong's lips twitched when his eyes reached my feet. "Big," he said simply, and somehow I felt repulsive.

I started to speak, but the younger bodyguard caught my eye. Recognition dawned on me. I knew the bodyguard. Hong Xiaohao and I had learned English together, at the Mission. Later, after my husband died, Xiaohao wanted to court me, but I was determined to remain a chaste widow. It had cost me much to choose a life of loneliness. Xiaohao had been one of the few who looked past my odd eyebrows and big feet; when he looked at me, he saw more than the exorcist's daughter, more than the young widow. And I had rejected him.

Xiaohao's eyes were always relentlessly bland, but his mouth revealed all those things other men express with their eyes. If he curled the edges of his lips one way, it meant he was feeling haughty; a slight difference in the lip-curl meant he was feeling shy. And right now, his lips were giving me a warning.

"Have a contract drawn up," Mr. Wong told his older bodyguard, and turned back to his parrot. Facing the bird, he said, "Three years. Thirty percent less than usual on account of the feet."

I stammered. This was going wrong, all wrong. "Mr. Wong, I—"

"Be silent," he said.

Hong Xiaohao's lips moved and he turned his shoulders so he faced the corner of the room. I followed his gaze.

A woman was standing in the corner, behind a table and chairs. She'd been so quiet and motionless that I hadn't even noticed her. Facing the wall, she wore a red qipao dress with long sleeves. Leaning against the wall near her was a bamboo cane. It looked sturdy, solid. It was about five feet long.

It had been used to beat her.

So that's how it was. In this place, where women under contract spread their legs for six bits, a woman who spoke out of turn would be punished with a caning.

Mr. Wong's parrot cooed, and he murmured a gentle response.

I found myself angered, though I knew it was not the time for anger. I had no wish to be punished, to be reduced before these men.

I stared for a moment, uncertain. If I spoke at all, I would be violating a kind of unwritten rule here, and I might anger Mr. Wong. If I spoke I might be punished.

"Daoshi Xian Zhengying has been injured," I blurted out.

Mr. Wong turned his face to me and I felt the weight of his gaze. Scrutinizing. Then he spoke. "You are the Daoshi's daughter," he said simply. I nodded.

He turned his body toward me. "I thought you wanted to be a contract girl," he said. He shrugged. "It is no loss of face for my friend the Daoshi. Will he be all right?"

I relaxed a little, and bowed. "Yes, Mr. Wong. He is recuperating at Dr. Wei's infirmary. Mr. Wong, Father wanted me to ask you about a man who recently came to Gold Mountain." Father had asked no such thing of me, but the lie would hurt no one.

He raised an eyebrow. "Hundreds of immigrants come here every year."

I bowed again. "Yes, Mr. Wong. This man has only one arm. His name is Liu Qiang."

An expression crossed Mr. Wong's face, like a cloud blown in front of the moon. He gave a gesture to his bodyguards. Hong Xiaohao and the older man strode out of the room, probably to wait outside. I heard the door swing shut and relaxed a little, out of the presence of the pistols.

Mr. Wong walked to the table in the far corner of the room, near where the contract girl was being disciplined. He sat down in a chair facing the wall and gestured for me to take the chair opposite. I sat, and he said, "Bring me a bottle of rice wine and a cup, whore."

Blood rushed into my head. I gaped at him. It felt like a slap across my face. I began to tremble from emotion. It was shame and fear but anger was bubbling too, and I found my hands hardening to iron, my fingers shaping Sword Trees. But then the woman at the wall shot into motion and I realized he hadn't been talking to me. She sped across the floor surprisingly fast for a woman with bound feet. I began to calm down, but then the other implications of his words sank in.

A bottle of rice wine and a cup. One cup. He would make the woman pour him a cup of rice wine, and he'd offer me none. Father had always been skilled at establishing his place in the social order. I was not.

If Mr. Wong had asked for two cups, and served me first, it would mean he was showing respect to a superior. If he'd served me second, he would have been addressing me as an equal who was a guest in his home. If he'd had two cups brought out and then made me serve myself, it would demonstrate that he considered me an underling.

A cup for himself and none for me meant one of two things. Either he saw me as a stranger who had come to his door begging for alms, or he saw me as an enemy. If he saw me as a beggar, he would drink the rice wine. If he saw me as an enemy, he would pour it out on the ground.

I was completely unnerved. I needed to find out more about Liu Qiang, and I needed to understand what Mr. Wong was planning to do with the corpses in the gold mines. But before he would tell me anything, he was going to insult me, and make me accept it.

I lowered my head. "Mr. Wong, sir, please will you tell me what you know about Liu Qiang?"

Mr. Wong began to speak, his voice deep and rumbling. "I will tell you in good time, girl," he said. "Do you see this badge?"

I nodded, puzzled and frustrated. Here, in Mr. Wong's place of business, the most powerful man in Chinatown was going to share information when he chose, if at all.

"This badge was given to me by the Governor of the State of California." He touched it with his fingers, and pride gleamed in his eyes. The badge was silver, and the word *Sheriff* was engraved in it. "I united Chinatown. I made order. Men came to Gold Mountain, and I provided them with shelter, found them work, and offered them protection. People called me the Mayor of Chinatown back then. Back when I could walk my streets without body-guards, without chainmail under my shirt."

The woman in the red dress returned, carrying a tray with a bottle and a cup. I sat tense on the chair, waiting to learn whether he saw me as a stranger or an enemy. The woman filled his cup and placed it on the table, then stepped away, waiting for further instruction.

She was good at this, I realized. She had a skill for disappearing from men's eyes. Subservience had taught her a kind of invisibility. In a different context, such vanishings could be deadly. It was a skill worth learning, I decided.

"Five years ago, a man came here. To this very room." Mr. Wong sneered, recollecting. "He stood here in this room and asked for half."

He paused. Mr. Wong was telling a story, I realized. He was waiting for me to ask the obvious. "Half?" I obliged.

"Half," he repeated. "Half of Chinatown. And who was he? He was nobody. He was piss. I laughed in his face, and then some of my little brothers beat him."

He picked up his cup and lifted it toward his mouth. It looked like he was about to drink from it, but he hesitated. "That man," he said, and placed the cup back on the table, while a look of total abhorrence crossed his face. "That filth. Prancing around in his American clothes. What kind of man names himself after a *vegetable*?"

I tapped my feet under the table anxiously.

Mr. Wong held his cup in both hands, running a finger over the rim as he spoke. "Bok Choy," he muttered darkly, and the name set Mr. Wong's parrot into a commotion.

"Bok Choy! Bok Choy!" the bird mimicked. "Fuck his ancestors to the eighteenth generation!"

I gaped at the parrot. The bird had shown me the depth of Mr. Wong's hatred, more than anything he could say. How many hours he must have spent in this room, dis-cussing business with his 438s, cursing Bok Choy's name so often that the parrot had learned his expressions. I turned back to face Mr. Wong.

"Within a year, my profits were down. It had taken me so many years to build the Ansheng tong, and so quickly it began to fail. My fantan tables were empty. Bok Choy and the Xie Liang tong took over gambling first. And he wanted the rest, he wanted it all now. A ship from China was robbed before we could unload our goods. Bok Choy stole our cargo, girls and opium, and I still had to pay for it."

Hands shaking with rage, he put the cup back on the table. "He found a Christian minister—a minister!—and started him on a crusade against vice in Chinatown. Bok Choy tells him where to find my gambling halls and opium dens, and then the minister shows up with constables and they shut me down."

"Why don't you have his businesses shut down too?"

His gaze fell on me like a weight. "Because he only tells the minister about my smaller businesses. If I were to retaliate in any way, Bok Choy would have my bigger ones shut down." He put his head in his hands, a helpless gesture. "And then one of his men and one of mine got into a fight, over something meaningless, like a woman. And the tongs went to war for five days."

"I remember," I said. For five days, hatchetmen ran through the streets, livid with vengeance. The tong war left a dozen men dead.

"Those were good men, my men. Do you know what I call the young men who work for me?"

"Little brothers," I said, allowing him to tell his story as he saw fit. I still couldn't tell what this had to do with Liu Qiang, but I had spent the years of my life among older men. They like to talk in stories.

"Little brothers," he repeated.

Mr. Wong let out a heavy sigh.

"I have sent assassins, of course. Bok Choy can't even shoot straight. Do you know what he does in a gunfight? He takes a .45-caliber pistol in each hand, and then he closes his eyes. With his eyes closed, he squats down and spins around, shooting at random. He could shoot his friends or his bodyguards by accident. He's no warrior. My assassins should have killed him." He looked down at the floor and fidgeted with his silver badge.

"He has their corpses brought here in the night. Here, to my restaurant. He leaves the corpses of my little brothers on my front step. My Daoshi makes sure their corpses are well treated, their names revered in the Hall of Ancestors."

He clasped his hands together. "I have the best Daoshi in America working for me," he said. "Fifteen years ago I brought him here from China. He was fleeing something, and he had his daughter."

I sat alert, suddenly interested. I hadn't come here today expecting to learn about my past. What did he mean, Father was fleeing something? This was something Father had never told me.

"The American officials wouldn't let him in. Not with a daughter. It was the Chinese Exclusion Act. I sent him letters. Leave the girl behind, I said. Sell her, there's always someone willing to buy a girl. But he wouldn't. He wouldn't come here without her."

I stared at him. My mouth was open in a perfect circle. What he was saying couldn't be true. If it was true, it meant I had misunderstood my father for a lifetime. If it was true, it meant he valued me more than he'd ever led me to believe. I had spent my life wishing I could make him proud of me, and Mr. Wong was telling me that my father valued me all along.

"He wouldn't leave me behind?" I asked in a tiny voice.

"He wouldn't leave you," Mr. Wong repeated. "So I had to bribe the officials to classify him as a merchant. It cost me a fortune. A fortune! It cost a fortune to bring the great Daoshi Xian Zhengying and his daughter to Chinatown."

I sat there, stunned. Father always seemed so severe, so distant. And yet Mr. Wong was telling me that Father risked staying in China rather than leave me behind. It didn't make sense at all. He had given his eye for me, but he had only done it to save face. What had he hoped to gain by refusing to leave me behind?

Mr. Wong picked up his cup of rice wine and took a sip. But it seemed casual, unthinking; did it mean he considered me no enemy? Or had he simply forgotten? I had no way to tell. I was full of hope and confusion, a mess of childish emotion, and utterly bewildered.

"All this I did for your father, and he would not do the one thing the Ansheng tong needed most. He would not summon evil spirits to kill Bok Choy."

I felt suddenly cold. Horror washed over me as the words sank in. I pushed back my chair, ready to run, ready to fight. My pulses were racing. "You asked him to unleash monsters in Chinatown?" Outrage was plain in my voice.

Mr. Wong raised a hand to silence me. "For three years I asked this thing of him. For three years he refused. 'It would go against the ideals of my lineage,' he said. It took me a long time to accept his position. Daoshi Xian Zhengying honors his lineage, his ancestors. He is a man who does not compromise. I hope to honor my ancestors as he honors his." Mr. Wong looked down and away. I felt my pulses begin to calm down.

"Some of my 438s did not feel the same way. They watched our businesses go under, they saw their glory extinguished, and they saw Bok Choy and his American ways gain in power. They have been saying I am too old. My ways are too Chinese, too old-fashioned, they say. There is one man in particular," he said, and I saw pain in his eyes, "one in particular who disagrees with me."

The pain made it clear to me. "Tom," I said. Mr. Wong gave a slow, heavy nod.

"Tom said I should not tolerate your father's insubordination. He said if your father refuses to summon monsters to kill Bok Choy, we should hire someone who will do as he's asked."

"Liu Qiang," I said. My hand involuntarily went to touch the cuts on my stomach.

Mr. Wong gave a barely affirmative gesture, and continued. "My son and a number of his friends are acting outside my authority now. They issue commands in my name but I have not asked them to do as they're doing. There is disharmony among the Ansheng tong. There are sworn brothers who follow my son and not me. I do not know how many. Others follow Tom's commands, believing they came from me."

I watched his face, weary and heavy. I could hardly imagine all the years he had spent building the Ansheng tong into what it was, both a surrogate family and a criminal empire. First he watched it lose power and status to the upstart Bok Choy, and now he was watching his organization fracture. How it must have broken his heart, and how much more it must have hurt him to know the man trying to overthrow him was his own son.

I looked at Mr. Wong, the great man of Chinatown, who had done so much for so many, including Father and me. He was lost in thought, and seemed alone. If I showed sympathy, I would cause him to lose face. I needed to take advantage of the moment.

"Will you tell me about the miners?" I asked.

"Miners?" he said, turning to me. He looked baffled.

"The corpses in the gold mine. I was told you had them exhumed to send their bones to China."

"No," he said, "I have ordered no such thing. It must be Tom's doing. But what would Tom want with corpses?"

"I don't know, Mr. Wong," I said.

"Whore!" he said. The contract girl and I both jumped. He turned to her. "Why did you bring only one cup for rice wine?"

"I . . . it was my mistake, Mr. Wong," she said. She fled to bring me a cup.

He waited for her to leave. Once the door was closed behind her, we were alone, and he looked at me with a gaze of centuries. "I will not help you fight my son, Xian Li-lin. If you need allies, go seek out the Xie Liang tong, and tell them Bok Choy is in danger," he told me.

"Mr. Wong," I said slowly, "the Ansheng tong is my whole world. I will not work with the Xie Liangs."

"Go to them if you need help," he repeated, and the next words he spoke felt like he had etched them in granite. "But if my son must be killed, I want you to do it, not some Xie Liang scum."

My eyes went wide but I said nothing. He had made certain no one else was in the room. He had advised me to seek aid from his enemies, he had given me permission to kill his son, and he had made sure no one would witness him saying these things.

I could not believe a rift had grown so wide between Mr. Wong and his son. Tom was a good man; filial piety had always mattered to him.

The woman returned with a cup and placed it down in front of me, full of steaming rice wine. Mr. Wong offered me much face with this gesture, so I had to drink it. I took a sip and the rice wine flowed into my mouth, warm and pleasant, and left a burning sensation when I swallowed. I loved it.

"Your face is red," Mr. Wong said with some amusement.

"Your rice wine is excellent," I replied.

"It is rice wine," he said. He stood then, and bowed. I stood also, bowed more deeply than he, and then I went to the door.

I walked out through the hall of whores, trying not to hear the sounds of men and women moving together on straw cots. A few moments later, I emerged into the pleasant clamor of men dining at Hung Sing, and the mouthwatering aroma of cooking.

Mr. Wong was a deep and strange man, I thought. He was caught up in conflicts both internal and external. He seemed to have little respect for women, but he showed me some respect. He encouraged me to go to his enemies for help, and yet I was certain he would show me no mercy if I did. He shared his rice wine with me today, but he had no intention of ever doing so again.

He asked me, as a kind of favor, to become his enemy. If I killed Tom, he would mourn his son. And I was certain he would owe me a secret debt.

My head full of doubts, I walked through the restaurant, out of Ansheng headquarters, and into the street.

There were seagulls crying and I heard my name among the seagulls' cry.

Four men loitered in the street. They'd been waiting for me.

One of them was Tom Wong. One of them was Hong Xiaohao.

And one of them was Liu Qiang.

FOURTEEN

Liu Qiang's arm should have ended in a stump. It would have looked that way to anyone who didn't have yin eyes. But now there was a spirit at the end of the stump. It was sickly white and thick as an arm. It moved like an arm, but also like a snake, and it was longer than an arm should be, six or seven feet long. The spirit arm was pale as mold and it writhed like a rabid animal.

Where a human arm ends in a hand, Liu Qiang's spirit arm ended in some kind of monstrous reptile head. A yellow forked tongue flicked out between needle-thin fangs. The snake's red eyes—all three of them—watched me with a cruel intelligence. Whatever it was, I had the feeling it wanted to make me suffer.

The spirit-snake looked like it had been grafted onto Liu Qiang's arm. My father's sword had severed the bone and muscle, and somehow Liu Qiang had interwoven this snaking, dangerous spirit with his own flesh. The bones and muscles of the man's spirit body had been torn apart and knit together into the body of this yaoguai. It must have been agony to endure the bonding.

Liu Qiang was dangerous, far more dangerous than my father had led me to believe. Powerful sorcery bound that arm to him, and I had no idea what it could do. He no longer seemed to be off-balance; his spirit arm balanced his movements, so he stalked with a predatory grace.

Somehow, earlier, when he walked into Father's temple, he left the arm behind. Father's talismans would have barred its entry. But that meant the snaking phantom was bound to Liu, and yet independent of him. They were two, and yet one. I had to treat Liu Qiang and his arm as two separate opponents until I knew more about the spirit-arm's abilities—and its mind.

The spirit-arm gazed at me, hatred evident in its three red eyes. Then it opened its mouth and spoke, in a voice like claws ripping against flesh and bone. "The baby means to fight," it said to Liu Qiang. The other men couldn't hear it, didn't seem to know it was there.

I stared at the monster and shuddered. "I want to eat the baby," it said, its voice sickening as the sound of nails being driven through eyelids.

I glanced around at the rest of the men. I didn't know the fourth man, but his short hair and shaved fore-head could only mean one thing. He'd gotten out of prison recently. Barbers had clipped off his queue in prison, and now he was growing it back. He stood stiff and alert, like a city guard. His face seemed hard, almost pitiless. It was the look of an enforcer.

The four of them had me surrounded. In a fair fight I might stand a chance against four unskilled men. But Tom Wong used to spar with Rocket, and Liu Qiang had trained alongside Father, so at least two of them had some training. And there was no telling what Liu Qiang's monstrous arm could do.

I do not hide from monsters, but facing them here, on the street, I couldn't hope to win. I could only fight and die, and then they would come for Father while he was still recuperating, and then there would be no one left who could stop their plans. I knew what I needed to do. I needed to get away.

"Tom," I said, facing him, "don't do this."

My husband's friend looked down and away, then looked back to me and shrugged. "Sorry," he said.

I turned to Xiaohao, whose lips were pursed and inexpressive. "Xiaohao," I said, "two years ago you wanted me for a wife."

He said nothing, only smiled; and in his grim smile I saw a world of confusion. Hong Xiaohao had no idea what he was doing here. He had wanted to become a little brother of the Ansheng tong, and now he was involved in schemes he didn't understand. I gave a frustrated huff.

The man without a queue leered at me. "My Tiger Style can kick apart your Crane Legs," he said.

Tom Wong backhanded him, knocking the leer off his face. "Never," Tom said to the other man, "never talk to her like that."

The other man wiped blood from his lips. "I don't understand," he said.

Tom's voice was hard as iron. "You can fight her, you can even kill her if you have to," he said. "But never forget that she's my friend's wife. You will show him respect. Do nothing, say nothing, that will cause Rocket to lose face. Do you understand?"

The short-haired man dropped his eyes and nodded.

I stared at Tom, taken aback by the intensity of his feeling, the contradictory impulses of a man who would allow me to be killed but protect me from insult. There was a part of me that still cared about my husband's friend, and maybe there was a part of him that still cared about me. But it wasn't about me, I realized; it was Rocket, my dead husband, who mattered to him.

"Tom," I said. "Let me go. You were my husband's friend."

"You think I've forgotten that, Li-lin?" Anger and pain distorted his pretty face. "I'm doing this *because of* Rocket!" Tom shouted.

"What are you saying?" I felt dizzy. I felt ill. It felt like a wound had been torn open, and all I could do was watch the blood seep out, oblivious of all else. "Tom," I began, "if you think my husband would support what you're doing, you never knew him at all."

"Of course he wouldn't support this, Li-lin! He was a hero. But there's no place for heroes anymore." Tom looked at me with anguish in his eyes. "Rocket was the strongest. No one could match his skill in kung fu. And none of it mattered, none of his strength and courage and brilliance mattered when they shot him, pow pow."

Tom Wong was quiet, facing me.

"My husband died, Tom, and no one mourns him more than I do," I said. "I am your friend's wife, and I have been faithful to him, his chaste widow, and yet you allowed a man to bare my skin and cut me. How can you justify the things you've done?"

Tom's eyes were hollow with old pain. "Everything is different now," he said, his voice bitter. "When they shot him, everything changed. That's when I realized the old ways aren't enough. We can't live by the old rules, Li-lin. Kung fu is useless when they have guns, and magic is worthless if you won't use it to kill your enemies."

"Tom," I said, shaking my head. "You don't know the horrors you're stirring up. A weapon is as good or evil as the hand that holds it, but magic doesn't work that way. Liu Qiang's magic is filthy."

The monstrous arm made a sound then, a hideous screech like iron against bone, and I realized it was laughing.

"Want to eat the baby's hands," it said, in its horror of a voice. It wanted to eat me, but it wanted to cripple me first. I didn't comprehend why anything would hate me so much.

Liu Qiang's lips were trembling. He stepped closer to me and yelled, "You call it filthy, but it's stronger! After tomorrow night, everyone will know my magic is stronger!"

Tomorrow night. I made sure I would remember it. And then Liu Qiang blew stupefying powder in my face.

I had been learning for as long as I could remember.

The women at the mission taught me English. They taught me to add, subtract, multiply, and divide, to weigh ounces and pounds, to measure inches, feet, and miles. Everything else, my father taught me.

My yin eyes were the result of an imbalance, and it was important to him to balance my yin with yang. So he taught me the martial arts of Mount Wudang, and he taught me the Dao.

He taught me through repetition and he taught me through scorn. I studied the Daolu Registers until I could name eighty thousand gods and demons. I could not count the hours spent practicing taiji postures, or the hours scribbling with my left hand, drawing down the moon through my closed eyes, until I could write in ghostscript.

Of all the forms of learning, I loved sparring the best. I loved standing up, facing an opponent, ready to strike or be struck. There was something about those moments facing an opponent, all my skill and intelligence pitted against another human being in a few minutes of all-consuming alertness.

But I also loved listening to my father when he would tell me stories. He told stories of the immortals and stories of the Daoshi. There were stories of men brave enough, clever enough, or hungry enough to overcome monsters. There was a man who sold a ghost into slavery, and another man who fried a ghost and ate it. He told me stories where men married foxes, women fought like men, outlaws stood up to injustice, immortals could speak in thunderclaps, and evil men practiced the forbidden skill called dian-si-shuei, the death touch—striking five points along a victim's body to cause instant death.

I was ten years old when my father told me about the scholar Wang Zhaosu. Wang made some philosophical arguments about the nature of the universe. His arguments made little impression on me. What I remembered of Wang Zhaosu was that he was capable of turtle breathing.

Wang Zhaosu could take a single breath and make it last for eight minutes. Eight minutes of heightened awareness.

I was ten years old and turtle breathing became my obsession. Slowing the breath, awakening the spirit. When Father was busy I practiced it. I would inhale deeply and let the vital breath fill me. The vital breath moved through me with an electric tingling to the tips of my fingers.

Twenty-second breaths. Thirty-second breaths. Ninety-second breaths. I got better and better.

I was up to five minutes. Two and a half minutes breathing in, two and a half minutes breathing out.

Liu Qiang blew a puff of yellow powder in my face. I had no time to inhale. That meant I had to hold the breath in my lungs. It meant I had two and a half minutes before I needed to gulp down air.

After so many years of training, holding my breath brought mental clarity. It brought instant-to-instant focus and a deep calm from which I could make decisions. A cloud of yellowish powder floated in the air near my face. And all these men thought I had been drugged.

A sudden elation burst through me. Finally, I held an advantage.

I let my eyes slip out of focus, and brought a drunken quality to my stance. Was this how it looked to be stupefied? I wondered. Would I fool them? And which of them would act first?

It was Tom. I should have known—he needed to assert his leadership. He reached an arm out and took a grip on my left shoulder. I looked up into his eyes and saw a hardness in his face that had never been a part of Rocket's pretty friend, and I took his elbow in my left hand and yanked him forward. Toward me. I forced out the last of my remaining breath and blew the stupefying powder at him.

If all went well, the powder would stun him, but I couldn't wait to find out if it worked. I drew my rope dart and swung my right knee up in a spinning jump. My knee took Tom Wong in the chest and I shot my rope dart out behind me, throwing it into a spin.

Liu Qiang's monstrous arm snapped at me, its jaws wide, its teeth needle-sharp and deadly. I dropped to the ground to evade it and its mouth clicked shut on the air above my head. I rolled backward, keeping my rope dart in motion.

Tom Wong was advancing on me. He hadn't been stupefied. But I wasn't surrounded any longer; there was no one behind me. The intensity of life-or-death combat filled me with a kind of burning focus. I knew where all four men were standing, I knew where Liu Qiang's arm was, and I knew what they were doing. I could feel them, sense their presence. There was nothing in my mind but them, nothing but me and them.

I spun my rope dart faster and faster. Its whirring motion formed a barrier, but Liu Qiang's spirit arm could pass right through the dart. With my left hand I drew my peachwood sword, holding it in reverse grip, like a dagger.

I faced the four men and the monstrous arm. For a moment everything was held in perfect stillness, like a painting, aside from the whirring rope dart.

Liu Qiang's arm coiled in silence, pale as dead flesh, opening and closing a mouth lined with needle-sharp teeth. Its three eyes studied me, unblinking. Its eyes were the red of fresh blood, and I had a sense that nothing would make it happier than seeing me suffer. Making me suffer.

Hong Xiaohao stood back from the other men, watching them, watching me. His lips curled in a way I couldn't interpret. He lifted his leather club, and suddenly I knew what the look on his mouth meant.

Tom turned back to face me. We assessed each other for an instant that felt like an hour. My rope dart was spinning fast enough that the iron weight could shatter stone, but Tom Wong was good enough that a rope dart wouldn't stop him. All he had to do was get the timing right and grab the rope at just the right moment.

He grabbed the rope at just the right moment. He gave me a pretty smile, and began to speak. He was probably intending to gloat. But then Hong Xiaohao brought his club down on the back of Tom's head.

There was a heavy thud and Tom stumbled forward. He turned to face his assailant, which gave me the opportunity I needed. I shot a kick at the back of Tom's knee. It connected and his leg gave out under him. He dropped to one knee and I coiled my rope dart's cord around his throat, cutting off his circulation.

"Li-lin," he choked, "please." He tried to drive a finger under the rope line, but he couldn't find a hold.

Xiaohao stood back, in a defensive posture. If he had any significant amount of training, I didn't know about it. The man from prison faced him with a look like stone, and Liu Qiang regarded Xiaohao and me almost idly. Deciding which one to go after first.

Liu Qiang's arm reared back, coiling like a snake, and it launched forward and struck at Xiaohao with a speed that was astonishing, almost too fast to see. Its jaws snapped shut on Xiaohao's neck. The young man's lips said nothing, but they spoke to me of hope and loss, of decency and effort. He reached a hand toward his throat, but his arm was already going limp. Bleeding punctures opened on his neck. The snake-arm lifted him four feet in the air and tossed him aside like a shovelful of dirt. What landed on the street was a corpse.

Watching Xiaohao die filled me with a sense of horror, and a kind of helplessness I loathed feeling. The man who'd recently been to prison looked at Liu Qiang, and there was fear on his face.

Liu Qiang's arm looked ecstatic, as though there were no greater rapture than murder. I was afraid of it, and I felt something inside me keening and mourning Xiaohao. He had sided with me, and it cost him his life. Another good man, another senseless death.

Tom Wong sprang to his feet. Raging, in a burst of motion, he yanked the rope from my hands and threw it to the ground. Foolish, Li-lin. I let a moment of grief rob my focus and now Tom Wong was free to attack me again.

He came at me like a thunderstorm. He was furious now, and his indiscriminate onslaught was all power and no finesse. I pushed aside a cross punch, elbowed him in the ribs, and took a step back.

Rage made him imprecise. That gave me an advantage. I needed to use that, to feed his anger.

"Oh, Tom," I said, taunting, "here you are in front of Hung Sing, your father's restaurant, in plain view of the street, and a woman forced you to your knees. Such a loss of face."

He looked around. People were walking by, pretending they had seen nothing. A corpse lay on the street and no one would ever admit seeing him die. Men climbed down from a cable car and immediately looked away from the street fight. The line of men in front of Hung Sing stared resolutely forward, not looking. No one was looking, but everything was witnessed, and everything would be told, and told again; where there are people, there is gossip.

"Such a loss of face," I repeated, shaking my head.

Tom's muscles were rigid. Self-control didn't seem to be one of his gifts. "Face," he said, "is the old way. This world has no place for heroes any longer, and there's no place for face, or filial piety, or sworn brothers. Only power matters. Power is the new way. Kill her, Mr. Liu."

I switched the peachwood sword to my right hand. Liu Qiang's spirit arm watched me, its three eyes cunning. It knew what peachwood could do to it.

"Power?" I asked. "You expect power from Liu Qiang?"

"Oh yes, Li-lin," Tom said, his eyes bright with a sense of glory. "More power than you've ever seen."

Keeping myself safe with the peachwood sword, I bent down and retrieved my rope dart. I faced Tom Wong and said, "You know, Tom, my father pissed in his face once."

Liu Qiang gave an enraged, inarticulate shout. I stuck out my tongue at him, then turned and ran.

Behind me I heard Tom Wong say, "Let her go. There's no way she can stop us."

I went home and added a name to the Hall of Ancestors. "Hong Xiaohao," I said, "I would not be your wife, but you were a good man. I will wail at your grave." I touched the paper with his name on it to my forehead, then lit a candle. "I will light a candle each day," I said, "for forty-nine days, and burn you paper offerings."

There were tears in my eyes as I thought of Xiaohao. He had wanted to marry me, but even though I had rejected him, he had stood up for me when I was alone among my enemies. He did it, knowing it would gain him nothing, knowing he would probably die for it.

"I will find you a wife," I said. "A woman who died young. And I will perform a ghost wedding for the two of you." He would be able to have a family in the lands hereafter. It was the best I could do for him.

I went next to the Tong Sheng, the celestial almanac. With both hands, I took the heavy tome and leafed through its thin rice-paper pages until I found the next day's charts. For a few minutes I studied the charts, committing the astrological relations to memory.

Then I walked to the infirmary and filled Father in on everything I had learned. I told him what Mr. Wong had told me, what Liu Qiang had said, and I told him of Hong Xiaohao's death.

"This is going to happen tomorrow night?" he said.

"Yes, Father."

He looked away, his expression contemplative, severe. "There must be a reason for that. I need to know what kind of spell would be most auspicious for tomorrow night. Ah Li, you will go and study the star charts in the Tong Sheng."

"Father, I—"

"I will need to know tomorrow night's readings, the ten celestial stems and twelve earthly branches in yin."

"Father—"

"Which of us speaks first?" he asked.

I hung my head. I felt ashamed for being disrespectful toward my father, but frustrated too.

"While you are there, make sure you learn the aspect of the moon and its location during the hour of the First Earthly Branch. Commit all that to memory and return here at once."

I took a frustrated breath and let it out. "Father, I studied the Tong Sheng before I came here."

He looked at me, startled. I let a moment pass, but I had learned, long ago, not to expect praise. I said, "Tomorrow night, it will be the Earth phase, Dog year, Autumn season, Mountain trigram. Tomorrow night the lunar month is Earth, the celestial stem yin is wu, and the terrestrial branch yin is xu."

He listened closely, doing calculations in his head. "Earth produces Metal, conquers Water, is conquered by Wood, masked by Fire," he said in a mumble. "Stem and branch in yin, born from stars and branching to earth, is wuxu." He seemed lost in thought for a moment, then he turned his eye toward me with a sudden sharp focus. "And the aspect and position of the moon during the hour of the First Earthly Branch?"

"The moon will be sparkling, in the palace of Wei."

"Wei, the Gateway of Man," he said. "Subconstellation?"

"Jishi, Father."

"Jishi . . ." A stricken look crossed my father's face. "It couldn't be. He wouldn't dare. And yet the corpses . . ."

"What, Father? What is it?"

He closed his eye. He sat, tense, in a silence so thick and woeful it seemed almost like he was trying to make the whole world change just because he wanted it to change. When the powers of shadow were at their strongest, the moon would be in the subconstellation Jishi—and Jishi means *Heap of Corpses*.

His eye shot open. "Liu Qiang," he said. "That rotten toad. I'm going to rip his intestines out and stuff them in his mouth."

I hesitated. "Father, what is he planning?"

Father said nothing. He turned his eye to the window and brooded. After a few minutes he looked at me.

"Do you know the story of the Kulou-Yuanling?"

Kulou meant skeleton, and a yuanling was a kind of vengeful wraith. But the terms, added together, meant nothing to me. "No, Father," I said.

He looked out the window again, and despair ruled his face. "I know of only one Kulou-Yuanling in all the history of China. There was a man who raised one once. It was seven hundred years ago, when the Song Dynasty ruled in China. Have I told you about the Song Dynasty, Ah Li?" Father was slipping into teacher mode.

"The Song was a period of great accomplishment, Father."

"It was the Chinese who invented the first compass, you know. During the Song Dynasty. We printed the first paper money. Even before the Song, it was one of the Daoshi who made use of the first Fire Medicine. Do you know what the white folk call Fire Medicine?"

"Yes, Father," I replied. "Gunpowder."

"The Song was a great period for the Daoshi. There was a temple in the north, called Golden Shrine for Contemplation of Spirit. And it was a marvel, Ah Li. It was resplendent in red and gold, and its smoke tower was a hundred feet high. There was a pond in the courtyard where it is said the deities would come to bathe. The adepts at Golden Shrine for Contemplation of Spirit spent decades consolidating the Dao Canon.

"Sometimes they found scrolls and books of vile magic. Wicked spells sprout like fungus, anywhere they can. They came along the Silk Road, like so much other commerce. The Daoshi at Golden Shrine for Contemplation of Spirit gathered foul magic from lands as far away as Japan, Malaya, and Siam. There were even instructions on how to perform dian-si-shuei, the death touch. Five strikes that kill a man in an instant." My father shuddered at the thought. Then he was quiet for a moment. "Golden Shrine's adepts locked all these evils away in a Plague Box. They cleansed the world of such vile forms of magic. It was a tremendous achievement, Ah Li. But then," he said, and his face tightened at the words, "there were the Nuzhens in the north of China."

He'd spoken about the Nuzhens before. The next words he spoke were going to be "dirty savages."

"Filthy savages," he said. "The Nuzhens refused the benevolent rule of the Song Dynasty. They united and began fighting back. They would kill people, patriots who stayed loyal to the Emperor. There were so many of the vermin, Ah Li. A horde of barbarians swarmed through the north like locusts.

"The Senior Abbot of the Shrine at Golden Shrine for Contemplation of Spirit wasn't going to let some dirty savages destroy such a marvel. So he unlocked the Plague Box where the yao shu scrolls were quarantined, and there he found a spell that would be strong enough to fight off the Nuzhen hordes.

"The spell required the corpses of a hundred men," my father said.

Things were beginning to make sense, in a sickening way. It was the logic of the Dao that appealed to me, the way everything added together in a system of perfection, a system of balance. It made me feel ill to think of a Daoshi who perverted the Dao. A Daoshi had resorted to yao shu, filthy magic. It was grotesque.

"To raise a Kulou-Yuanling," my father continued, "it takes the corpses of a hundred men who died badly. A hundred men who were murdered, who were crushed or starved to death. But even that isn't enough. Those hundred men must be unremembered. A hundred men whose corpses are unburied, whose names are not intoned in any Hall of Ancestors."

"Hao Xiongdi," I whispered. Good Brothers, a euphemism for angry ghosts.

"Yes, Good Brothers. But more than that," he said, "for their manner of death must remain with their corpses. A red miasma must linger where they died. They need to have died so badly that their death contaminates the very land."

He was quiet for a few moments, contemplating. When he spoke it sounded like he was giving a lecture. "The spell to raise a Kulou-Yuanling is similar to the spell to make a quanshen. A quanshen is dangerous enough, and it is only a single dog that died badly. Ah Li, can you imagine a monster comprised of a hundred men who died badly?"

I shook my head. He turned his eye toward the window again. "It was an Earth Dog year, in Autumn, governed by the Mountain trigram. On a night when the stars were aligned in yin, ten celestial stems to twelve terrestrial branches in wuxu, the Senior Abbot of the Shrine gathered the corpses of a hundred men. When eleven o'clock arrived, the moon was sparkling in the court of Jishi, and he performed the ritual. He raised a Kulou-Yuanling. The monster was taller than temples, and it made a noise that shook the hills.

"When the Nuzhens came to pillage Golden Shrine for Contemplation of Spirit, they found a giant monster waiting for them. The Kulou-Yuanling crushed them, Ah Li. The Nuzhen hordes fell before its onslaught as though they were insects. It ate them alive, and the sound of human bones crunching in its teeth made even the bravest of them flee.

"But the Kulou-Yuanling remained hungry. The Daoshi's control over the giant monster had its limits. The monster went out at night and devoured whatever it could find. Cows, horses, and people. The Kulou-Yuanling took them in its enormous hands and ate them alive. And still the giant monster remained hungry.

"So the Senior Abbot of the Shrine set out to destroy the Kulou-Yuanling. He was of the Seventh Ordination but his spells were not enough. He recruited every farmer from the countryside, and they fought it with spears, shovels, and hoes. The Senior Abbot used his magic and rallied the Five Ghosts, but they could do no more than slow it down.

They used Fire Medicine. Rockets, fireworks, and even primitive flamethrowers. But nothing worked, and all the Kulou-Yuanling needed to do was shout, and men would double over, clutching their heads with pain.

"Eventually, somehow, the Senior Abbot managed to defeat the Kulou-Yuanling."

"How, Father?" I asked.

"It is not known," he admitted. He was quiet for a long moment. On his face I saw the signs of old pain, internal struggle. "Do you know the name of the Senior Abbot at Golden Shrine for Contemplation of Spirit, Li-lin?"

I shook my head.

"His name was Li Zhenren," he said.

My eyes widened. "Li Zhenren, the founder of the Maoshan lineage?"

"Yes," he said. "The founder of my lineage. Li Zhenren defeated the Kulou-Yuanling. When the Nuzhens came again, he gave up Golden Shrine for Contemplation of Spirit, and fled to the south of China, with the Song Dynasty. There he founded the Maoshan lineage, dedicated to fighting spirits and suppressing yao shu."

He lay quiet, and I thought about what he'd just told me. All of it. For seven centuries, our lineage had been fighting monsters. We guarded the Ghost Gate, we appeased spirits or exorcised them, we fought monsters and sometimes we died fighting them. And this, all of this, eighty generations and more, all of it, was the result of one man trying to undo the harm he'd done. Li Zhenren raised a Kulou-Yuanling. He violated a hundred corpses to craft a monster.

Thinking of the corpses, thinking of a hundred dead men, gave me a sick feeling. I touched my stomach, and felt where Liu Qiang had cut me. The cuts still stung. Anger still coursed through me. I still wanted vengeance for what he had done to me, but somehow, that seemed small now. The cuts were small.

I wondered what Tom Wong would want with a Kulou-Yuanling. He was going to kill Bok Choy, that much was obvious. But a simpler spell could do that. A spell that didn't require a hundred corpses.

Then I remembered something Tom had said to me. "Power is the new way," he told me. Power. That's what Tom was after. He had watched my husband die and then he started thinking about power. Craving it. My husband's death taught him that guns are more powerful than martial arts. And Tom wanted something more powerful than guns.

I knew what he was planning. Tom Wong wanted to go to war, and he wanted to have the better weapon this time. The Kulou-Yuanling would be his weapon. He'd start small. He'd kill Bok Choy and slaughter that side of Chinatown. The tongs would line up behind him, terrified to do otherwise.

Constables would come. They'd bring muskets and pistols. Fire Medicine had failed before. The Kulou-Yuanling would slaughter the constables.

The army would bring cannons. They would face a giant monster, and whatever evil spirits Liu Qiang could summon. Cannons are slow to load. Iron might have no effect against a Kulou-Yuanling. It would be a massacre.

Tom wanted to teach the world a lesson. He wanted to punish the world for Rocket's death.

Something went whirring past me. I looked to the door to see what had caused the sound. When I turned back, Father was clutching his chest in pain. There were three spirit darts buried in his chest.

FIFTEEN

My father writhed, and a small moan escaped his mouth. Then I saw him exert self-control. His eye became clear and focused. Between gritted teeth, Father said, "It's just an itch. No more than that."

It was worse than an itch, I knew. Spirit darts are not a major affliction, but they are more than a nuisance, more than an itch. My father was in agony.

I should have seen them coming. I should have protected him. I had failed him once again.

"Father, it's—" I began, and then cut myself off. I looked at him on the infirmary cot. He was half-blind, swaddled in bandages, with his neck immobilized in a plaster brace. What would he do if I told him about the spirit darts? He'd probably storm to the temple and try a counterspell. The last time he'd left the infirmary, a monstrous dog had mauled him. I didn't want my father to charge out again. I decided not to let him know about the spirit darts in his chest.

Darts, not arrows. That was puzzling. A sorcerer looking to harm someone would fire spirit arrows. The darts cause pain, but they do no real damage. Three of them would cause a lot of pain, but no number would be sufficient to kill.

Father was under attack, but his attacker meant only to torment him, not to do him any real harm. It was strange.

And then I realized something else. The spirit darts had somehow been fired through the talismans outside Dr. Wei's infirmary. That shouldn't have been possible; they

were my father's talismans, and they were nearly impen-
etrable. Something must be wrong with them, and if spirit
darts could get through, so could other forms of attack.
Spirit arrows. Quanshen. Liu Qiang's arm.

The image came to mind of the spirit-arm snaking
out at Hong Xiaohao, chomping down on him with its
rows of needle-sharp teeth. Its pale white, fleshy scales. The
cruel intellect in its three eyes. The sense that it knew me,
knew me and hated me.

The infirmary's defenses had to be reinforced before
some terrible attack took place.

Father rubbed at his chest with a scowl. I stood and
bowed. "I will go and get Dr. Wei, Father," I said.

His gaze met mine, acknowledging.

I needed to find out how the spirit darts had made it
through my father's defenses, so I went downstairs to the
infirmary's front door. Outside the sun was shining. Street
vendors lined up along Dupont Street, selling their wares.
A man called out to all in range, offering to repair metal
knives, forks, plates, bowls, and cups.

I examined the string of talismans outside the infirmary's entrance. They were triangular pennants, made
of yellow cloth. There were three check marks at the top.
The white hare of the moon, the three-legged raven of the
sun, and the names of the Five Ghosts—Father's orthodox
spirit-generals—warped into ghostscript, in vermilion
ink. The Seven Stars of the Northern Bushel, the names of
gods, the bagua, Father's seal. Everything was complete.
Everything was flawless. Of course it was: my father had
made it.

Nothing from the spirit world could have crossed it.
Not yaoguai, not ghosts, and definitely not spirit darts.

I went back in through the front door. Inside, on a
wall facing the door, was a bagua mirror—a round mirror
in an octagonal wooden frame, its eight sides etched with
the trigrams of the Yi Jing. It had been positioned impec-
cably. If something had somehow made it past the row

of talismans, the bagua mirror should have deflected any spirit attack back out the door.

I found Dr. Wei in an inner room. He was leaning over a big book of herbal recipes, following their instructions to measure herbal powders into remedies. His wife was with him, and she eyed me with a suspicious look. Her jaw was square, her lips pursed, and big bamboo earrings dangled from her lobes. Her ears had been pierced, several times.

"I trust your father is comfortable, Li-lin?" asked Dr. Wei, adjusting his spectacles.

"He has an itch," I said. "It seems severe. Dr. Wei, is there a rear entrance to the infirmary?"

He gave me a long, analytical look, and then he removed his spectacles. And then he smiled.

"Why Xian Li-lin, it sounds like there's a young man out front you'd rather avoid," he said, grinning.

I blinked at his response. Then I blinked some more. "Yes, Dr. Wei," I lied, "that's it exactly."

"You should come here early in the morning sometime," he said with a smile, wiping his lenses with a cloth. "There's one of my apprentices you might find appealing."

I said nothing. This was not where I wanted the discussion to go.

"You don't intend to remain a chaste widow, do you, Li-lin?" he said, and I winced.

"I intend to honor my husband's memory."

"Rocket was a fine man, Li-lin, but he was never the kind of person who would want anyone to be unhappy for his sake. You are in your twenty-second year?"

"My twenty-third."

He shook his head. "A girl your age really ought to remarry, Li-lin. We are living in a new world now, and there's no reason for you to live by old rules. You are young and beautiful. Chinatown is full of men who would appreciate a wife like you, even one with your temper."

"My temper?" I said. "Would you like to see it, Dr. Wei?"

He smiled. "No need, I've seen it before. You're practically my niece, Li-lin, you'll behave."

I glared at him, hating the truth of it. He was someone I held in high esteem, and I would not be harsh with him, especially with his wife there.

"Don't you want the opportunity to give a man sons?" he said.

"I wanted to give Rocket sons, Dr. Wei, because the world needs more men like him. But he was gone before that happened. Now please tell me, Dr. Wei, where is there a rear entrance?"

With a disappointed look, he put his spectacles back on his face. "Yes, yes, right through there," he said, and gestured toward a hall.

I bowed, then raced down the hall and out the back door. It opened onto an alley. Hanging over the door was another string of my father's talismans. I studied them; the ink was not so fresh as the talismans at the front, but their power was intact. Nothing short of a deity should have been able to get through.

I stepped inside the door and saw another bagua mirror, perfectly positioned.

I chewed my lip and thought. If nothing could have gotten in, then it could mean only one thing: the spirit darts had been fired from inside the infirmary. The person who fired them would have need of magical tools. The patients had nothing with them but infirmary clothes. The apprentices would not have enough privacy to perform a ritual. That left only Dr. Wei and—

I sped down the hall, making sure my equipment was ready. My peachwood sword, my rope dart, my bagua mirror, my paper talismans, and some matches. I drew power into myself, what little power I could draw, and steeled myself for a confrontation. I was nervous, on edge. I had no idea what she could do.

I burst back into the room. "Dr. Wei, I need to speak with your wife. Now."

My eyes locked onto hers. She suppressed a flinch.

"Whatever for?" he asked, and before I could reply he said, "Oho, female matters."

"That's right, Dr. Wei," I said. "I need to ask your wife some questions about those female matters."

He stood and closed the book of herbal recipes. "I should check on your father's itch now anyway," he said, and pushed his glasses higher up on his nose. He left the room and closed the door behind him.

Swift as an arrow I crossed the room and shoved Dr. Wei's wife against the wall. Her back slapped against the boards. She looked terrified. "What did you do?" I demanded. "What did you do to him?"

"I don't know what—"

"Don't lie to me, woman. I'll tell your husband if I need to. He'll search your things. What do you think he'll do to you when he finds your yao shu tools?"

The look on her face slipped from fear to outrage. She said, "It's not yao shu," and spit the last words.

"Tell me what I need to know," I said.

"I will tell you nothing," she said, "you Hanzu witch."

I stared at her. "People have cursed me for a witch before, but it was never a witch who made the accusation."

"I am no witch," she said.

I hesitated. I had focused on the wrong word. "You called me Hanzu," I said. Most of the Chinese people in Gold Mountain were Hanzu.

Hate seemed to steam from her eyes. "Hanzu! Always shitting on the rest of us. No ways matter but your own."

I looked at Mrs. Wei, pinned against the wall. I looked at her ears. The big bamboo earrings, the rows of piercings, the knots in her hair. "You come from one of the tribes," I said.

Her eyes squinted. "You think that makes me less than you, child? You think that makes me a savage, a witch?"

"No," I said, holding her in place. "Attacking my father makes you a witch."

"Your father," she said, and there was venom in her tone. "The Daoshi deserved it."

I looked at her in disbelief. "Father protects China-town from evil spirits. His talismans hang over this infir-mary's doors, keeping you safe."

"Pfaugh," she spat. "I heard him. I heard him talking about the Nuzhens. Filthy savages, he called them. Just like the Hanzu said about my people."

I kept my eyes on her and thought. Mrs. Wei had acted from old hostility. She brought hurt and anger here from another country, and all the old resentments sparked into a flame when she heard my father express his scorn for an entire people. If she was telling me the truth, she had attacked in response to hearing what he said a few minutes ago.

If she was telling me the truth, she wasn't part of Liu Qiang's broader plans.

I released her and took a few wary steps back, remain-ing in an alert posture. I watched her hands for stupefying powder, for magic gestures.

She crossed her arms, regaining her composure. "The Hanzu came to my tribe and said, 'You are Chinese now.' They made us pay taxes to the Emperor. And the Hanzu brought the Daoshi with them, and the Daoshi said no one was to do Wushi anymore."

"Wushi?" I asked, surprised. "You practiced wild magic?"

"My mother was our tribe's Wushi woman," she said, her voice husky and intense, "like her mother before her. She taught me to be a Wushi woman as well."

"Wushi rituals are unorthodox," I said. "They invite chaos. Wushi practitioners call demons, ghosts, and gob-lins into their bodies. They dance all night, screaming and howling like feral animals."

Hearing my words, she looked at me with pain. "That's not how it was, child. My family's spirit servants protected our tribe for hundreds of years, but the Daoshi said they were strange monsters. The Daoshi killed the spirits who protected my people."

I took a breath. Mrs. Wei wasn't working with Liu Qiang. I believed her. I even felt sorry for her.

"Mrs. Wei, what you did to my father was unacceptable. A man came here for healing, and you sent spirit darts to afflict him. You bring shame upon your husband. You bring shame upon this infirmary, and you bring shame upon your ancestors."

Then she did something I never would have expected. She burst into tears, and then she prostrated herself on the floor. "It's true!" she said, knocking her head against the floorboards. "It's true. I have chosen a path of disgrace." She hit her head on the floor again.

I crouched down beside her, embarrassed. "Stop that," I said, and took her by the shoulders. "Stop hitting your head, Mrs. Wei."

"How can I make things right, Li-lin? How can I recover from such a loss of face?" The woman was sobbing now. I felt uncomfortable.

"Just," I said, "just break the spell. Remove the darts. And never do this again."

She looked up at me. I was still holding her shoulders. Her face was wet with tears, and her nose dribbled. She nodded. "Yes," she said, "I can do that."

She led me into her sleeping chambers. I looked at the spacious room, the large soft mattress, and envy stopped my breath. Dr. Wei had enough money that he and his wife could sleep in separate rooms. I grew up sharing a small room with my father; it had two cots, a table, a stove, and some shelves made out of scrap wood. My idea of home was a room where there were no chairs. There were workers in Chinatown who lived close together like fish in a net, twenty or thirty men in a single apartment. I was amazed to see that Mrs. Wei had a room of her own.

She reached inside a closet and withdrew a small wooden chest. Within the chest there were gongs and strings and colorful strips of cloth, long sticks of incense, ornate bells and thick candles, packets of herbs and balls of powder. She took an indigo strip of cloth and tied one end around the doorknob. She held onto the other end.

I watched her set up an impromptu altar, stacking two empty crates. Their open ends faced us; the altar had two stories. She walked to the door and placed a length of bamboo over the frame. "Copper girder," she said, and there was pride in her voice. She walked back to the altar. She placed another length of bamboo on top of the boxes, and said, "Iron girder."

This was not so different from Dao magic, I thought. Then, taking a bamboo spike in one hand, she pushed back her sleeves and began to shake. Spasms moved across her body. Every part of her, arms and legs, twitched like a man in agony. I watched her tremors in horror. "Stop this, Mrs. Wei," I said, but she continued to convulse.

Her eyes were open. They stared blankly and were clear as glass. She grunted, over and over, rhythmically, as one might sound while being beaten. She shook, but it looked almost as if something was shaking her. Her loss of control was absolute. She twitched all over. "Stop this now, Mrs. Wei," I repeated.

Still grunting, she gouged at her arm with the bamboo spike. "Stop this!" I cried. She yanked the spike back and forth along her arm, and ribbons of blood began to appear. Simply watching it made me feel violated, like Liu Qiang cutting my stomach. What kind of magic demands its practitioners to degrade and harm themselves? "Stop this now!" I shouted.

And then it was done. Her fit of spasms died down, her grunting came to an end. Her eyes returned to normal, as though a fog had cleared. She smiled at me and I found it ghoulish. "I needed to attach my bridge to the world of spirits," she said.

"Then you should find a different way." I felt scorn harden in my voice. "A clean way."

Her smile vanished, and now she pursed her lips. Shaking her head, she took the other end of the indigo cloth and tied it to her altar. The cloth stretched out between the altar and the doorknob. I gasped.

"The altar," I said. "You tied your altar to the world."

Her square-jawed face broke into another creepy smile. "Yes, I suppose that is what I did. This is a spirit bridge, Li-lin. The altar is the center of my power, and the spirit bridge is the path I follow when I want to bring my power with me to the world of spirits. But you can see that, can't you?"

I nodded, and then I caught myself. I had just admitted that I had yin eyes. Somehow I had begun to trust this strange woman, and I didn't think I wanted to.

She shook her head, and her bamboo earrings shook with her, making a faint clatter. "My mother would have been so happy to train a girl with your gift."

I stared at her, and then it all hit me like a fist, all the isolation, the misery, the freakishness, that came from being what I was. "A gift?" I cried. "Having yin eyes is a curse. My condition loses face for my father, brings shame upon his ancestors. I see monstrous spirits all around me, and I can never shut them out, no matter how hard I try. I see loneliness and pain and anger where they've been festering. I've tried every possible remedy to get rid of this 'gift.' I drank water infused with talismanic ashes every day for over a decade and still my yin eyes afflicted me. A woman with yin eyes will lead a painful life. It is no gift."

Mrs. Wei's eyes were wide, and she shook her head. "There are so many worlds," she said. "China and Gold Mountain. The Hanzu and the rest of us. Men and women. The spirit world and the world of the living. Where do you belong, Li-lin?"

Nowhere, I thought, but I said nothing. I belonged in my husband's home. That should have been my life, wife of a great man and mother to his sons. But he was gone, and my world went with him.

She sighed. "Here, Li-lin. Watch what I do next," she said, and her hands moved deftly over the spirit bridge. She made finger gestures that reminded me less of Daoist shou-jue and more of sewing. With delicate motions, her fingers found wisps in the air, so slender that they were nearly invisible. There were three wisps. She wound them around her fingers until they were tightly coiled, then she took a firm grip on the wisps with her other hand. She yanked her hands apart, and I heard the faintest of snaps.

"There," she said. "The spirit darts are no more."

The ending of the ritual had been simple and straight-forward. Like a punch.

"I need to go," I said.

"Will you . . ." she said, and then she trailed off. "What are you going to tell my husband?"

I gave her a long look and considered what I should say. "Nothing," I said. "Not now. But if you ever hurt any-one again, I will tell him, and I will tell everyone what you've done."

She nodded. Not meeting my eyes, she untied her spirit bridge from the doorknob.

SIXTEEN

Evening had fallen by the time I left the infirmary. I thought about Mrs. Wei. Sometimes it's easy to forget that the people of Chinatown are not a single people. She might be alone like me, practicing a magic that had no place here, but there was a difference. She could stop being what she was. She could remove her bamboo earrings, but I could not remove my yin eyes.

My father's eye was waiting for me on a staircase near the infirmary. I lifted him up onto my shoulder and then I started to walk the three blocks toward my home. While I was walking, I filled the little spirit in on all the things I'd learned.

"A Kulou-Yuanling," he said. "That sounds bad."

I nodded my agreement. "Tom Wong is making a show of power," I said. "He considers Bok Choy a threat to the Ansheng tong, and he thinks his father hasn't been strong enough to stop him. So he's going to demonstrate a kind of power that has never been seen in Chinatown before. He's been gathering corpses from the abandoned mines, and probably from other places too, and tomorrow night he and Liu Qiang will raise a Kulou-Yuanling."

"But that would be madness," Mr. Yanqiu said. "A monster like that could destroy half of Chinatown."

"Yes," I said. "That's what they want. They'll aim the Kulou-Yuanling at the streets that belong to the Xie Liang tong, and it will demolish everything. Tom will aim it at the businesses that defected from the Ansheng tong to the

Xie Liang. The Kulou-Yuanling will demolish buildings, devour men, and leave others destitute.

"There will be no Xie Liang tong anymore," I continued. "Everyone will be clamoring to earn Tom's favor. He thinks his father's 438s will see the wisdom of his ways and they'll make Mr. Wong step down. He thinks filial piety is an antiquated notion, just another of the old ways that must be changed."

Somehow my father's eye managed to give a sigh. "But there are people outside Chinatown, aren't there? Lots of them. They won't just sit back and tolerate some giant monster running loose in their city."

"It will start a war," I said, "and that's exactly what Tom wants. The corpses will be stacked half a mile in the air."

Mr. Yanqiu stroked a tiny hand along the place of his absent chin. "And he's doing all this for power."

"For power, and revenge," I said. "I don't think Tom has recovered from Rocket's death any more than I have."

"Yes," the eyeball said, choosing his words with care. "Will you tell me about that?"

We had arrived outside my father's temple. Mr. Yanqiu wouldn't be able to enter. "Let me get you a cup of tea," I said.

The eye looked at me with a gaze like iron. "I would love a cup of tea," he said, "but when you get back, I would like it if you would tell me about what happened."

I sighed. I didn't want to talk about it, didn't want to think about it. But my husband's death had started Tom Wong on this path, and I needed to understand Tom if I intended to fight him. "I will tell you, Mr. Yanqiu," I said. "I promise."

I went inside and began to prepare two cups of tea, one for me to drink, the other for the eyeball to soak in. I kept my emotions distant while the water heated. I didn't want to feel the pain again. I didn't want to talk about the day Rocket died, so I made my feelings go numb.

When the tea was ready, I brought it outside. I sat down on the front step and leaned my back against the brick wall. I pushed one of the cups over to Mr. Yanqiu, and he climbed inside, bathing with a contented look. "Are you ready to talk, Li-lin?" he asked me.

"It was just two years ago," I began. "Rocket was the tallest man in Chinatown, and his martial arts were beyond compare. Even his magic was amazing, since my father had ordained him to the Seventh. He had never learned any English, which made him 'a real man of China' in my father's eyes. He worked as my father's assistant. Early every morning he and I would climb to the roof of my father's temple and watch the sun come up. I was so happy. We were saving money to move to Berkeley, where Rocket was planning to open a Daoist temple of his own."

I looked away. The silence was painful. As it stretched on, I found myself wishing I hadn't started to tell the story. But I do not hide from monstrous things. "One day some white men came to Chinatown. They had worked at a boot factory, but the factory shut down and they all lost their jobs."

"So they blamed the Chinese competition," my father's eye said, fitting the pieces together. "They must have come to Chinatown looking for trouble."

I took a sip of my tea, and nodded. "They were harmless, really. They just knocked men's hats off their heads, or pulled on men's queues. They were bullies, stupid bullies, but that's all they were. Tom Wong went to find some constables. And Rocket walked up to the men.

"There was a hat lying on the boardwalk, where the men had knocked it off of someone's head. I can still remember the look on my husband's face. He was pretending to be a fool. He said, 'Look, someone lost a hat!' And then he bent down to pick up the hat, and he deliberately made his ass into a target. One of the men tried to kick him, but he stepped out of the way, as if by accident. The man fell. Still pretending he didn't know what was going on, Rocket put the hat on his head. One of the men tried to knock it off, but Rocket moved out of the way, again making it look like an accident. Over and over, the men tried to knock the hat off my husband's head, but Rocket remained just out of reach, bobbing and ducking and dodging. He never even tried to strike back. Dozens of men crowded around, watching. Rocket was playing. But the men were humiliated. The crowd was laughing at them.

"The men grew angry. They started throwing punches but they still couldn't hit him." I sipped more tea, and the memory of that day went on in my head, unfurling like a long prayer scroll. "One man tried to hit him but he bobbed to the side, and the man wound up punching his friend in the face. He broke his friend's nose.

"The men were completely unprepared. Rocket was younger, stronger, faster, more agile, and better trained. They never stood a chance. Without even striking anyone, my husband wore them down and battered them. One of them pulled out a hunting knife and Rocket pinched his wrist and disarmed him.

"I loved him so much in that moment," I said. "I was so proud of him. He defeated four bullies without ever resorting to violence. He stood there over the exhausted men, holding the hunting knife, and I thought he looked like a xiashi, a knight from the old stories.

"That was when Tom Wong returned with the constables. They took one look at the scene, a man with a big knife standing over four men who looked like they'd been thrashed, and the constables pulled out their pistols, and they started to shout at him to put down the knife, but they were shouting in English, and Rocket, he . . ."

"Had never learned English," the eye finished for me.

I started to sob. I cried like I had so many times since that day. It felt like there would never be an end to all my weeping. My father's eye spoke soothing words but they were incomprehensible to me.

I could not bring myself to tell the rest of the story. I remembered how Tom stood there shouting for the constables to stop, people were shouting at Rocket to put down the knife—but some were shouting in Guanhua and others in Yue and there were the dialects of Fujian and Wu, some with a Taishanese accent. Rocket stood there in the cacophony of shouting voices, comprehending nothing. Then thunder struck. The first bullet hit him in the shoulder, spinning him sideways. The second took him in the stomach.

The next thing I remembered, he was prone on the ground and I was holding his hand. Dr. Wei was on the other side of him, speaking slow and calm words that made no sense. Rocket looked in my eyes. There was a little blood around his lips, but he tried to smile. "Li-lin," he said. "Did I . . . ?" And then he spoke no more.

The constabulary was quick to issue a formal apology. The constables who shot him came to his funeral, bringing flowers. Flowers have no part in our customs. We wailed and burned paper offerings at my husband's grave, while the policemen stood there, awkward, with their arms full of flowers and their eyes full of regret.

The bullies came to speak with me later. They offered to do labor for me for free. They brought wood for the stove. They brought me chickens from their yards. I refused them, I refused everything, but I knew their remorse was genuine.

It was a cruel, ugly, stupid world that slaughtered my husband for no reason, and left me with no one I could hate for it.

With my husband gone, I stopped climbing to the roof to watch the sun rise. Part of me believed that dawn would never come again in a world where my husband was dead.

My father grieved as deeply as I did. He had loved Rocket like a son. My father grieved, Tom Wong grieved, and I grieved, but never did we grieve together.

Nothing made sense, nothing ever made sense since that day, and nothing would ever make sense again.

Nothing made sense but the Dao.

The Way, and its power. The perfect order that underlies the universe. I had studied the Dao all my life, because my father wanted me to study; but for the first time, I studied the Dao by my own choice. It was important for me to understand the interconnections between all things. The Dao brought harmony to the discord between yin and yang. The Dao made sense. It gave me something to believe in, and that was all that mattered.

I asked my father if I could take Rocket's place as his assistant. He reluctantly agreed. I chose to carry on my husband's mission as my own. I would become a protector, as a tribute to the man I loved.

Tom Wong grieved differently. I remembered seeing him now and then, in the months that followed. Maybe he felt guilty for bringing the constables. Maybe he blamed himself for having faith in the authorities. Tom seemed as lost as I was. He looked like his higher soul had been diminished. He lost weight, maybe twenty pounds. The color left his lips. I wanted to console him, or maybe I wanted him to console me, but somehow even talking with my husband's pretty friend would have felt like a betrayal.

No one consoled me, and I immersed myself in the Dao. Now I realized Tom had found something different to believe in. He would never trust any authorities to protect him again. Instead he had come to believe in standing up to his enemies, gaining power at any cost, and proving that power to the world. After tomorrow night, all the people of Chinatown would tremble at his name. Soon enough the whole world would quake in fear. Tomorrow night, a Kulou-Yuanling was going to rise. An old terror would re-enter the world.

"Unless I stop it," I said out loud, and it was then I realized I had stopped crying.

"Stop what?" Mr. Yanqiu asked.

"The ritual. That's the weak point. If Liu Qiang manages to complete the ritual, then the Kulou-Yuanling will rise. It will kill everyone in its path. It will destroy everything. And no one will be able to fight it."

"Stop the ritual, and you stop the monster," the eye mused.

"That's a plan," I said.

"That's not a plan," the eye said, turning in the teacup to face me, "that's an idiot telling a moron to do something stupid. You can't fight them, Li-lin, and you know it. You don't even know how many of the hatchetmen are following Tom Wong. And then there's Liu Qiang! It would be dire enough if you had to fight a Daoshi of the Fifth Ordination, but he went and became a soulstealer and learned some yao shu and he can call upon evil spirits, and did I forget to mention something? Oh yes," he said, "his arm is a great big snake monster! With three eyes!"

"You think I should let my father handle this."

"Obviously."

I scowled at Mr. Yanqiu. He was clearly my father's eye. "Why haven't I destroyed you yet?"

He shrugged. "I'm giving you good advice here, Li-lin."

"You're still trying to save me," I said.

"It's my nature."

"You could find a hobby."

"Saving you is my hobby. It's like gambling—a reckless, self-destructive hobby that only a fool would pursue."

I smiled, glad for a little levity. "Mr. Yanqiu, my father is resting in an infirmary bed. He was still recuperating from gouging out his eye when a big dog monster chewed him half to death. He shouldn't even be standing up right now, let alone going off to fight."

The eye appraised me from his cup. "So what do you think you should do?"

"I'm not sure," I said, taking a sip of my tea. "I can find allies."

"Mrs. Wei offered to teach you her magic."

"I won't be taking her offer," I said. "First, her magic rituals involve shen-da, activities which harm the body."

"Like gouging her arm?"

"Yes, like that, but if I were to perform shen-da, I'd also probably need to slit my tongue, pierce my cheeks with a spike, or beat myself with a barbed rod. I might need to burn my fingertips until they lose sensation, or roll naked over thorny branches."

"I see," Mr. Yanqiu said.

"With a bloodied tongue, my incantations would be weaker. With burned fingers, my shoujue gestures would be less precise. After beating myself or rolling in thorns, I would not fight as well."

"That all makes sense," the eyeball said. "But what if her magic would give you what you need to beat Liu Qiang?"

I smiled. "That brings me to my second point, Mr. Yanqiu. Her magic wouldn't give me enough."

"How do you know, Li-lin?"

"Mrs. Wei said as much. She offered to teach me her people's magic, and she offered to help me find her people's spirit servants. But she also told me the Daoshi defeated her people's spells and killed their spirits."

"I see," Mr. Yanqiu said. "Asking for Mrs. Wei's help would mean inflicting harm on yourself, and all you'd get in return would be spirits too weak to fight Daoshi."

I nodded.

"So when you said you could find allies," he said, "who did you have in mind?"

"I was thinking of Bok Choy."

My father's eye sputtered in the teacup. "Li-lin, if Bok Choy helps you, you'll be cast out from the Ansheng tong. This whole side of town will be off-limits to you. Half the gangsters in town will raise their hatchets at the sight of you."

I sighed and turned my head away. Not far from me a man was selling fireworks from a cart. Across the street a woman with bound feet was haggling with a butcher, while two small children waited behind her.

These were the people who lived in Chinatown. They crossed an ocean in pursuit of a dream. And I imagined them dead. I imagined their bodies crushed or torn to pieces by the Kulou-Yuanling. The image filled me with a nauseated feeling, a feeling of helplessness and horror. I made up my mind.

"I have to do something," I said. "In the morning I'll go to Xie Liang headquarters," I told the spirit. "Tomorrow I'm going to talk with Bok Choy."

The eye dipped underwater and somehow blew little bubbles. When he came up, he said, "Could you do me a favor?"

"What do you have in mind, Mr. Yanqiu?"

"Could you destroy me now? Please?"

"Excuse me?"

"You're going to destroy me sooner or later," he said. "I'm a monster and it's your duty. But my duty, my only duty, is to keep you safe. So I would greatly prefer it if you would destroy me now, so I don't have to watch you get murdered by gangsters."

I stared at him for a long moment, and then I began to laugh. With my thumb I dunked his head under the water. He bobbed back up with an undignified look on his eye.

"You don't ever give me face," he said.

"You haven't got a face, Mr. Yanqiu."

He harrumphed.

SEVENTEEN

When the sun went down I stood on the steps to Father's temple and called for Mao'er. He did not come. I went back inside and came out with a flask of lamp oil. "Mao'er," I called again. A pair of red lacquered lanterns hung outside the temple. I refreshed their oil and lit them. All down the street, other people had done the same. Passersby would walk between shadows, lit by the glow of lamps and lanterns.

I sat on the bottom step and poured my remaining lamp oil into a ceramic saucer. This time, when I called, a small orange shape came sauntering out of the shadows. Mao'er's two tails were high. He carried himself with a deliberately casual air, as if he just happened to be walking nearby.

"Miao," he said. He stretched himself on the board-walk, his eyes focused on the saucer full of oil.

"Don't be shy, Mao'er," I said, pushing the saucer closer to him. "It's for you."

"Mine-mine?"

I nodded, but still he approached the oil warily, as though some other cat might leap out of the darkness and take his treat from him. He inched toward the saucer. When he reached it, he lowered his head and began lapping it up, with a kind of gusto.

After a few moments, he sat back, in a posture that seemed to be intent on reclaiming some of his dignity. "Dao girl fighty now?"

I looked at him. "I've seen you fight, Mao'er. You were like a whirlwind of claws and teeth. Those boys ran away, covered with bites and scratches."

He preened. "Mao'er fighty!"

"You weren't holding back when you fought them, were you?"

"Hrah!" he said, or something like it, a cat's proud laugh. "Me be jungle cat, Dao girl, me be fierce. Hunty, fighty! No hold back."

"So what you're saying, Mao'er, is that you fought with all your might, against children, and only managed to give them some scratches?"

He glared at me, his posture shrinking from pride to sullenness. "Mao'er fighty," he said. "Hunty, fighty."

"Mao'er, I'm sure you are a mighty hunter, and I would not insult your prowess," I said. "But I do not think you should join me in my fighty. I mean, my fight."

Sulking, he went back to lapping up the fish oil.

When there was none left, I burned paper mice. Mao'er hunted the mice, taunted and toyed with them, for minutes, before he killed them with a savagery that surprised me. He was chewing spirit-meat from their bones when I climbed back up the stone steps into the temple, and down the rickety wooden stairs to Father's quarters.

To prepare myself for what was coming, I needed to pray and meditate, to perform prostrations and move through taiji sequences, if I was to have any hope of succeeding tomorrow.

Tomorrow. The day was approaching, second by second, and it frightened me. I didn't see how I could face my challenges, but I still had to try. Tomorrow morning I needed to try to recruit the help of gangsters I had always held in contempt. Tomorrow night I needed to try to stop Liu Qiang's ritual.

At eleven o'clock it was quiet in the empty apartment, and no wind was blowing outside. I wouldn't have heard the sound if there hadn't been silence within the apartment and silence outside. That's how soft the tap was. I looked toward the door and waited. There was another tap. A few moments later, another.

I walked to the door, gathering my peachwood sword and my rope dart on the way. There was no way I could know what was out there.

I swung the door open and saw nothing, just another night in San Francisco's Chinatown. Then a small pebble landed on my toe. I looked down, and my father's eye looked up at me.

Mr. Yanqiu stood just outside the line of talismans over the door, with a heap of pebbles stockpiled nearby. "Li-lin," he said, clearly out of breath from the effort it took to gather the pebbles and throw them.

I squatted down to look him in the eye. "What is it, Mr. Yanqiu? What's the matter?"

"There's something you ought to see," he said, panting.

"I need to rest for tomorrow, Mr. Yanqiu. I have to gather my energy. If you've found some sort of steam vent . . ." I let my voice trail off.

"I've found something that might be able to help you," he said.

I blinked at him, then placed my wooden sword in my belt, my rope dart in my pocket, and scooped up the little spirit. "Let's go," I said.

Mr. Yanqiu guided me down the streets of Chinatown, as he had in the world of spirits, telling me where to turn. The traffic on Pacific was as it often is, men walking to work or from work, some going to pay visits to whores or spend the night at gambling houses. And then I heard something odd. There were voices coming from around a corner, from an alley between Dupont and Lozier.

"What . . ." I began, my head reeling.

Chinatown was a mere twelve blocks. There were neighborhoods I avoided, but here, at Pacific and Dupont, I knew where everything was located. I could find my way around if I were drunk in the dark.

And there is no alley on Pacific between Dupont and Lozier.

I turned to face the impossible alley. Market stalls lined the lane, lit by paper lanterns. Vendors were selling, customers were buying, it was business as usual in many places in Chinatown.

Except none of these vendors, and none of these customers, were human.

There was a pig-nosed ghost selling a bottle with a blue flame swirling inside of it, and nearby I saw an animal tall as a man, with red fur and an anteater's trunk. It was standing on two feet, and it held a sign that said, "DREAMS EATEN FOR TWO BITS." Perched on an awning was a large bird with a woman's head. An old man was browsing through the stalls, or at least something that looked like an old man; he had white hair and a long white beard, but bats were flying in circles all around him, and he didn't seem to mind.

I took a breath. Panic threatened to rush through my body. I wanted to turn around, run away, and never come back. There were ghosts and goblins all around me. Though not so horrific as those that dance with the Night Parade, these were still freaks of spirit, outlandish monsters going about their business near the world of men, where they had no right to be. An old umbrella hopped around on one leg, with a long red tongue protruding from its face. Two thin wicker arms extended from the umbrella's side.

"What is this place?" I said.

"This is Gui Shi," Mr. Yanqiu said. "Ghost Market is on the border between Chinatown and the spirit world. It appears somewhere different every night."

"Mr. Yanqiu," I said under my breath, "that makes no sense. It could not appear so often in such a small community without my knowing of it."

"This isn't the only Chinatown, Li-lin."

"You're saying this Ghost Market moves between Chinatown in San Francisco and New York?"

"And Hawaii, Boston, Chicago, Toronto. Every Chinatown in the world. Wherever your people have gone."

"Because no one leaves their ghosts behind," I said. "It makes sense. Wherever we go, we are outsiders. Laborers looking for work, far from our homeland, we lose touch with our ancestors and our traditions. Strange beings haunt us, as flies follow horses."

Mr. Yanqiu nodded. "Ghost Market is in them all, and in none, Li-lin. Madmen stumble upon it sometimes, and smokers of opium. You can see it, but even you cannot find Ghost Market without a spirit leading you here."

"Mr. Yanqiu, why would you bring me to an alley full of ghosts and goblins? I can't perform such a massive exorcism."

The eyeball laughed. "What makes you think you need to exorcise them?"

"It's what I do," I said. "What I must do."

"What you must do is stop Liu Qiang from creating a Kulou-Yuanling," he said. "Look around you, Li-lin. You might find something that can help."

I scowled. "Anything I find here I will have to buy, at the cost of consorting with spirits. Any agreements I enter into will move me further out of the human social order. I have no wish to become one more freak of the spirit world."

Mr. Yanqiu was quiet. I imagined his lips would be pursed if he had any. I sighed. I hadn't meant to insult the eyeball.

I looked up and saw an old woman walking toward me down the alley. She was wearing a large cloak. There were *things* moving beneath the cloak, where her body should have been. Jagged shapes pushed out against the cloak, darting like knives or shards of glass beneath the fabric. And I saw, bulbous and protruding in the woman's forehead, a third eye.

The crone stepped closer. Her head was crooked on her neck, as though someone had taken a statue apart and put the pieces back together at the wrong angles. She smiled at me from a mouth that had no teeth, her beaklike nose twitching. There was a sparkle in her dark beady eyes, all three of them. She said, in a voice of laughter and grief, "Xian Li-lin."

I could only gape. I knew that voice. I'd known it for years.

"Jiujiu?"

"Aah!" the old woman said, the sad and laughing voice of a seagull cackling from the old lady's mouth. "Aah!"

"Jiujiu, you . . . What are you . . ." I couldn't figure out what I should say. I had known this bird lady for most of my life, but I'd only ever seen her in the shape of a seagull. I wasn't even aware that Jiujiu had any other forms.

"Here," she said, "Aah! Here to bargain."

"Bargain? What for?"

"Protection, Xian Li-lin. The Haiou Shen need a protector."

I gazed at the three-eyed old woman. Spirit gulls can see the future, so it could be important to find out what she meant. "Protection from what?"

"Aah!" the old woman said. "Those who will come."

"And who are they, Jiujiu?"

Her head went further awry on her not-quite-human neck. "Those who come, Xian Li-lin," she repeated. "The Haiou Shen would bargain with you, aah!"

I tried not to let my surprise show. The gull spirits had always come to warn me of their own accord. Now Jiujiu was trying to make some sort of deal with me. I didn't understand what had changed. "What kind of bargain do you have in mind?"

"Bones are swirling in the world of spirits, Xian Li-lin," the old lady said, "click clack, go the bones of a never-was, aah! You will need us when the bones grow hungry."

"Bones," I repeated. "Skeletons. You're talking about the Kulou-Yuanling."

"Aah! Aah!" the old woman shouted. "Protect us, Xian Li-lin, and we will follow you."

Mr. Yanqiu spoke from my shoulder. "What do you mean when you say you'll follow her?"

"Aah! The Haiou Shen will be your soldiers, Xian Li-lin. Protect us, lead us, we will follow you."

"Protect you from what?" Mr. Yanqiu asked.

The old lady scowled. "From those who will come, aah!" she said. "Already said so, didn't we."

"How long?" I asked. "How long must I protect you if I agree?"

"From the time of ten suns to the time of none. Aah! Aah!"

I blinked. In the early days of the world, in primordial times, there had been ten suns. Archer Yi slew nine of them, leaving only one sun in the sky.

Mr. Yanqiu shook his eyeball. "Don't do it, Li-lin. They want you to be their guardian for all time, and in exchange for that, all you'll be able to do is lead some seagulls into battle."

"Spirit soldiers," I said to him. "I can still ask the Xie Liang tong for their help, and then I would have men and spirits at my back."

"That's some army you're building there," the eyeball spirit said. "I'm sure Liu Qiang will quake in terror when he sees you've recruited the help of seagulls and undisciplined gangsters."

I grinned. "How could we lose?"

"They're *birds*, Li-lin," said Mr. Yanqiu, a frown distinct in his voice. "They're just birds."

"Aaah!" cried Jiujiu. "Such an insult, from just an eye."

"Enough," I told the both of them. They settled into quiet sulking. I turned to face Jiujiu. "Long ago, you and I hid together at the bottom of a well. Back then neither of us could protect, neither of us could fight, so we hid. But there will be no more hiding. If you will follow me, I will protect you."

Mr. Yanqiu sighed. "You accept the bargain, Xian Li-lin?" Jiujiu asked.

"I accept the bargain," I said. "How do we seal the agreement?"

The old lady reached inside her shifting cloak and took out a rectangular piece of blue paper. She handed the paper to me. It was blank.

"I don't understand," I said.

Then Jiujiu drew back her cloak. Gulls flew out. There was a noise of wings, and the birds poured forth by dozens, and then by flying hundreds, a raucous crowd of white and blue-gray feathers. The three-eyed gulls kept coming, more than could ever possibly fit beneath the cloak. They flew up to the sky, circling in the bruise-dark night, and they kept coming.

Up and down the lane, the monsters had paused their business to watch the spirit gulls fly out from the cloak and form a cloud in the sky. Bird by bird they came forth, flapping innumerable wings, and I gaped watching their flight.

It seemed to last for minutes, the skyward procession of the gulls, and then the cloak crumpled to the ground, empty.

The stars were no longer visible. All that could be seen was the dark of stormclouds, a storm of birds, and then the gulls rained down.

Down from the sky they flew, and right at me. The first three-eyed seagull came at me with such speed that I flinched, but with the sound of wings it flew against the blue paper in my hand and vanished.

The bird was just gone. "What was that?" I said, mystified.

And then the next gull flew against the paper and was gone, and the next, and the next. The flock of them had blackened the sky, and all streamed now toward the blue paper, vanishing when they touched it.

At last, eventually, the wings were silent. There were no more gulls to be seen.

"Okay, *that* was impressive," said Mr. Yanqiu.

I looked at the blue paper in my hand. It was no longer blank. In row after orderly row, small birds had been stamped in black ink. "A talisman," I said. There was a blank space at the bottom for me to sign it with my name and lineage.

Staring at it, I began to realize what I'd done. I'd made a bargain without taking the time to understand it. I had agreed to protect the spirit gulls, without even knowing what I was supposed to protect them from. There would be consequences, and I couldn't even guess what they might be.

I became aware of something. A silence up and down the alley. Raising my eyes from the blue paper talisman, I saw them, all of them. The strange monsters that had business on Ghost Market had watched the flight of the Haiou Shen, and now they were watching me. All of them.

The man circled by bats. The dream eater. A man's head the size of a man. A red pear with a man's face. A white ape standing on one hand and one foot, its head to the side. All of them, an alley thronged with ghosts and goblins, and every freakish eye was watching me. I was terrified. I wanted to crouch down and make myself small, I wanted to apologize for having offered offense. I tried not to let the spirits see me shaking.

One of them moved toward me. He looked like a man with no eyes in his face, but he didn't have empty eye sockets. There was just a blank stretch of skin where most men have eyes.

"Is he blind?" I asked Mr. Yanqiu, and then the man held up his hands.

The gesture was one I'd ordinarily associate with peace, since open hands do not carry weapons. But on the palm of each of this man's hands, he had an eye.

I blinked, and the eyes on his palms blinked back.

The weirdness of the spirit bewildered me, made me feel dizzy, as I stared into the man's palms and the palms stared back. It was as if a man had been mutilated, his body parts rearranged, and between the disorientation and the disgust, I felt as though I might vomit.

"It's one of them," the man with eyes in his palms said, his voice slow but clear. "A person. One of the living."

I heard breaths drawn all around me. There was hissing, and something growled, low and guttural.

A tall man with a frog's head walked toward me. "It shouldn't be here," he said, shaking his froggy head. "It doesn't belong here."

I do not hide from monsters. By reflex I reached for my peachwood sword and began to draw it out of my belt, but then I glimpsed the eyeball on my shoulder. It was an odd little monster, and it was also my friend. Perhaps I had choices aside from hiding and fighting.

It wasn't easy to push my sword back down into my belt. My pulses were racing. I turned to face the frog-headed man, and opened my hands to show I carried no weapons.

"This is Ghost Market," I said. "Where the world of spirits borders upon the world of men."

The bulge on the frog-man's neck inflated and deflated before it spoke. "What of it?" it asked. "You belong in the world of men."

"Do I? I have yin eyes, and I have seen and talked with spirits since I was a small girl."

The eyes protruding from his frog head seemed to widen at that. He glanced at me for a moment that stretched on and on. "You have killed spirits," he said at last.

"Yes," I said, looking down. And suddenly I felt ashamed of myself, of my life. I felt justified for killing some of the spirits; they had threatened human lives, and I'd had no choice but to destroy them. But there were others I could have appeased, or driven away, or made more of an effort to understand.

The frog man watched me, and I thought I saw a form of sympathy on his face. "You shouldn't be here," he said, more gently now. "You belong in the world of living men, not the world of ghosts and goblins. Why don't you go home now."

"Yes," I said with a nod. I turned back toward the alley's entryway and began to walk away.

"He's right, you know," Mr. Yanqiu said from my shoulder. "You belong among your own kind."

I stopped walking. "And what about you?"

"What do you mean, Li-lin?"

"Shouldn't you be with your kind, Mr. Yanqiu?"

He huffed. "I should be with you," he said.

I looked at him for a long moment, then lifted him off my shoulder with one hand. "Li-lin!" he cried. "What are you doing?"

"I'm sorry, Mr. Yanqiu," I said, as I placed him on the ground. "Father wants me to destroy you. Here in Ghost Market I don't have to."

"What do you mean?" Mr. Yanqiu yelled, shaking his hands. "What are you saying?" Tears began to flow from his face. The teardrops were the size of his hands.

"I can exorcise you here, in Ghost Market," I said, taking out a paper talisman, "and you won't die. You will no longer intrude upon the human social order, and yet you'll be able to go on living here, among your kind."

"Li-lin, please! I'm begging you. Please don't do this."

Inside me I felt a barren space grow wide. It threatened to make me break down in tears, but there was no doubt in my mind. By exorcising Mr. Yanqiu here, in Ghost Market, I could honor my father's wishes without doing harm to Mr. Yanqiu. It was the best of possible outcomes.

"I'm sorry," I said, and I lit the talisman of exorcism on fire.

EIGHTEEN

In dreams I ran through fields and forests on the strong legs of an animal. My paws touched down and I sprang forward with a kind of fundamental joy. The air carried the smells of danger and the smells of meat, and often they were the same smell. My fur bristled.

Something growled and I realized it was me. My voice. A fierce pride went through me. I swished my tail. Flexed my claws. Climbed over stones. Padded over earth. Water made me cautious. Hunger made me mad.

The new blue ghost made me mad too. Hovering by my shoulder. Telling me to kill.

The new ghost made me dream what he wanted me to dream. Dream of men. Their taste, their meat, their blood. "Find people," the blue ghost said. "Kill them."

A man moved between trees. "Kill him!" the blue ghost said. "Tear him apart."

I growled at the blue ghost, but I felt it course through me. The bloodlust. The kill hunger. "Kill him, kill him, kill him," the blue ghost said.

The man ran from me. Ran like a frightened little mouse. It was too much. I leapt into action. Hunted him, caught him, killed him. Ate. I was sated and happy. I licked the warm wet sticky stuff from my paws. His ribs had a lot of meat on them. I chewed and licked and chewed.

A new ghost stood up. Looked at his hands. Shivered.

The blue ghost was gone. I chewed the flesh from the dead man's bones. "What is happening?" the new ghost said.

I licked my chops, in my dream. I knew nothing would change. The new ghost would be my blue ghost now. He was the freshest soul of the human meat, so he would follow. He was going to hover by me, following me like another tail. He'd talk to me. He'd speed my blood. Urge me to kill. Kill kill kill, he would say. Always the same.

"Kill," he said. "Kill kill kill."

Days sped forward in my dream, became weeks, weeks became months. Then blood wet my claws again, human meat died screaming, and a new ghost came. But there was something strange about this new ghost. He was different.

I was dreaming. Light streamed through the trees, and it was a wrong light. It was the light through windows, through closed eyelids. I wasn't a tiger.

"Hush," a man's voice said. "Go back to sleep."

I licked blood from my paw. The new ghost looked at me. He was different. No hair.

His meat was lean. I chewed his corpse, swallowed the chunks of man, and his ghost watched me. His blue face was smiling.

I prowled through the woods in my dream. The new blue ghost talked. Blue ghosts always talk. They always say, kill. Kill, kill, kill. Kill someone else so I can be free, they always say.

This blue ghost did not say, kill. He talked. He told me things. He spoke of old age, disease, and death.

"Change is the origin of suffering," the blue ghost said.

"Buddha," he said.

"Enlightenment is the end of suffering," he said.

"First become human," he said, "then become enlightened."

I woke from dreaming. My mind spun. I took a moment to make sure I wasn't a tiger. My hands reassured me that my anatomy was my own. I touched my face, my hips, and both my legs. It was me, all right.

I walked to the books at the other end of the room. Father's Daoist books were upstairs in the temple's back room, but here in our basement apartment, Father kept the others. He had literary classics and popular stories. Stories full of strange tales.

I chose some of the older books and began paging through the thin sheets of rice paper. There were stories of foxes, walking corpses, sorcerers, tigers, and ghosts.

It didn't take me long to find what I needed. There were plenty of stories about chang gui, compensation ghosts. A man may drown in a lake, and his spirit will remain trapped there until someone else drowns and takes his place. There are rooms where women hanged themselves and became ghosts, and now these ghost women are always trying to convince other people to hang themselves. To take their place.

I found the stories I was looking for in old books of strange tales. They were stories about tigers. Tigers, and the murdered spirits that haunt them.

Story after story described a tiger accompanied by a ghost. Sometimes the ghost wore blue clothing. Sometimes the ghost had blue skin. One sentence made me catch my breath.

A tiger's compensation ghost had the ability to communicate with humans in their dreams.

I was sure of it now. The dream was a message.

I had been dreaming about the Buddhist monk, Shuai Hu. The man with a tiger's shadow. If I understood the dream correctly, Shuai Hu had a chang gui. He was a tiger, and his compensation ghosts drove him to kill. He killed many men, and each one took the place of the last. Then he killed a Buddhist monk, and the monk became his chang gui, but the monk hadn't urged him to kill people. The monk urged him to seek enlightenment.

I needed to wash, so I put a pot of water on the stove. When the water was warm, I removed my clothes and washed myself with soap and a warm cloth.

Guilt. I was amazed to feel it. Shuai Hu was a three-tailed tiger spirit, and I felt guilty for attacking him. It was absurd, but it was how I felt. As if I had done something very, very impolite.

And he had been polite to me. He'd addressed me respectfully, even remembering to call me Daonu, the formal title of a female Daoshi. There was no one else I knew who addressed me by title.

He had been born a tiger, but he was a baldie now. What had been a monster was now trying to be a man. He followed the Eightfold Path of the baldies, meditating and abstaining from meat. Shuai Hu wasn't just trying to be a man; he was trying to be a righteous man.

It amazed me that an animal would even want that. That was the kind of monster I wanted for an ally.

I dried myself off, and dressed in the sand-yellow robes of a Daoshi, to go and talk to the tiger.

The baldies stood on the Flower Lane, performing martial exercises. Their motions were crisp and straight and regimented. Strong, direct movements. A dozen Shaolin warrior monks stood in front of me. They were strong men, men of peace, and they knew how to fight.

So this is Shaolin, I thought. I marveled at the idea of Shuai Hu. Such a powerful animal. By nature a tiger is the fiercest of predators. A tiger with two tails would gain power, and this tiger had grown three tails. His power would be immense.

Take that powerful monster and train it in Shaolin. Teach it the discipline and deadliness of martial arts. I didn't need to see Bok Choy after all. I was going to recruit a three-tailed tiger trained in Shaolin kung fu, and no Daoshi of the Fifth or army of hatchetmen or evil snake-arm could hope to stand against it.

Shuai Hu would rend my enemies with monstrous claws. I didn't know what I would do while I watched. Maybe I'd bring a flask of rice wine.

The martial exercises came to an end, and the warrior monks dispersed. Some went to meditate, others went to work. Shuai Hu gave me a suspicious look. Wiping sweat from his forehead, he walked toward me. He peered all around to see if I had anyone hiding to ambush him.

"Daonu Xian," he said with a wary tone, and inclined his head in my direction.

"Shuai Hu, I fear I have done you a disservice."

His look could have stopped a wild stallion in its tracks. "What have you done?"

"I thought of you as a monster," I said. My throat felt dry. "I did not understand your aspirations."

His eyes narrowed. "What aspirations do you mean?"

I looked in his eyes, and saw a depth in there. "You want to live like a human. You want to pursue the Buddhist Eightfold Path, so that you can be reborn as a human and achieve enlightenment."

"Where did you hear of these things?"

It was a strange question. I didn't understand what was going through his mind. "In a dream," I said.

He turned away as fast as a stone launched from a slingshot. "Lan Ge!" he yelled. "Show yourself, ghost!"

On an awning at the left side of the street, a small blue man stood up and stretched. He was two or three inches tall, only a little bigger than Mr. Yanqiu. His skin was the rich blue of the ocean. There was no hair on his head. He yawned.

So this was Shuai Hu's final murder victim. The little blue man had given up the possibility of finding peace and a happier rebirth in order to work toward the enlightenment of an animal. Of the animal that killed him.

"Lan Ge," Shuai Hu growled. "You've been sending dreams again."

The blue man said nothing. He yawned once more.

"We must not force others to see those things they do not choose to see," the tiger monk said, his tone scolding. "That is the way of Mara, father of illusions. It is not our way."

The blue man yawned again. Then he said, "The Dharma is no rigid thing, Brother Hu; you know there are eighty-four thousand doors to the Dharma."

What was going on here? It seemed as though the blue ghost's morality was more flexible than the tiger's. Maybe the tiger needed to follow a rigid moral code, in order to remain on his path.

"Why have you done such a thing, Lan Ge?"

"It needed to be done, Brother Hu. This girl can change everything."

Startled, I said, "Me?"

The little blue man turned to face me. His gaze was lethargic and sleepy. "For more than a hundred years, my tiger friend Shuai Hu has followed the Buddha's teachings. He has been a good man, Xian Li-lin, pursuing right actions, and yet, still, wherever we have gone, the Daoshi have come after him with their weapons and their spells. He would have killed them if they fought, so he fled from town to town, from monastery to monastery. He fled to protect the men who wanted to kill him."

"I think I understand," I said, "but what does this have to do with me?"

"You are a Daoshi, Xian Li-lin, and the daughter of a Daoshi. And yet you are friends with a monster. You are friends with a talking eyeball."

I blanched. "Mr. Yanqiu saved me when I was trapped in the world of spirits."

The blue ghost's smile was irritatingly serene. "You made an exception for him."

"There are no exceptions," I said. "It's why I exorcised Mr. Yanqiu."

The blue ghost looked surprised, and then he looked intrigued. "You exorcised a spirit that saved your life?"

"I did as I must."

"*Thieves may harm thieves, and enemies may harm each other, but a poorly directed mind can do much greater harm.*"

"You quote the teachings of the Buddha, Blue Ghost, but I do not follow them."

"Well then," he said, "'*Nowhere can be found a principle that is right in all circumstances, or an action that is wrong in all circumstances.*'"

He had quoted the *Liezi*, one of the major scriptures of the Dao. I was slow to respond.

"I am a daughter and a student. My father, my teacher, decreed that Mr. Yanqiu must be destroyed."

"And yet you came here today, Daonu Xian, to talk with Shuai Hu. You know he is a monster, but you did not come to make war, did you?"

"He is trying to be a righteous man."

"So it's not enough for you to say a monster is a monster. You see a monster trying to better himself as a human being, and you respect him for that."

"I do," I said, slowly. "And I have come to seek his help. Men are going to die if he doesn't help me."

"What is happening?" the tiger-monk asked, a serious demeanor on his round face.

"There is a soulstealer in Chinatown," I said. "He intends to raise a giant monster and use it to massacre hundreds of people."

"What does this have to do with me?" he asked, his voice a growl.

"I need to fight him," I said. "He's going to perform a ritual tonight. I need to stop the ritual before he can call forth the monster."

"That sounds like something you and your father should be able to handle, Daonu Xian."

"Father is wounded," I said. "The soulstealer anticipated my father as a threat and sent a monster after him. A quanshen."

"But still," said the tiger, "you nearly knocked me over when you kicked my shoulder, and you seem lethal with that rope dart. I cannot imagine you would need help to fight one man."

"He isn't alone, Shuai Hu. He has allied himself with hateful spirits. One of his arms is some kind of demon. He has the force of the Ansheng tong behind him—up to forty armed men."

"There are men?" he asked.

"Yes, a number of men. I don't know how many."

A significant look passed between the tiger and the blue ghost. "What is it you want me to do, Daonu Xian?"

"Fight them," I said. "Join with me and fight them at my side. Will you do this thing?"

"No." The word came out crisp, emphatic, and final. I took an involuntary step back.

"But you must," I said, looking into his face. His eyes were deep and unreadable.

"No," he repeated. "I am a monster, Daonu Xian. At every moment I am choosing to be better than my nature. I follow the Five Precepts. I will never take another life."

"You can fight them without killing them if that is what you need," I told him.

Shrugging his massive shoulders, he turned away. "At every moment I struggle to control myself. Soulstealers and yaoguai may be your enemies, but passion, aggression, and ignorance are mine. It is too easy for me to revert to my nature. I have chosen not to be a beast. Were I to join in this battle as a man, Daonu Xian, I would not be of much assistance to you. You are asking me to fight as a monster. This I will not do."

I stamped my foot in frustration. "So fight as a man! I can't fight them alone."

"And if I should kill one by mistake?"

"Then one of them dies by mistake. Is your oath more important than the lives of hundreds of men?"

"No," he said, "it's more than the oath. Daonu Xian, you know I was born a tiger. Tigers grow up to nine feet in length. We weigh as much as six hundred pounds. We are among the deadliest of beasts. And we seldom live longer than twenty years." His eyes were as clear and ancient as any I'd ever seen. "In my fiftieth year I grew a second tail, and I grew in power. In my hundredth year I grew a third tail, and my power increased again. In all my years in China's forests, I never saw a tiger with more than two tails. My power is already terrible. And soon I will grow a fourth tail. I do not know what I will be capable of."

"You're almost two hundred years old," I breathed.

He nodded. "When a tiger kills a man, the man's ghost stays with the tiger. The most recent victim's spirit remains trapped until someone replaces him."

"Until you kill someone else," I said.

"Yes. I do not know how many I killed. I killed men and I killed women. I killed children, Daonu Xian. Each of them hung on me like a weight. Each of them drove my aggression."

"They wanted you to kill someone else."

"So they could move on, yes, they wanted me to kill again. Until I killed Lan Ge."

The blue ghost turned to me, yawning. "I had taken an oath," the blue man said. "I had sworn to work toward the enlightenment of all beings."

"Do you understand, Daonu Xian? Do you understand yet?"

I looked at him. I saw it beneath his big happy cheeks, his warrior shoulders. I saw sorrow, and guilt, and fear. He had no fear for himself. He was afraid of what he might wind up doing to other people. "I think I do understand," I said, my voice resigned. "You are one of the most dangerous beings in the world. Soon you will be more powerful. If you kill someone else, even by accident, he will take Lan Ge's place. You think without a Buddhist ghost at your side, you will stray from your path."

The monk looked down. "I will become a killer again, Daonu. A mindless, murderous animal, driven to violence by ghost after ghost of the people I will murder."

I looked away, feeling weary. The vigor drained out of my voice. "And once you have your fourth tail, human weapons and magical spells may not be enough to bring you down."

He nodded.

"Thank you, Shuai Hu," I said. I felt genuine sadness for this man, this monster. I bowed and turned away.

"Wait, Daonu," he said. "What are you going to do?"

I faced him.

"I'll fight them," I said, "of course. But first I will ask my father for guidance."

NINETEEN

It was early afternoon when I reached the corner of Pacific and Dupont. I saw the infirmary door and gasped. An ugly knot of spirits clustered outside the door. Little black fists crawled around on spider legs, creepy and cackling. Each of them had the face of a human baby. My shoulders were tense. I took a deep breath.

"Aiya," I said.

Yaozhizhu, goblin spiders, had crawled onto the streets of Chinatown, out of folktale and nightmare.

For now the yaozhizhu crowded around the infirmary's doorway, their cries grotesquely human. The talismans, I realized; Father's talismans were keeping them out.

To the side of the infirmary's door I saw three squirming shapes. They reminded me of cats that boys have trapped inside bags, to toy with and torture, but they were human spirits. Three people had lost portions of their souls here, trapped in the gray-white webs. The goblin spiders would suck out the essence of spirit at their leisure. It was a horrifying fate.

I walked closer, to get a better look. The yaozhizhu had spun an enormous spirit web. It covered the entire entryway with gossamer strands and a filthing of the air. I guessed they had spun another one over the back door. No one would be able to enter or leave the infirmary without getting caught in the sticky, fleshy webs of the goblin spiders.

I looked at the baby faces of the yaozhizhu and felt my skin crawl. They were foul creatures. Vile mockeries of humanity. Looking at them, I wanted a different life. I wanted to be someone who didn't have to see such monstrosities.

The goblin spiders skittered and giggled by dozens or hundreds. Drool and snot dripped from their childlike faces.

One of the webbed bags of human spirit squirmed, struggling inside its snare. No human thing should be so degraded. The spirit portion would last hours or days, slurped down like milk by the baby-faces of the goblin spiders.

"Get out of here, Li-lin!" Dr. Wei stuck his head out of the second-floor window. "The infirmary is under quarantine! Go away!"

So the residents of the infirmary were aware of the yaozhizhu. They were treating it like an epidemic.

"Is Father inside?" I called up to the window.

"There's nothing you can do for him. Go away from here!"

"Is he well?" I called up.

Dr. Wei pushed his spectacles higher on his nose with a weary look. "The infirmary is under quarantine, Li-lin! Do you understand me? You need to go away, now."

"Is my father well?"

The doctor hesitated. "If I tell you, will you go away?"

"Of course I will, Dr. Wei," I lied.

"He's gotten worse," he called down. "He came down with an illness."

A wave of horror washed over me. "Did he try to leave?" I asked Dr. Wei.

"He took two steps out the door and collapsed," he called back.

I stared up at him, my mouth open. My father was one of the yaozhizhu's bundled victims, a webbed captive spirit to be fed upon. Missing a significant portion of his spirit, he would weaken, sicken, and eventually die; but not before he was lost and broken.

The sight of the goblin spiders made me feel ill. Liu Qiang must have sent them to harm my father, or keep him out of the way long enough for him to complete his ritual and raise the Kulou-Yuanling.

Once again Liu Qiang saw my father as an obstacle, and once again he saw me as nothing. The yaozhizhu were here, but they hadn't been sent for me. I didn't even need to face them.

Looking at the grotesque monsters, I realized I could turn around and walk away. I could still find a way to stop Liu Qiang's ritual, without facing the baby-faced spiders. There was no need for me to fight them.

The goblin spiders had trapped a portion of my father's spirit, but it was merely a third. He would wake up and still be two thirds of what he was. He'd be strong enough to kill the yaozhizhu by himself. Once Father knew what he was facing, he could incinerate the goblin spiders with five syllables and a two-handed gesture. He could reclaim the missing portion of his spirit without my help. Even diminished by a third, my father was still stronger and more experienced than I could ever hope to become.

I stood at the corner, thinking. I could walk away. The thought of it felt like a breeze on a hot day. It felt like freedom. Let someone else handle this. I didn't need to scar my mind by confronting the yaozhizhu.

I stood still, watching the skittering spiders and hearing their babyish cries. Behind them, webbed up, a portion of my father's spirit was struggling, trapped.

When my spirit was trapped, my father sacrificed his eye to rescue me.

Drawing my peachwood sword, I charged at the goblin spiders. The closest locked its infant eyes on me with a false look of innocence, and it died on the point of my peachwood sword. I impaled a second, and a third, and the twitchy crowd of monsters turned on me. Hundreds of baby eyes, thousands of hairy, skittering spider legs, the entire horde of the yaozhizhu advanced.

I stepped back, and swung my sword to clear it of the guts and parts of goblin spiders. The rest of the yaozhizhu were coming after me. There were too many of them. One girl with a sword would never be enough to hack her way through this disgusting swarm. My arm would tire long before they were finished.

I needed to fight them on my terms. From a better vantage point. But where?

I continued stepping back, one step back and then another, while all of the goblin spiders swarmed toward me.

Then an idea occurred to me. I could fight them from behind the doorway, protected by a string of cloth talismans.

The only problem was, the yaozhizhu were massed between me and the door.

I bolted to the left and the goblin spiders sped after me, a multitude of clicking legs and crying faces. Angling my feet toward the wall, I began the dynamic shifts of weight and motion that make up qinggong. I only needed to lighten my body a little. My feet hit the ground, lighter from one moment to the next, and I had done enough by the time I reached the wall.

One foot against the wall, push up, and spring off: I flipped over the seething moat of goblin spiders. They had all come at me together, and I was behind them now. Their animal intelligence was basic, but cunning. One alerted the others to my whereabouts with a warbling screech, and the mob of baby-faced monsters pivoted toward me again.

But I had already crossed to their other side, and I was running. I sped toward the door of the infirmary, wielding my wooden blade in both hands. I heard Dr. Wei's voice. He called down warnings from the second floor. But I saw things he could not see, and I swung my peachwood sword at the pale fleshy web the yaozhizhu had spun over his doorway. The peachwood sliced down, and the web shredded into flimsy strands of gossamer.

I burst in through the doorway, panting. The goblin spiders charged after me, but when they hit the perimeter marked by my father's talismans, they stopped in their tracks. I heard them chitter in their rage and frustration.

Dr. Wei ran down the stairs. "What are you doing, Li-lin? You said you'd go away."

"Yes, Dr. Wei," I said, catching my breath. "I did say that. I was lying."

He stopped and stared. "You are a very strange girl," he said. "You shouldn't have come back. You'll have to stay inside the quarantine now."

"It's not an epidemic, Dr. Wei. It's yaozhizhu. There are goblin spiders outside the door. They can't get past the string of talismans, but they put up a web outside the door. They've caught some spirits in their webs. Father's spirit is caught."

If a bird had been flying through the infirmary, it might have flown into Dr. Wei's mouth at that moment. His eyes bulged wide behind his spectacles as he pieced the information together, then he snapped his mouth shut and gave me a firm look.

"Li-lin, why didn't you ever tell me you have yin eyes?"

"There's no time for this, Dr. Wei. I need to kill the yaozhizhu outside, and I need to save the soul portions that they've caught. How much lamp oil can you spare?"

"Lamp oil?" he asked.

"Yes, Dr. Wei. Lamp oil."

He pushed his spectacles farther back on his nose with a sigh. "A lot?" he said.

"I need oil," I said. "And matches."

I poured fish oil over the goblin spiders, and lit them on fire. Pedestrians watched and gaped. I heard one say, "That's the girl who beat up Tom Wong in the street!"

In the spirit world, flames took the baby-faced spiders. They coughed and cried and fled in circles, spinning on their hairy, segmented legs, burning. Mucus dripped down their baby noses. I felt none of the elation of victory. This wasn't a fight; it was merely an execution.

I carried the buckets of lamp oil to the back door and executed the rest.

When it was done, I went out front. The captive spirits were nearly weightless. Encased in cobweb, their essential matter diminished by hungry goblin spiders, my father's spirit and the others had started to shrivel.

They would survive. Thanks to me, they would survive, but none would ever thank me for it. We would put all this behind us. For once I was glad of it. I wanted the yaozhizhu gone and forgotten.

Carefully, with my peachwood sword, I sliced the webs off of the spirits. I kept my arm steady, making sure I didn't even nick the soul portions with the blade. They emerged from the webbing like puffs of steam. I watched them float, indistinct as clouds at night. They would drift back to join the rest of the spirit that had been fractioned. I watched a piece of my father's spirit pass into the infirmary, unimpeded by his own talisman.

Mrs. Wei approached me from inside the infirmary. I eyed her with suspicion. I never wanted to talk to her again.

"I have been thinking about you, Li-lin. There is so much I could teach you," she said. Her words came out in an excited rush. "I could teach you to walk the spirit bridge like a Wushi woman. I could show you how to recruit spirit servants."

I recoiled as if she'd kicked me in the gut. "I am a Daoshi, Mrs. Wei. I am the daughter of a Daoshi, and I am the widow of a Daoshi. I will not shake and gouge my skin, and I will not learn your witchcraft or claim your demons."

Her body went stiff and her face cold. "They are not demons," she said. Old anger hardened her voice.

I walked past her to the cot where my father was resting. Fresh bandages covered the side of his face, where he had torn out his eye. For me. He was breathing slowly.

Dr. Wei sat on a stool at his side, checking his pulses. He looked up at me. "Your father's vital signs are stronger," he told me. "He was breathing shallowly, and four of his pulses had failed. But now he's stabilized. He just needs some rest."

I smiled, nodding. "You can call off the quarantine," I said.

He gave me a steady, regarding look, and nodded. "Does your father know about your yin eyes?"

"He did know, once. He thinks he cured me." I paused. "You won't tell him, will you?"

"I've taken the Hippocratic Oath, Li-lin," he said, "so I will never divulge a medical secret. But one of these days you and I will need to talk."

I knew what he would say: women with yin eyes die young. A woman with yin eyes will lead a painful life. Drink this water infused with talismanic ashes. Let me stick needles into your meridians. Drink this herbal tea. Let me touch your meridians with this hot moxa stick. I'd been hearing it from my father ever since I was a little girl.

"I should check on my other patients now," the doctor said. "But do come talk to me soon, Li-lin."

"I will return tonight, to see how Father is doing," I said.

I walked back toward the apartment, feeling tense. Edges grew indistinct in the hazy six o'clock light. Liu Qiang was going to perform his ritual at eleven. It was only five hours away. I needed a plan. I needed allies.

Mrs. Wei offered to help me find spirit allies, but really she was offering to corrupt me. She practiced a forbidden magic. Those ways were wild and ruinous. I had seen Mrs. Wei perform a ritual. She shook and cut herself. Generations of scholars and Daoshi had taken magic and made it civilized. They cleansed it of its madness, its grisliness, and its contaminations.

Mr. Wong had suggested that I go to the Xie Liang tong and ask them for help. But he made sure no one could hear him when he said it. The Xie Liangs were supposed to be reckless, and dangerous in the way of undisciplined men. If I went to the Xie Liang tong for help, I could expect to be shut out from the world I knew.

Even Dr. Wei worked for the Ansheng tong. I thought of him for a moment, how he would react to me if I was no longer welcome among the Ansheng. The thought of him turning away, treating me like some kind of stranger or an enemy, was nearly enough to make me start crying.

And yet I had to do something. I couldn't sit back and let Tom Wong slaughter innocent men. Rocket would never tolerate such a thing. I could not allow him a legacy that he would find shaming.

I turned and began to walk away from the Ansheng territory. Away from everything I had ever known.

Crossing into the southwest side of Chinatown felt like passing out of one country and into another. My father had always worked for the Ansheng tong, so the territory of the Xie Liangs felt like a hostile foreign land.

It looked the same. The same grungy, boxy buildings. The ramshackle balconies and rickety stairways looked no different. On Sacramento Street there were greengrocers and street vendors. Men walked past with the resolute and tired eyes of those who work hard, and their queues swished behind them as they walked. Nothing here was truly different. There were the same suspicious glances, the same whispers, the same odd mix of vibrancy and despair. The high-pitched music of an erhu floated through the air. Chinatown took its own shape, and neither Mr. Wong nor Bok Choy could force it to take a different one.

It felt to me like the world was sinking. My father—the invincible, the powerful protector of Chinatown—lay in bed, feeble. There was no one else who could stand in his place. No one but me. It was up to me to protect Chinatown.

My father and I had always been with the Ansheng tong, so the Xie Liang tong had always been our enemy. Now Tom Wong wanted to destroy the Xie Liangs. I found myself wondering why I would want to stop him.

I stopped walking. I wondered if I was doing the right thing. The Ansheng tong had sheltered my family since we first came to Gold Mountain. They were good people. They provided Father with his temple, and they paid for my husband's funeral.

I took a deep breath. I didn't need to do this. I didn't need to do anything. The Anshengs were my people. And who were the Xie Liangs? Strangers. I could simply go back to my life, pretending there was nothing else I could have done. The Anshengs were my people. Why would I step outside the social order? Why would I fight against men who helped raise me?

An old man sat on the corner, playing music. The mournful sound of his erhu made me feel doomed, like the whole world was drowning.

"Pretty girl," the old man called to me. He gave me a gentle smile that had no teeth. "Let me play you a song."

I stopped and looked at him. There was so much to read on his face. A wrinkle below the mouth showed me someone who frowned often. The crinkles behind his eyes denoted laughter.

"Is it a happy song?" I asked.

"I know some happy songs."

"Tomorrow," I said. "I will come back tomorrow and ask you to play me a happy song."

I bowed to the old man and walked deeper into Xie Liang territory. Maybe I was throwing my life away for an old man playing an erhu, but I wanted to hear a happy song. If Liu Qiang were to raise the Kulou-Yuanling, the musician would die and I'd never get to hear his happy song.

I smiled at my own foolishness. For a happy song, I had decided to go to war with the Ansheng tong.

I was wearing the full outfit of a Daoshi—yellow robes embroidered with black trigrams, and a square black hat. I would walk into Bok Choy's headquarters and no one would mistake me for a contract girl. I had decided to let them see me as powerful, a person of consequence, who must be taken seriously.

"Are you lost, little girl?" called a young man with a cruel face. Beside him, two friends laughed.

"Are you with the Xie Liang tong?" I asked.

The three of them stood in front of me, barring my path. "Why does it matter to you?"

I touched the pocket where I kept my rope dart. I might need it. "I want to talk with Bok Choy."

The young men glanced at each other uncertainly, and then the hatchet-faced youth spoke again. "What do you want with him, little girl?"

I sighed. Such a juvenile way to taunt me. "If I don't talk to Bok Choy, his gambling halls will burn, his brothels will lie in wreckage. The Xie Liang tong will be no more, and each man who refuses to acknowledge the power of the Ansheng will be hunted down and shamed, broken, or killed. Bok Choy will probably be allowed to live, but the Anshengs will cripple him, cripple his arms and legs, so he will have to earn his living as a beggar, selling listeners the story of how he rose to such a height and fell so far so fast," I said. "And all this will come to pass, and it will come to pass tonight, if you do not bring me to him, right now."

The young men had gone as pale as corpses. They exchanged glances, and then the first one spoke again. "We'll take you to him," he said.

There were no talismans over the door. No Door Gods, nothing to protect against spells or spirits. That was odd. Foolish of them, to leave their business so exposed. Goblins, ghosts, and curses had free rein to wreck the place.

The young men led me down a flight of stairs and into a big, poorly lit chamber. In the dim room, I could see men gambling at the tables, playing fantan, pai jiu, and ma jiang, as well as white people games with playing cards and dice. "Wait here," hatchet-face said to me. "I'll go talk to him."

I watched the faces of the men at the gaming tables. There was so much hope, and also so much devastation. I saw excitement, but I also saw exhaustion—the exhaustion that comes from living for small victories, forever waiting for the next one.

Tiles clinked on the tables, and dice rolled. I heard the sound of pouring liquid and looked over to see a woman serving rice wine to a group of gamblers. She wore American makeup, but the brightness of her face, the relaxation in her posture, and a gentle sense of contentment made her shine with an inner beauty. Behind red lips, rouged cheeks, and shadowed eyes, she had the bearing and expression of a woman who is profoundly loved. I had looked that way once. Yet here she was, looking a few years older than me, and still she radiated.

The waitress met my eyes with a curious look. Who are you, her eyes seemed to be asking, what are you? I wondered the same. But I realized who she was. For such a beautiful woman to circulate among gangsters without being bothered, she could only be the boss's wife.

A whore was circulating among the men. Her dress was cut shorter than the ordinary style, and I saw men flirting with her. She turned, and I saw she was wearing a great deal of makeup.

And under the makeup, I could see, clearly, it was a man. I stared. In his face I saw something surprising. He didn't look defeated.

We faced each other for a moment, and then he walked over to me. "Four bits to feel," he said with a smile, "six bits to do." He made no effort to conceal his male voice.

I blushed and looked down. "You," I said to him, and looked back at his face, "you haven't been doing this long?"

His face was smothered under makeup, and he began to laugh. "I'm the whore today," he said. "I lost more bets than anyone else yesterday. Someone else will have to dress up as a whore tomorrow."

I looked at him. "So you're not really . . . six bits?"

"For you, I'd only charge four bits," he said with a leer. I couldn't help it, it was so absurd I broke out in laughter.

Then Bok Choy came charging out from a back room. It was hard to miss him. He was wearing a white American suit with diamonds glittering on the lapels. A short man and skinny, he moved quickly, as if he was rushing somewhere.

He saw me and smiled. Gold flashed among his teeth. I knew better than to trust this man's smile. His hands fluttered like birds in motion. The whore of the day stepped back into the crowd.

"Let me see her, let me see," he said to his men, and when they stepped aside he looked at me and laughed. "How precious," he said, "how darling!"

I blinked. So this was Bok Choy, twitchy and failing to be charming, alive with spastic energy. I had gone to school with the missionaries, so I knew a little of the culture outside Chinatown, but I had no idea how I should behave around a tong leader in an American suit.

I bowed. "Mr. Choy," I began, but his shrilling laughter cut me off.

"No need for us to be so formal," he said. "But come on, let's go somewhere private."

I looked to his men for guidance. They only shrugged. I wondered if there was something wrong with him. He acted like a crazy man.

They led me to a room in the back. As soon as I stepped through the door, someone threw a net over me.

I never learned to grapple, so any one of the men could have wrestled me down. Especially since I was caught in a net and had been taken by surprise. But the Xie Liangs went in for overkill. Four or five men dragged me to the floor and held me there. A man held each arm and each leg, and a fifth man squatted on my hips. I struggled but it was useless under all their weight.

I felt terror come over me. I wanted to run but I couldn't even move. I heard myself whimper in the net.

Bok Choy stood about six feet away, tapping his feet. He was wearing white American shoes. I watched from the ground, from inside the net, as another man walked close to me. He lowered his foot toward my face, and I turned my head to the side.

Apparently that was what he had wanted. His foot pinned my head in place, facing Bok Choy. I felt my teeth clench together, a feral expression. My muscles were tight all along my body, pressing hard against the weight that held me pinned.

Bok Choy lit a cigar. "I lost two dollars thanks to you," he said in a nasal tone. "Everyone knew you were setting me up. My men Chicken and Locomotive—" he gestured to two of the men near him—"said you'd come here tonight, but I thought you would wait a day. We made a bet, and I lost."

"What are you"—it isn't easy to speak with a foot on your ear— "talking about?"

Bok Choy squatted down near me. "Mr. Wong sent you to kill me," he said.

I groaned. People could be so stupid. Nothing made sense but the Dao.

"As soon as I heard that a girl beat up his son, I knew I was being set up." He puffed on his cigar. "So you could get close enough to kill me."

The stupidity of the accusation made me angry, but underneath the anger I felt so weary. By coming here to speak with the Xie Liang tong, I had betrayed my own people. And even the Xie Liangs considered me an enemy.

I felt the men tie my ankles together, winding the rope in and out of the netting, and then they tied my knees. "I didn't," I said, struggling to breathe, "come here . . . to kill you."

Bok Choy laughed, and it was a shrill, deranged laugh. He gestured to his men and I felt them pull my arms in front of me, inside the net. They tied my wrists together, the rope weaving in and out of the mesh.

Cigar in hand, he leaned over and reached his arm out to me. "Would you like a puff?" he asked.

It was a nightmare. I was pinned to the floor and a madman was trying to get me to smoke his cigar. "What are you saying?" I asked.

"Come on, now," he said, and gold glinted in his smile. "Just take one puff on my cigar."

"Maybe later," I said, to be polite. What kind of game was he playing?

He waited a few moments and then withdrew the cigar. He took a puff himself. "It's a pity," he said.

The door opened and someone came in. I heard a woman's voice. "You wanted to see me?"

Bok Choy straightened up and said, "I always want to see you, darling dove," he said. "But it would help me if you would search this girl for weapons."

I heard footsteps, and felt a new pair of hands on me. A gentler touch moved down my arms, squeezing every inch of my sleeves. It was Bok Choy's wife, whose beauty had astonished me. Her hands brushed down the front of my body. The men shifted positions to accommodate her. She removed the peachwood sword from my belt and the rope dart from my pocket. Her hands lingered over my thighs, where people commonly conceal knives. Her touch was thorough, careful, and businesslike. Then the men rolled me over onto my stomach and held me down so she could continue searching me. She started at my feet, frisking up along my body. She removed the bagua mirror from my back.

When she reached my head, she leaned over and whispered in my ear. "If he offers you a cigar, smoke it," she said, soft as breathing, and then she withdrew.

"She couldn't have said so before?" I muttered, glaring at her back as she walked out of the room.

The men pushed me onto my back again. They climbed onto me, keeping me pinned down with their weight. The man's foot came down over my face again. I turned my head to the side and he pressed down, immobilizing me.

They were skillful. Experienced. They didn't let me have control of any part of my body—not even my head.

I looked up at Bok Choy. His feet were tapping. A man's foot pinned my head to the floor. Bok Choy shook his head and sighed. "You just cost me another dollar. I bet Chicken you'd be carrying knives."

He lay down on his side and faced me. Bok Choy lounged in a mockery of my posture. I scowled at him.

He took a slow puff on his cigar, and then he blurred into a stream of movement.

I stared into dark, blurry circles. It took me a moment to realize what I was looking at.

Guns.

Bok Choy was aiming two pistols at my eyes.

I hate guns.

"I like you," he told me. "I really like you. Normally you'd be dead by now. But I like you a lot. Do you know why I like you so much?"

Looking into the barrels of his guns, pinned in place, I felt small and frightened. I thought about men like Mr. Wong and his son, and I knew the answer to Bok Choy's question.

"You like me because I'm powerless," I said.

"Wrong!" he shouted, shaking the pistols in front of my eyes. "I like you because you remind me of my daughter."

I reminded him of his daughter, and he was pointing guns in my eyes? I was baffled.

"A sorcerer is going to destroy your part of Chinatown," I said.

The guns shook again. He giggled once more. The foot pressed down harder. I winced, my cheekbone forced to the wood floor.

It was too much. The foot in my face made me boil with rage. There's only so much I can tolerate before I snap. "You," I said, "the one with the foot in my face. I'm going to beat you to a pulp."

The men laughed. The pistols withdrew. Bok Choy said, "Do you think you could?"

"What do you mean?" I said, staring into the gangster's eager face. This man's behavior had baffled me since the moment I met him.

"Do you think you could beat my man Chicken in a fight?"

I didn't know. I didn't know what he looked like, I didn't know what training he might have had, and I didn't know how young or old or good or fast he was. But fury had taken over and I wasn't thinking. I was a bundle of anger. In the last few days I'd been tricked, attacked, pushed around, held down, tied up. And now I had a man's foot in my face and I wanted to beat him until he wept and bled.

"Yes," I said.

Bok Choy held out the cigar again. "A puff?" he asked.

Remembering what his wife had whispered, I said yes. He placed his cigar between my lips. I closed my mouth and puffed on his cigar.

I had expected the room to erupt in raunchy laughter, but there was silence.

Bok Choy withdrew his cigar and rose up to his feet again. "Let her go," he told his men, "untie her."

All at once the weight came off me. The rope was pulled free next, and then the net was removed. I sat up. It was nearly dizzying, to be free to move again. I rubbed my wrists where the rope had bound them.

"A dollar on the girl," said Bok Choy.

"You're on a losing streak, Boss," one of his men said. "You might be the whore tomorrow. I'll take that bet."

"Good," said Bok Choy. "What are you waiting for? *Fight!*"

TWENTY

I shot to my feet in time to duck below a powerful punch. Staggering back, I tried to regain my balance, but my leg hit a chair and I stumbled to the floor. The man kicked at my face. I dodged his kick, rolled to the side, grabbed the chair by its leg, and yanked it in front of me in time to block another kick. I turned the chair and caught his ankle between the chair's legs, then I pushed it away from me, knocking him off balance. I sprang back up to my feet.

His side was facing me. I chambered my leg. Short, hard kicks to his ribs. One kick, two kicks, three. He groaned and stifled a cough.

Men were shouting all around us. They were cheering. A fierce joy surged through me, an elation. I wasn't even sure what my opponent looked like, but it didn't matter to me. I was free and swift, and fighting, and I wanted to pound somebody.

I began another series of sharp kicks to his midsection. He brought his elbow down on my ankle. It connected. Pain shot up my leg. I took a few steps back and he advanced toward me. There was an opening: his stance was slightly too wide; his left knee was defenseless. I roundhoused the knee, striking it with the heel of my left foot. He bent over to clutch it and I brought an elbow down at the base of his skull.

Crying out in pain, he stepped forward and grabbed hold of my robe. Grappling isn't a strength of mine. If he got me down to the floor, he'd beat me.

But he'd already had me on the floor. His foot in my face. I aimed a stomp-kick at the same knee. My kick landed with a clapping sound, and I pushed off, out of the man's grasp.

I didn't waste any time. I came back hitting. A blizzard of fists and kicks. He held up his arms in front of his body for protection and I hit him some more. He backed away and I pursued, continuing to hit him. He backed up against the wall. Eventually he stopped holding his arms up, and I kept on pounding away at his chest.

I became aware of voices. "You can stop," the voices were saying, "you won."

I landed punch after punch on the chest of the man who had put his foot in my face. Men grabbed at me and I blocked, dodged, weaved to the side and continued to pummel this man. I wasn't going to let anyone treat me like that. I was tired of it, tired of the cuts in my stomach, the feet in my face.

They managed to pull the unconscious man away from me but I wasn't ready to stop fighting. I turned and attacked the gangsters with a flurry of strikes. I was a blur of violence. Men grabbed chairs and held them up as weapons. Or maybe to protect themselves. I kicked a chair and it slammed into the man holding it, knocking him over backward. I advanced to the next man. Hardly more than a boy, he held a chair up in front of him. He looked frightened. I yanked the chair and he held onto it, stupidly, and tipped forward. I landed a fist on his throat. He made a gurgling noise and dropped to the floor.

The men circled me, wielding chairs and knives. I didn't care. Rage drove my pulses, rage and a kind of predatory ecstasy.

A little girl's voice came from the side of the room. "What's happening, Papa?" she said. At the sound of her voice, all the men in the room dropped their chairs and took casual poses.

It was bizarre enough to snap me out of my blood-rage. What was going on? I stood in a haze, like a waking dream. I felt the anger begin to drain from my body, and my own behavior bewildered me.

At the other end of the room, Bok Choy squatted on his haunches, facing a little girl. She was about five years old. "There's nothing to worry about, little one," he said. "A new friend is showing us some of her kung fu skills."

The girl clapped her hands together and jumped up and down. "I want to see! I want to see!"

Bok Choy reached out his arms and drew her into a hug. He lifted her up in his arms and twirled around. He was grinning. His gold tooth glinted in his smile, a genuine smile. Bok Choy seemed delighted to have this little girl in his arms. It was as strange as seeing the gangsters sitting nervously in the chairs they'd been holding moments earlier to defend themselves against my onslaught.

Still holding the girl tight, Bok Choy turned to me. "My daughter wants to see you do some kung fu maneuvers," he said. "Will you give her a demonstration?"

The world had gone mad. My pulses were still pounding from the pummeling I gave that man, everyone in the room was pretending to be relaxed, at ease, while the gang leader was doting on a little girl. I had never seen a man show such affection toward a daughter.

"A demonstration for my daughter," he repeated. "You cost me two dollars tonight. A little show is the least you could do."

The girl's eyes met mine. She seemed so innocent, so full of hope, so happy in her father's arms. She was what I was here for. She was naïve and open-hearted, in need of protection. I could remember it, almost, the innocence. For someone like her I would fight men and monsters. For someone like her I would hop around like a trained monkey.

In that madhouse, I decided to show off my martial arts skills. I pushed two chairs together. From a standing position I jumped over the chairs, kicked out with both feet, and executed a three-point landing. I retrieved my rope dart and spun it around, showing the girl how I can wrap the line around my calf to speed it up, and disengage it to shoot it out. I put the rope dart back in my pocket and ran to the wall; when I reached the wall, I ran two steps up and pushed myself off in a backflip. I went through the first third of the rounded motions of taiji, the twelve animal forms of xing yi, the stepping pattern of bagua.

The girl clapped and squealed with delight. "Teach me!" she shouted. "I want to learn."

Bok Choy, the madman, the killer, tickled her under the chin and said, "Hua, our guest just put on a show for you. Isn't there something you should say?"

The girl turned to face me. I had to wonder if my eyes had ever looked so bright and eager. Her name was Hua, Flower. Of course it was. "Thank you!" she said.

Bok Choy was teaching his daughter American customs, not Chinese. Everything here was unpredictable, bizarre. Deciding to offer both worlds of manners, I bowed and said, "You're welcome."

Bok Choy looked at me, sizing me up with his quick eyes. "Was that bagua you were doing at the end?"

I nodded.

"That's bodyguard training," he said to Hua. Bok Choy kissed his daughter's forehead and said, "Papa will tuck you in soon. Ask Mama to tell you a story, and remember to say thank-you when she's done. I need to have a grown-up talk with these people."

He let her stand on her own feet and shooed her off through a door. Before she left, she turned and said, "I love you, Papa!"

"I love you too, Hua! Tell your Mama I love her more than diamonds."

As soon as the girl was gone, Bok Choy said, "Get Chicken to the infirmary." He turned to face me. "If you didn't come here to kill me, what do you want?"

Sitting at a table like civilized people, I told him what was happening. Finishing, I said, "Every merchant who pays you instead of the Ansheng tong is going to die. Every building you own is going to be destroyed. This will happen tonight, in just a few hours. I can't stop it alone."

Bok Choy mulled it all over. His eyes flicked back and forth, up and down, like a gambler calculating the odds. Moments passed that felt like hours. Finally he looked at me again and said, "I'm not a Daoist, Li-lin."

It felt like I suddenly deflated. So that was that, then. He thought everything I was telling him was bunk and nonsense, superstitions left behind in the old country. I let out a tired breath. I had endured so much here tonight, for nothing.

"The only gods I believe in are the gods of gambling," he said, his gold tooth shining in his smile. "So. Thirty men."

"I don't know what you mean," I told him.

"Thirty men. They will come armed with knives and hatchets."

I watched him, waiting to hear the catch. He couldn't just be offering them to me.

"Thirty men is an army in Chinatown. Thirty men means tong war," Bok Choy said. "Thirty men means the Xie Liang tong is committed to making war against the Anshengs."

I started to smile. I had no idea the Xie Liang tong had grown so powerful. The well-established Ansheng tong could rouse at most forty fighting men.

"I am willing to commit a force of thirty men," Bok Choy continued, "and all you have to do is beat me in a game of pai jiu. We leave the decision in the hands of the gods of gambling."

My arms dropped to my sides in mute surprise.

"Hundreds of people will die if you don't do something," I insisted. "Hundreds of *your* people."

Bok Choy shook his head. "I don't know if I believe you. Even if I do believe you, I don't know if I'm willing to start fighting the tong wars again. This is why I'm going to let the gods of gambling make my decision."

I took a breath. "And what will happen if I lose?"

"Well then you'll work for me," he said. His smile gleamed like a knife. "On a three-year contract."

I stared at Bok Choy. I imagined my life as a contract girl. A sick sensation coursed through me.

My husband and I made love, frequently. We shared such an intense bond. We were passionate in our hunger for each other. I couldn't imagine putting that kind of intimacy on sale. Two bits to see me, four bits to touch me, six bits to . . .

I stared at the grinning man who wanted to turn me into a whore. His gold tooth gleamed. A feeling of horror moved from my gut out to the rest of my body. If I accepted this challenge, if I played his game and lost, I would be committed to years of misery and degradation.

But I had spent years watching my father play pai jiu with Dr. Wei. Both were brilliant men. I knew all the strategies. Bok Choy was certain to underestimate me. Half of Chinatown needed to be protected, and I needed to avenge myself on Liu Qiang. I couldn't imagine how bad things would be if Liu Qiang managed to raise a Kulou-Yuanling. A whole town would be screaming.

And I'd heard a whole town scream once before.

"Let's play pai jiu," I said to Bok Choy, and my guts turned upside down.

TWENTY-ONE

The tiles clinked on the table. He had played *za jiu*, a mismatched pair of dominoes with nine pips each. It was a good play, worth nine points, but I was still a point ahead. Just barely, I was winning.

Holding my cigar between two fingers, I studied my tiles. I needed to win. The consequences of losing were beyond belief.

Bok Choy sat across from me, twitchy and hyperkinetic. Puffing on his cigar, he grinned his gilded teeth at me. "Might as well start calling me Boss, Li-lin," he said.

Sparring had taught me enough to know when an opponent was trying to make me lose composure. The crowd pressed closer, watching us play. I didn't want to let them see how nervous I was.

Bok Choy smirked at me. He was trying to make me lose composure. It was working. I was so tense I was nearly hallucinating. Staring at the pips on the pai jiu tiles, my vision blurred till I thought I saw a contract. I remembered Mr. Wong's contract girl, facing the wall in silence, the apparition of a cane over her. I remembered the grunts and moans behind the closed doors. I knew they spent years like that, in those fetid, dingy rooms, paying off a contract.

My breathing grew shallow and quick. I shouldn't have taken the bet. What was I thinking? I'd been thinking of the men on the southwest side of Chinatown, decent men who labored twelve hours every day and slept three men to a bed so they could send money to their families in China. I had been thinking of my father, who sacrificed one of his eyes to save me.

"You can still forfeit," said Bok Choy, his smile wild and golden. "Forfeit now and there's no contract. I'll let you start leaving me red envelopes, but you won't have to come work for me if you forfeit."

I opened my mouth. I wanted to say yes, I forfeit. Yes, I've had enough of this game. I was terrified of what would happen if I lost. It shook me to my core.

And yet forfeiting the game would mean I'd lose a chance at getting his support. With thirty armed men I might be able to stop them from raising a Kulou-Yuanling. With thirty armed men at my side I could descend on Liu Qiang and his allies as an army.

I took a deep breath and placed the next pair of tiles. I played *meihua, mei pai*, a matching pair of dominoes, with ten pips each. It was a strong hand, worth ten points. I began to feel a little more confident. I was eleven points ahead. Hands worth eleven or twelve points are very rare.

Bok Choy began to giggle. He stood up, nearly knocking his chair over. With a flourish he placed one domino down. Twelve pips. I felt the contents of my stomach begin to come up as the gangster grinned his gold-pocked smile, and placed his other domino. Also twelve pips.

Tian pai. The License of the Sky. The rarest, most valuable hand.

The only hand worth twelve points.

Vaguely I was aware of cheering all around me, but I had entered a deep silence, like the silence of opium dreamers or drowned men.

Bok Choy leaned over the pai jiu table. A gold smile gloated at me. "You work for me now," he said.

The world came to a stop. If I refused to honor my bet, then the Xie Liang tong would be coming after me. I wouldn't live long. No one would trust my word ever again.

The room was still cheering. I hated these people, cheering Bok Choy's victory. Cheering my defeat, my degradation.

"Do you know English?" he asked me.

"Yes," I said, and then the implication hit me. Some contract girls work in bathhouses catering to white San Franciscans. The men who came there were often opium addicts, or workers who resent the Chinese competition. They were rough with Chinese women. How long would I be able to last before I was broken?

Someone brought a sheet of paper over to my side of the pai jiu table. A contract. My eyes were wet with tears, but I would not weep.

The men in the room were lining up to congratulate Bok Choy. The man dressed as a whore congratulated him. Even the waitress, his wife, who had helped me, came up to congratulate him on his victory. My eyes glazed over. I was ruined.

"Sign the contract, Li-lin," Bok Choy said with a smirk. I had already begun to hate his smirk.

I met his eyes. Once I signed the contract, I was his. They're called three-year contracts, but it's a lie, to trick gullible girls into signing them. It costs money to live—rent and food. For three years, a contract girl works on her back, but she develops a debt. When the three years are over, the contract girl thinks she's free to go, but she now has to work to pay off all the money she owes. Usually, the only way a girl can get out of a contract is when another man buys it.

I fought back my tears. "Sign the contract," he said. I stifled a sob.

"It will give you much face to have the girl who beat Tom Wong working for you, won't it," I said.

"Sign the contract," he said.

I stared at him, and heard the cheering of the Xie Liangs in the room. They weren't my people. I hated them, hated each and every one of them. I wasn't going to let them see me cowed or craven, trying to renege on a bet.

I took the pen and signed the contract.

Bok Choy handed the signed paper to one of his men. I felt so defeated. His wife came over to him. Glaring at me, she counted out five dollars and handed them to Bok Choy.

He grinned at me. "I bet her you would sign the contract without reading it," he gloated.

A sick wave went through me. I had made yet another mistake. The last days were a roadmap of my errors. Trusting Liu Qiang, failing to protect my father, and now coming here. I scowled at myself.

"Wait," I said to Bok Choy, "please. Give me tonight. Let me finish this. Let me stop the ritual."

"And give you time to run away?"

"I will not run away," I said, choking on the words. It was the truth. If I ran, word would get out. Everyone would know I was a runaway whore, someone who couldn't even be trusted to honor a contract. My father would disown me. There was no one who would take me in. Even my spirit powers would diminish, since talismans are contracts too. "Give me tonight. Tomorrow I will come and work for you."

Bok Choy gazed at me, sizing me up with the mind of a gambler. He was wondering, I knew, if I was worth betting on. He was teetering on the edge of a decision.

It was up to me to tip him so he'd fall where I wanted. He might even send men to help me after all. It was outlandish, but I thought I knew what was most important to him

"Your daughter's life is in jeopardy, Bok Choy."

The gangster gestured to the table, where the pai jiu tiles spelled out his victory. "You lost, Li-lin. Accept it."

"But this is serious," I told him.

"You want to know what's serious?" he said, with a maniacal gleam in his eye. "I worship the gods of gambling, and you lost the damn game. Now go out there and do your thing. Jump up and down. Ring your little bell, burn some funny paper, and shout 'yo ho.'"

I stared. Bok Choy was out of his mind. Bai mu—white-eyed from blindness. He was mocking all that was sacred. What kind of man risks his future on the roll of a die?

"Go on," Bok Choy told me with a smirk. "Get out there and chant your nonsense and burn your phony money until your scary giant monster goes away."

"Yo ho," I said with a scowl. I stood. The Xie Liangs made room for me as I strode out of the gambling hall and into the night.

TWENTY-TWO

A breeze blew westward from the Bay, bringing a chill to the dark San Francisco night. I shivered. There were only three hours left, three hours before Liu Qiang performed his ritual.

No matter what happened, I was in a position now where there was no way I could win. If the one-armed sorcerer managed to call forth a Kulou-Yuanling, there would be such a reign of destruction I could scarcely imagine it. And if I stopped the ritual, if I defeated the man who cut me and ruined my father's eyesight, then the sun would come up in the morning, and I would go to work as a whore for the Xie Liang tong.

I wanted to cry at the injustice of it. I remembered how my life had been, once, young and hopeful and married to a hero, when my future seemed as if it were going to be spent in day after day of contentment with the man I loved.

What would happen if I did nothing? I didn't have to oppose Tom and Liu Qiang. I didn't have to try to stop their ritual. The Kulou-Yuanling would rise, and my life would go on. Simply by doing nothing, I could escape a whore's fate.

And yet, if I did nothing, Liu Qiang would triumph. He wouldn't allow my father to go on living. The one-armed man would come for him with a monster that could slaughter armies, a monster that even the Senior Abbot who founded the Maoshan lineage was not strong enough to fight. Father would be killed.

Thinking of Liu Qiang made me go stiff with anger. If he managed to raise the Kulou-Yuanling, he'd kill my father, but he'd probably let me live. That's how insignificant he considered me, no threat to him in any way. Fury bubbled inside me. I wanted to see the one-armed man broken and defeated.

I had to defeat Liu Qiang. No one else was going to do it. Even if it meant I was going to live a life of degradation, I needed to stop him.

Liu Qiang. His monstrous arm. Tom Wong. Evil spirits. Gangsters from the Ansheng. Men and monsters were arrayed against me, and I had to face them alone.

I didn't even know where the ritual was going to take place.

I thought for a moment. To perform the ritual, Liu Qiang would need to burn a hundred corpses. They wouldn't do that indoors, so it had to be somewhere out in the open. They had to bring the corpses there somehow. Chinatown is too small to carry dozens of corpses around without people noticing. Smuggling that many dead men to one place is bound to attract attention.

Was there anyone who'd be willing to tell me? Maybe. But I only had three hours. There was no time to go poking around in the hope that someone would give me information.

I needed a more direct approach.

I arrived at the monastery and found Shuai Hu. In the austere quarters, he was eating, using a windowsill as his table. My eyes bulged. The tiger monk's demeanor had shown so much discipline, composure, and self-control. But he'd never learned to eat with utensils.

There was sauce dripping from his hands and smeared on his chin. There was rice scattered along the windowsill where he was eating. He stuck out his tongue and licked sauce from his fingers the way a cat laps water from a bowl. I wanted to laugh at the absurdity of it.

"Shuai Hu, I need your help," I said.

"No," said the tiger-man, shaking his bald head. "I already told you, Daonu Xian. I will not fight, and I will not kill."

I smiled. "Are you willing to scare people?"

He pondered for a moment. He wiped sauce from his mouth with one big hand. His face broke out in a cheerful, lopsided grin. "I can do that," he said. "If you promise me something."

I walked to the territory of the Ansheng tong with Shuai Hu at my side. Beneath the painted balconies of Tian Hou Temple Street we found what we were looking for. Six of the Ansheng hatchetmen, traveling together. They were men in their teens and twenties. They had hatchets at their belts. They wore layer upon layer of heavy cotton shirts to protect against knife attacks. I had repaired some of those shirts when they'd been torn.

"There's a ritual tonight," I said to them. "You're going to tell me where it is."

The men glanced at each other. What they saw in each other's faces reinforced their confidence. They thought they could take a girl and a baldie in a fight. "Why would we tell you anything?" one asked.

The monk spoke, his voice serious, solid as iron. "People will suffer if you don't tell us."

The men laughed. "Shut your mouth, Baldie," one of them said.

A ripple moved through Shuai Hu's tiger shadow. The ripple rose out over the monk in a wave. His shadow pulsed with unnatural darkness, as though it were breathing. At each pulse the monstrous shape around him grew larger, more physical. The men watched, their stances growing less and less certain.

It took only moments. They were facing a man; seconds later there was a tiger standing in his place. A tiger with a man's shadow.

But not any tiger. Shuai Hu was huge, bigger than any tiger on record. He must have been as tall as a horse. Nothing human could stand against him. I staggered back, startled by the size of the wild beast. He could crush a wooden carriage between his paws, rend brick with his claws. And behind him, visible to all eyes in the ten o'clock light, three tails waved like banners of war.

Shuai Hu growled, baring fangs the size of small swords. A feral smell blew from his mouth. The men scattered, fleeing in panic.

I managed to grab hold of one by the collar of his shirt. "Now," I said, with the enormous supernatural tiger glowering behind me, "you will tell me where the ritual is taking place."

The man screamed and tried to pull away. I gripped his wrist with my other hand. "Tell me," I said. He screamed again.

I turned to the tiger. "Brother Hu," I said, "his screams are hurting my ears."

A pair of eyes focused on me, huge, green and gold and inhuman. Suddenly I was afraid. Was the monk still himself behind the monster's eyes? I would not want to go into combat against that beast, not even with my father leading the charge and an army of men with pistols and muskets. If Shuai Hu lost control of himself, there would be no stopping him.

Dark stripes and orange stripes poured into his shadow. The tiger vanished as though a chalk drawing had been wiped off of a blackboard. The monk staggered in its place, bald and silent. Muscles clenched and unclenched in his jaws. He seemed to struggle for awareness and self-control.

I watched his transformation and decided I would not ask him to do this again.

The hatchetman screamed once more, his voice hoarse by now, and then was quiet. His eyes had gone wide as saucers. He stared at the monk and began to shake.

"Where will the ritual take place?" I asked again.

The man looked at me with glassy eyes and shook with fear.

"Where?" I demanded.

"I," he began, his voice meek, "I don't know."

I stared at him. He didn't know? I had less than an hour to find Liu Qiang and this man didn't know.

"K-keep it away from me," he said.

"Tell me what I want to know and he'll let you live."

Shuai Hu smiled at the man. "Grr," he said, in a human voice drenched in wit. It was enough to push the man over the edge.

"I don't know about any ritual," he said, desperation in his voice, "I just got back to town!"

I looked at him. "Where were you?"

"Wyoming!" he shouted. "I was in Wyoming!"

I had a sick sense. Horror crept through me with the comprehension. I knew where he'd been, and I knew what he'd done there. But I needed to hear him say it. "Where in Wyoming?" I whispered.

"Rock Springs!" he said.

I took a deep breath. Some years back, there was a massacre at a Chinese settlement outside Rock Springs. Dozens of men were slaughtered. Their bodies were buried without ceremony in a mass grave. The mob that murdered them went unpunished. Liu Qiang would have his hundred corpses. It wouldn't be so hard to find a hundred Chinese men who died badly, here on Gold Mountain.

"You went on a mission to bring corpses back from Rock Springs," I said.

"Yes," he cried, "yes! Six of us. We dug them up and brought them back in carriages. It's an auspicious under-taking. The corpses are going to be buried in China, with their ancestors."

I rolled my eyes. This man believed what Tom Wong's men had told him, as my father had believed it. Sometimes it is easier to believe in the goodness of men's intentions.

"Where did you deliver the corpses?" I asked.

"A warehouse," he said. "There were other corpses there, not just the ones we brought from Wyoming."

"Corpses from Oregon and Los Angeles," I said, because I knew Chinese workers had been massacred there as well. "Where is this warehouse?"

"On California Street."

Something clicked into place. "California and Pike? They dry fish there?"

The man nodded. I cursed and let him go. With one last glance at Shuai Hu, the man ran off. He did not look back.

"You know something about this warehouse," Shuai Hu said.

"Yes," I said. "Mao'er brought me there a few days ago."

"Who is Mao'er?" the tiger monk asked.

"A cat spirit, with two tails. Mao'er is almost like a friend to me. I don't think you'd like him. He loves to fight."

Shuai Hu ignored that. "And this warehouse?"

"It's an Ansheng building, warded by my father's talismans, but Mao'er brought me there," I said, taking a breath, "because there's a back door."

Shuai Hu gave me a steady gaze. "A back door, meaning that spirits can cross past his talismans."

"Yes," I said. "Liu Qiang must have done something to Father's talismans. He may have taken them down and replaced them with copies that had no investiture of power."

"Why would he do that, Daonu? It seems like a lot of work to accomplish very little."

"When I first met Liu," I said, slowly, "his arm was an ordinary stump. This was at my father's temple. He must have temporarily removed his demonic arm. I thought it was due to my yin eyes. They knew I'd be able to see the monster, and they wouldn't have been able to trick me. But now . . ."

"Now you think it was also because your father's wards would have prevented his arm from entering the temple?"

"That's it exactly, Shuai Hu. If Father's talismans retained their power, Liu would need to remove his arm every time he entered the building. To prepare for the ritual, Liu Qiang needed to go in and out, with his spirit-arm whispering secrets in his ear."

"Daonu Xian," the monk said, bowing, "I take my leave."

"What do you mean?" I said. "You can't go. I need your help. Their ritual will begin in less than an hour. I don't even know where it's going to take place."

"Very well," he said. "Let us reason. If you were performing such a ritual, at such an hour, where would you do it?"

I mulled it over. "In a graveyard. But it would take a long time to carry a hundred corpses out of the warehouse. Constables would catch them."

"So they'll perform the ritual in the warehouse?"

"No," I said. "It will need to be outdoors, under the moon.

"So . . ."

"The ritual will be performed on the roof of the warehouse."

"You know where the ritual is going to be held. I have completed my end of our agreement. You will keep your end of it?"

"Yes," I said, trying not to let him hear the reluctance in my voice. "I will not kill any human beings tonight."

He gave me a lopsided smile that was somehow more human than any I'd ever seen. Without saying a word, he turned and walked away.

I watched him go. Shuai Hu was a strange man, I thought. Then I reminded myself, *a strange monster*.

TWENTY-THREE

I'd seen massacre before. I was six years old. I was a coward then. I saw the White-Haired Demoness, I saw her eerie, horrifying beauty, and I ran away. The town's guards confronted her. She said "Give me your hearts" and the hearts burst out of their chests. She floated through our village, killing my friends, my cousins, everyone.

I will never forget the screaming. I hid at the bottom of the well while my people fled, screamed, and died.

The next day was warm and sunny. Arms, legs, and human heads dangled from the branches of the trees, each suspended by a white hair. A stench rose from the mutilated corpses. They had been my friends, my uncles and cousins, my neighbors. My mother.

I had stuffed Mother's innards back into her body. Her eyes had been gouged out. Looking into the hollow sockets of her eyes, I swore that I would never hide from monsters. Never again.

Crowds of men parted around me as I strode through Chinatown. A man stood at the street corner with a barrel, selling rice. Another called out to everyone, offering to repair dented pots. These were hard-working men. Some of them were saving their money. Others were sending their earnings to support their families in China. I would not allow another massacre. I would die before I let that happen. To keep this Kulou-Yuanling from rising, I would risk my life a thousand times over. I would accept the fate the Gods of Gambling had dealt me.

I was carrying my paper talismans, a bagua mirror, my peachwood sword, and my rope dart. Liu Qiang was out there in the night. I was going to find a way to stop him. To stop him, and to punish him, I thought, brushing my hand over my stomach. His cuts itched.

Rage pounded in my ears. I walked faster, intent. Everything that happened in the last days, everything happening now, all of it started decades ago. Before I was born. In China, a group of young bullies harassed a boy. They'd been cruel to him, for no reason. Anger and rejection twisted that boy until he became a kind of monster himself; first a soulstealer, and now something worse.

The monster grafted to the stump of Liu Qiang's arm terrified me. I could still see Hong Xiaohao at the moment of his death, his body twitching and going limp when the serpent arm bit through his throat.

Half a block away from the warehouse, I stopped. The traffic of Chinatown continued as always. The men's queues swished from side to side as they walked. It was a different kind of movement that concerned me.

Here and there in the crowd were men who didn't seem to be in a hurry. A teenager in a black cap paced a dozen steps back and forth. An older man stood just inside a grocer's doorway, watching the crowd. I picked out a third, a fourth, a fifth.

They were guards.

The moon was rising, vast and somber. It was nearly eleven o'clock, the hour of the First Earthly Branch, when the deathly powers would be at their strongest.

And the warehouse—the entire building—was surrounded by guards.

There could be forty men between me and Liu Qiang. It might be the entire force of the Ansheng tong.

"Ai!" a man shouted. It was the man in the grocery shop's entryway. He was pointing right at me. Instantly men shot into motion—the teenager, another man I'd seen, and three more I hadn't. Drawing their weapons—knives, hatchets, iron bars—they looked to the older man, and saw him pointing in my direction.

The ritual was only minutes away. I didn't have time to fight a group of men. Even if they had no training, even if they came at me one at a time, an armed man would gut me the instant I made a mistake.

I turned and fled.

"Don't let her get away!" a man cried. I ran down Dupont Street. To my left I saw a carriage drawn by a white horse; I considered jumping aboard, or panicking the horse, but neither one was a definite escape. I needed to get away, and I needed to do it fast.

I heard their steps as they ran along the cobblestones. I sped for the wall, beginning to lighten my steps with qinggong. Each step was lighter than the one before it, and when I reached the wall I kept on running. One step. Two steps. I grabbed onto a wooden awning and pulled myself up.

There was cursing down below me while I climbed up the side of the building, finding handholds in the joints of wood or on balconies. I had escaped.

It was probably eleven by now. Liu Qiang would have started performing his ritual. I climbed to the roof and looked out over Chinatown. Below me on the street, a yellow trolley came to a stop. Some men climbed off, some climbed on, and it continued on its way. Its bell chimed more quickly as it picked up speed. At one corner, a man was hawking a basket of vegetables that had been fresh this morning. Throngs of men flowed below me. Some headed east, toward the granite facade of the Sub-Treasury Building. Others congregated around street vendors. A few stood eating rice porridge, engaged in animated conversation. It struck me how peaceful it all seemed, how normal. These men should flee for their lives, but they had no idea of the terror that was about to be unleashed. I watched them living their lives, and I was consumed by the knowledge that I'd failed them.

It was frustrating. Chinatown was in danger, and no one could help. Bok Choy refused to help. Shuai Hu refused to help. My father was too fragile in his current state—because of me, because of my mistakes. Rocket would have done something, but Rocket was dead.

There was no reason to hope. The forces of evil were closing on Chinatown—a soulstealer with a demon for an arm, a giant monster, and a dark undercurrent of the biggest criminal empire in the city.

I looked out, across the street. On a rooftop across the way I could see light, and movement, and a very large pile. A fire was burning, and there were men standing on the roof. It was them. I realized what the pile was. It was a pile of dead men. A hundred corpses who died of hunger or violence.

The ritual was already underway. I stamped my feet in frustration.

I needed to interrupt Liu Qiang before his ritual was complete. I examined my options. I could climb back down to the street, and try to sprint past the Ansheng guards. But the guards had seen me already. They knew where I was. They'd close in on me before I even reached the ground.

I could fight them, I supposed. I'd try to take them one at a time, but it was unlikely that would happen. No, they'd attack me all at once. Even though the attack would be uncoordinated, there would be too many fists and feet to account for. Even if I fought my way through, I'd emerge so battered that I wouldn't be able to stop the ritual.

I looked across the street, to the other roof. The street divided me from where I wanted to be. The street flowed between us, like a river. My eyes went up to the sky. The full moon's brightness kept me from seeing the stars, but I knew they were still up there.

One of my favorite legends involved a weaver girl and a farmboy who loved each other. They could not be together. They became stars, on opposite shores of the Silver River in the sky. Their love was eternal, and so was their loneliness. But what I loved about the story, what made the story bittersweet rather than simply tragic, is that one night each year, on the seventh day of the seventh month, all the magpies in the world would gather to help the lovers reunite. On this one night each year, the lovers come together, crossing the Silver River by walking on a bridge made of magpies.

I flipped through my paper talismans until I found the one I wanted. Blue paper stamped with row after row of birds.

I lit the talisman on fire and watched it burn. Smoke rose from the burning page, in wisps at first. The flame crackled. The old, familiar, sooty smell filled my nose. The smoke billowed from the sheet in dense black puffs. A bird burst through the smoke. A seagull. From a hook-shaped, pale orange beak, it gave out a cackling noise. Others followed, flapping out of the smoke. In moments there were hundreds of gulls. Moments later there were thousands, and all of them wailed, keened, or cackled like maniacs. Some made guttural murmurs. Plumages of white and gray, or blue, or black, encompassed the roof I was standing on and the sky above me. The commotion of their beating wings accompanied the trills and squawks.

The roof I was standing on was covered in birds, and so were some of the adjacent roofs. Hundreds of birds took to the air, circling me. Each gull of the multitude had a third eye in its forehead, a dark bead in a vertical slit. All around me I heard the grief and laughter of their cries: Aah! Aah! A kind of crazy joy met my anger in the wild spinning bird-filled night. I began to laugh like them. It was heartbreaking laughter.

The hatchetmen on the roof saw me and gaped. The Haiou Shen are visible to everyone, but they look like seagulls; no one sees the third eye. The men on the roof saw seagulls, a cloud of seagulls, and the gulls were holding a rope.

It was the line from my rope dart. I held the weight and dangled. Still murmuring their pandemonium, the gulls ferried me over California Street. I clenched the muscles in my stomach to keep the rope from spinning. My legs, crossed around the rope, were tense.

When I had seen hot air balloons aloft over San Francisco, I'd wondered how it must feel to drift like that, between earth and sky. I do not know how those ballooners felt, but looking down at the street below me, the human activity and the perimeter of guards, I felt terrified—and exhilarated. I could not stop laughing. My laughter, like the caws of gulls, sounded mad.

We reached the roof of the fish warehouse. Dropping the dart, I landed lightly, on three points. The scent of sweet incense reached my nostrils. A man's voice was chanting. I heard the flapping of wings. The spirit gulls were flying off. Though I could not say how I knew, I knew they wouldn't go far.

The roof was flat, made of red bricks. At the opposite corner from me, Liu Qiang stood next to a pile of corpses. Somehow I'd thought a hundred dead bodies would take up more space than that. So much tragedy demanded more room, somehow, and yet they'd been heaped together, with no respect for the sanctity of dead men.

Four hatchetmen stood between me and the corpses. Before I could stop the ceremony, I needed to get past them. The gulls had flown off with my rope dart. I drew my peachwood sword.

One of the men advanced toward me, smiling. "Look, it's the girl," he said, lazily raising his hatchet.

No killing tonight, I'd promised. I waited for my attacker to take a swing. I stepped inside his guard. With the pommel of my wooden sword, I smashed his mouth. Teeth broke and I swept his ankle. He crumpled to the roof. I stepped back into a low side-bow stance. The other three hatchetmen closed ranks, coming at me.

Something brushed against my leg. Looking down, I saw Mao'er. The two-tailed cat spirit had taken one of his human shapes. He was male for once. Today he looked like a little boy, aside from his mouth. Purring, grinning, he bared cat's teeth, long and sharp. "Fighty now, miao?"

Seeing Mao'er made me smile. "My friend," I said.

He huffed at me.

"Yes, yes," I said. "A cat has no friends. Be careful, Mao'er, these men are dangerous."

He didn't seem to care. With a suddenness that surprised me, Mao'er shifted into a feline shape. He pounced on the closest hatchetman, clawing at his face. The man cried out, flailing. The other hatchetmen gaped, seeing a big cat rip bloody slashes across their friend's face. But then Mao'er's expression changed to a look of surprise. With one hand, now human, he touched the throwing knife that had pierced his neck. "Peachwood," he said, dribbling spirit-blood from his mouth. Then he yanked the hatchetman backward. The two of them toppled together off the roof.

Just like that, so quickly, my friend was gone. "Mao'er," I whispered.

Liu Qiang lowered the arm that threw the knife. "I can see your demons, Li-lin," he called. "I wear a dog's eyes over my own."

I glanced at Liu Qiang with fresh hatred. The soulstealer had thrown a knife into Mao'er's throat and killed a dog for its spirit sight.

He lit a paper talisman on fire. No doubt he'd prepared a number of spells in case he had to defend himself against my father. The spells would work just as well against me. I thought swiftly: slash his spell with my peachwood sword, or deflect it with my bagua mirror? Spells and spirits would merely bounce off the mirror but my sword would end them. But some magic would slip like vapor past my sword. I couldn't afford to let the soulstealer infect me with a magical disease. Slipping my sword into my belt, I grabbed with frantic fingers, trying to unsling the octagonal mirror from my back.

Liu Qiang dropped his burning talisman and drove a spirit at me. The spirit was a long stretch of smoky darkness, full of faces, screaming. From their terror and despair, I understood how this spirit worked. It devoured its victims, digesting them into its dark spirit-body. If it caught me, I would live forever, terrified, trapped, and alone.

It came at me like a shooting star. Somehow I managed to hold up my bagua mirror in time. The spirit struck the mirror with enough force that I stumbled a few steps back, but I managed to deflect it. The spirit streamed away from the mirror, but it had already started curving its trajectory, turning its long smoky body around so it would face me again. I estimated I had a few seconds before it could attack me again.

So long as the two remaining hatchetmen hadn't been trained in kung fu, it should only take me a few seconds to disarm them. Shifting the mirror to my left hand, I drew my peachwood sword and charged at them. The first man swung his hatchet. I ducked under his arm and stepped past him. The second man was holding his hatchet too far from his body, a mistake made by men who over-rely on brute force. I lunged for him, dropping into a low forward strike, and yanked my sword's wooden blade up from behind his hatchet. His weapon flew from his grip, clattering onto the roof. His face and throat were exposed, so I chopped at his jaw with the heavy bronze mirror in my left hand. Bone cracked and he fell backward. I spun to face the first man, but I'd been too slow.

The scream spirit struck me like a hammer. It carried so much force. Being hit by a locomotive might feel like that. I went sprawling toward the edge of the roof, with black miasma clinging to me. The spirit billowed, swathed me in inky blackness. It burrowed into my mouth, my nostrils, my ears. I could not think. I felt darkness burning at my spirit like acid. My self, my soul, felt like it was being destroyed.

Unnatural quiet came over me, then darkness. I was inside the spirit now. It was dissolving my memory, my identity. Before long, I knew, I wouldn't be able to recall my own name. I refused to scream.

TWENTY-FOUR

No time. There was no time left. I was beginning to lose consciousness. The scream spirit was eating my memories. That profound darkness etched deeper into me.

Etched. Liu Qiang had cut a spell into the center of my stomach. My father had cut a spell into my left side. Now the scream spirit was erasing me.

I began to drive a fingernail into the right side of my stomach. The pain was sharp and sudden. I needed three words to find myself again once I'd been lost. I needed three characters carved into my skin so I could climb out of this pit. I needed Jing, Qi, and Shen.

Jing came first. Fourteen strokes for the perfected essence. I gouged it into my stomach. My fingernail met my skin with a biting pain. Then came Qi, ten strokes for the breath, the vital energy that moves in two directions through all living things. I drove my thumbnail into my skin, writing Qi. The pain made me squirm. Warm blood trickled out onto my fingers. Shen, the character for spirit, came next. I stopped. How many strokes did the character Shen have? It was a simple word, but somehow I couldn't remember how to write it.

My mind felt hazy. I was feeling oddly relaxed, falling asleep. I lost track of whatever I'd been doing. My arm felt heavy. Soft, warm, and heavy. I felt it flop down at my side. It was heavy. I was tired. So tired.

Small and frightened. Memories flitted through my mind like minnows in a stream. So many memories. The sensation was of something sifting through me, of things being torn from my grip. But what? I felt a loss but I couldn't remember what it was or why it mattered.

Ha, once there was a little girl. Singing a little song. Sing, sing, singing. Hahaha! Was that me? Ha. Father's gaze hit me harder than a slap. "Where did you hear that song?"

"A turtle was singing it, Father."

His eyes aimed at me, tense as arrows in bows, ready to shoot. "What kind of turtle was this, Ah Li?"

"It was a silver turtle. The kind that floats in the air. It had an eye in the middle of its face. It was pretty."

He gave a tortured sigh. "It wasn't pretty, Ah Li. It was an abomination. Do you see things like that often?"

"All the time, Father."

He burned a yellow paper talisman, gathered its ashes, and stirred them into a cup of water. "Drink this," he said. "It should blind your yin eyes."

I drank the water. Gagged it down. He looked at me gravely, his face sharp as the point of an axe.

"You will drink talismanic water once a month, like a tonic, to keep you well."

"Yes, Father," I said.

He gave a quick nod. His right eye was twitching, moving, like it wasn't part of his face at all. Looking at me, it said, "There are three treasures."

But wait, no, that didn't happen. That wasn't what happened. I felt confused. His eye didn't say anything to me. What had happened?

The ash-infused water worked. That afternoon I saw no spirits, anywhere.

That night, my father brought paper offerings to burn at the corner of Dupont and California. He carried an iron basket and a satchel of paper offerings. I followed close behind. The streets had never felt less haunted. I looked at the crowds of Chinese immigrants. For the first time I could remember, I saw no swirl of misty faces around any of them, even though the sun had set. My father's spell had worked. Ancestors, ghosts, and goblins, all the creatures that come out at night, were hidden from me.

My father placed First Treasure at the bottom of his iron basket. First Treasure was coarse paper painted with purple and green stripes. Moving with the soft, rounded motions of a true taiji master, my father lit a match. He held the first of the Hell Bank Notes over the match's flame. Fire took the printed sheet by inches. Each movement was perfect, because perfection mattered to him. When the bill had begun to burn well, he dropped the flaming bank note onto First Treasure. He lit another bill.

I had seen my father perform this ceremony before, many times, but the spirit world had always been visible to me. I'd watched my father's performance and seen the spirits respond. This was the first time I'd ever watched him without being able to see the other side. My father had never seen the spirits mill around him, groping for money. He'd never been able to see the gratitude in their pale, no-longer-quite-human faces.

The meaning of my father's actions changed. Seeing him like this reshaped my notion of my father as a man: unsmiling but generous, smoke and sparks swirling around him, he labored every night to bring riches to dead men he would never see. The depth of his devotion moved me. So much effort, so much sacrifice, and all of it on faith. He spent his life protecting the living, assuaging the dead, and at the end of the day he had no one to love him, no one but me.

I looked up. It was getting dark out. Fog and smoke obscured the streets. In the haze I saw something glowing. It was a rich amber glow. It came from a pair of eyes.

The water dragon was longer than a man's height, but no wider than a man's thigh. His fur glistened, blue and white, like foam on the sea. There was an unearthly beauty to his sea-blue mane. His whiskers streamed like a kite in the wind.

With a barking laugh, he peeled back and away, surging up off the street and into the air. He flew upward in coils and dove into the clouds. The fog twisted as it accepted him. He flowed into the clouds foot by foot until there was no sign of him but a glowing pair of amber eyes only I could see.

I shouldn't have been able to see it at all. Not anymore. My father's spell had failed.

I turned to face my father. Focused completely on his ceremony, he noticed no other world. He was proud of his work, proud of the perfect execution of his rituals. He started burning another thousand-yuan bill. It blackened into cinder. I witnessed the change. What had been paper was transformed, by fire, into a thing of spirit. It became real money in the spirit world. Ghostly arms reached out from the shadows to gather the wealth. I could see them.

Tears tried to come out of my eyes, but I held them back. I never forgot that moment, the fire and shadows, the magnificence of the water dragon, the paper-smoke smell of an older country's magic. Watching my father, I knew to my core that I would rather live a painful life than tell him that his spell had worn off. My yin eyes had returned, and I was going to keep them.

At that moment I found my Jing. My refined essence.

Where am I? I wondered. I felt stronger. My legs began to twitch. There were people screaming all around me. Something was fighting me. And I had started to fight back.

A dark worm was eating my memories. I felt them go—a spring day, a cold morning, a conversation, an encounter. Gone. Snow fell over a village and something happened, but I forgot what it was. In the place of the memory, there was only haze. The steamer surged across the Pacific, someone said something, a barrel of rice began to bleed, and then fog rolled over the memory. I felt small losses as my history flitted away, an hour at a time.

Sparring with Rocket—no.

It couldn't have that.

Not that.

His fist came flying at me. He could break bricks, my husband, yet I knew he'd never hurt me. I dodged his hammer-punch and spun to face him. I was too slow. His knee raised up to crunch my chin but somehow he stopped himself an inch away. I laughed and thrust both hands at him, gouging with my thumbs. He caught my hands, pressed them to his lips, and flipped me over. I landed rolling and sprang up to face him. His eyes were so soft, and his mouth was so serious.

He launched a forward kick at my stomach and I dove in below his leg, yanking back at his ankle. Somehow he dropped his other leg and used his arms to propel himself into a flying kick. Both legs hit me and we landed in a sprawling laughing heap. I wrapped my ankles in front of his neck and shoved him off, and in instants we were back on our feet. I wasn't close to being his equal in a fight—no one was—but he was the greatest man I'd ever known, the greatest fighter, and I was going to make myself the best woman I could be. I was going to be a woman who deserved a man like him.

An eye was standing on the ground. "There are three treasures," it said. I blinked. That wasn't right. I looked again. There was no eye there, and there never had been.

I launched myself at the man I loved. My flurry of jabs and kicks forced him to take a step back, and then another. He smiled at me, impressed. His approving smile filled me with vigor, so I shot after him again. I was going to give him the best fight of his life.

I wouldn't let go of that memory, the one time I ever fought Rocket to a standstill. The one time anyone ever did. Something was trying to take the memory away from me, trying to tear it away, but I refused to let it go. I held on with a kind of determination that only those who have loved and loved deeply could understand. I had lost my husband, but I would not lose the memory. Not that one. I dug in, and it felt as though a wind were pressing at me. For that memory, I would be a mountain against the wind.

The wind came to a stop. And with that, I found my Qi, the vital energy that animates the body and the universe.

I felt invigorated, stronger, and more certain. Voices were screaming all around me. I was in trouble, I knew that, though I didn't know why. But I also knew that I was going to find a way out of it.

Suddenly, somehow, I was no longer inside the scream spirit.

I was lying on my back on the roof. The scream spirit was trying to climb on top of me again, a centipede of dark smoke.

And then the sky tore open and Father stood over it with a wooden staff.

TWENTY-FIVE

The scream spirit unfurled in the air. Its dark wormy length shot out at my father, but he was ready for its attack. Even missing an eye, even recovering from severe injuries, he sidestepped the charging worm and struck out with his goosewood staff, gouging a massive wound along its side.

I pushed myself up to my elbows and watched my father fight the scream monster. It attacked him, he stepped away, he hit it again with his staff. With each strike the monster grew more enraged and more reckless. Then it died.

Near the mass of darkness, other men sprawled around. The hatchetmen were dead. Liu Qiang was dead. I looked at Father. "You did this?" I asked, and there was awe in my voice. "You did all this? Alone?"

He gave a curt nod and offered a hand to help me up. "Well," he said, "not really alone. Your help was valuable."

I flushed at the unexpected praise. "I did nothing important, Father."

He flashed a fierce little grin. He looked immensely proud of himself. "Look behind me, Li-lin."

A tall man was standing behind him. And my world turned upside-down.

"Rocket?" I said. Tears began to stream down my face. "Gods and ancestors, you must be a ghost."

My father grinned. "Among Liu Qiang's possessions, he had a number of books. One of them had a spell that allowed me to bring your husband back to life."

"What are you saying?" I said amid sobs. "How could this be? Is this real?" I looked around me, at the rooftop. "Please let this be real," I whispered.

"It's really me," said my husband, young and serious, handsome, caring, and concerned. My husband.

"Husband, I wailed at your grave for forty-nine days. I have cried myself to sleep every night for two years."

"I am here now."

My husband was alive. I couldn't believe it. It made no sense. He died. His corpse was buried. His name was intoned with the ancestors. In a few months it would be time for us to unearth his bones and have them smuggled to China, where they would be buried alongside his ancestors.

I gazed in his face, the face of the boy who had always wanted to protect everyone, the face of the serious young man he had grown into. It was my husband's face. I loved seeing his eyes and mouth again.

"How . . ." I began. "How can you be here, Husband? Long ago you should have drunk tea with Lady Meng Po. You should have forgotten me. You should have forgotten your life, and been born afresh somewhere else."

He gave a brief sigh, as he had so often before. "The questions you ask are for philosophers to answer, Li-lin. If I were a wise man I could answer you, but I'm only a fisherman's son who likes to jump and kick."

I stared at him, tears welling in my eyes. These were my husband's words, and I'd heard him say such things many a time. His face, his posture, his eyes, no different from the bold young man who loved me until the day he died.

I couldn't believe it, but it was true. My husband had come back to me.

The next morning we climbed to the roof of Father's temple and watched the sun come up. Purple and orange streaks painted the dawn sky, while I hunkered down in the security of my husband's arms.

In the afternoon Rocket and I went to see Bok Choy, and he told me I'd been released from my contract. "I made peace with Mr. Wong," he said. The two tongs worked together and created great prosperity in Chinatown.

Father found a spell that cured me of my yin eyes. Never again would I be afflicted with the horrors of the spirit world.

Rocket and I moved to a little house in South Berkeley. Every morning he held me tight while we watched the dawn break. The sun rose each day through wisps of fog, rising over the tall buildings of the San Francisco skyline. Each day's light renewed the world.

One day Dr. Wei told me that my husband and I were going to have a baby. I was so happy. The man I loved was back in my life, and we were going to start a family. "I hope I can give you sons," I said.

"Sons or daughters, it doesn't matter to me, Li-lin," Rocket said.

My father rolled his eyes. "Idiot," he said affectionately.

I stared at my father's face. I felt like I was forgetting something. His eyes sparkled. He seemed happier than I could remember. I smiled, content.

Shuai Hu started coming to our house to play fan-tan with Father and Rocket. The Buddhist sat at our dinner table eating with his hands. A mess of vegetables sprawled across the table and spattered his jolly face. "Daonu Xian, I'm not a tiger anymore!" he said. "Your father cured me."

"I'm not a Daonu anymore, Brother Hu," I told him, smiling. "You were the only one who ever seemed to realize that I was."

"I want your babies to call me Uncle Tiger," he said in a booming voice. I laughed with delight.

A voice said, "There are three treasures."

"Did you hear that?" I asked the monk.

"Hear what?" He and Rocket looked at me with concern. My father locked his eyes on my face, his gaze intense.

I swallowed. "I thought I heard someone say that there are three treasures."

"Be careful, Rocket," Shuai Hu said to him with a lopsided grin, "I think your wife is hearing things."

I touched my stomach. It was swollen with child. The cuts had almost healed by now. There were Liu Qiang's cuts, Father's cuts, and there were mine. Months ago I had tried to cut three characters into my skin. The characters were supposed to be a kind of ladder for me to climb, so I could return to myself and escape from a spirit that had me trapped.

Months had gone by but I could still trace those three cuts on my skin. There was Jing, and Qi, and I had started to carve a third character, Shen. Together they were known as the Three Treasures.

"What are you doing, Li-lin?" my father asked, his voice solemn and disapproving.

I turned to face him. "That night on the roof, Father," I asked, "how did I escape from the scream spirit?"

He shrugged. "That was months ago," he said. "You awoke your mind."

I gave a slow shake of my head. "That wouldn't have been enough. There were three rungs on the ladder. I needed to climb three rungs to get out. And I only managed to carve two of them into my skin."

My father, my husband, and Shuai Hu pressed close around me. All three of them wore the same concerned expression. Their expressions were *exactly the same*. I looked at my father's eyes. I stepped back from the men and faced my husband. Tears welled in my eyes, but I would not let them fall.

"It's hard to believe that even a scream spirit could be this cruel," I said.

"What do you mean?" the thing with my husband's face asked.

"You are not Rocket," I said, "though I hate the fact with rage and passion, though I wish, how I wish, it were otherwise. My husband is dead, and he is buried. You are not my husband." I drove a fingernail into my stomach and finished the third character.

Shen, or spirit.

I watched my husband's face melt. I kept my eyes on his face while the whole world melted around us.

My spirit woke. The scream monster's spirit-flesh held me like a cocoon, its substance cold but so soft it was nearly liquid. I punched through its skin. The monster burst apart. Its spirit-matter splashed outward, convulsing. I fell from its torn body, dropping a few feet to land on my hands and knees on the roof, while the scream spirit erupted over the roof, spattering the surfaces with smoky fluid.

I wiped my face clean. I took a long, slow breath. My time of screaming was done, and now I shouted with rage.

There were fires burning everywhere I could see. And over the buildings, eclipsing the moon, I saw something tremendous and terrible, gleaming, undead, and fifty feet high.

The Kulou-Yuanling had risen.

TWENTY-SIX

In the moonlight, its head and shoulders loomed over the buildings of Chinatown. The Kulou-Yuanling was a human skeleton on an enormous scale, ten feet higher than Chinatown's tallest buildings. It had a skull for a head—a giant, human skull. A sick greenish glow shone from its empty eye sockets, and blood dribbled from its teeth and its jaws. In the spirit world, I could see lines of qi circulating around its yellow bones. Streams of energy flowed in two directions, glimmering around the monstrous skeleton.

The sheer size of the monster was terrifying. Looking at it strained my neck and made me feel dizzy. I stood gaping. Yes, it must have taken armies to bring this kind of monster down. There could be no reasoning with a creature born from so much misery.

Sympathy would only hinder me. I needed to cut off this line of thinking, or my emotions would cripple my tactics. No matter its origins, it was a tool in the hand of a man I despised. An automaton under his control. I watched its shoulderblades pivot with the swinging of its arms. The movement was slow and mechanical. Life-energy circulated outside its body in glowing ribbons of yin and yang.

In the streets people were fleeing in a panic, shouting and screaming. A man, or half a man, dangled from the giant's skeletal right hand; it looked like the Kulou-Yuanling had bitten off his upper body. In the monster's left hand, another man was sitting, serene and composed.

It was Liu Qiang. The spirit in place of his right arm coiled like white smoke, and its three eyes lit an angry red. I didn't know what manner of creature the arm was, but it was clear that the spirit was enjoying the destruction as much as Liu Qiang was. It was the arm's triumph as much as the man's.

I had failed to stop the ritual. All of Chinatown was going to suffer the effects of my failure, and I had no idea how I could stop the Kulou-Yuanling now.

In the street below me, the monstrous skeleton lowered a tremendous bone foot onto a carriage. The buggy crunched to boards and splinters under the monster's weight. The horse panicked and fled down the street, dragging its trace and neighing wildly.

Slow and shaky, I rose, first to my knees, and then to my feet. Around me on the rooftop were scattered globules of gray-white slime. It was all that remained of the scream spirit after I burst out of it.

Mr. Yanqiu stood near me. I looked at the spirit of my father's eye and knew the truth. I had exorcised him, exiled him to the world of spirits. But when I was losing myself to the scream spirit, the authority of my spells had begun to fade. Feeling the exorcism weaken, Mr. Yanqiu had crossed into the world of men. I was in trouble, so he climbed inside the scream spirit to rescue me. It was his voice I heard, over and over, reminding me that I needed to finish scratching the third character into my stomach.

"You saved me, Mr. Yanqiu," I said. "You saved me again."

He beamed at me. "You're all right, Li-lin?"

I hesitated. I had thought I'd been reunited with my husband, but it was all a lie, and the loss of that dream would torment me for a long time. "No," I said. "I'm not all right. But I have to find a way to stop the Kulou-Yuanling anyway."

Mr. Yanqiu started to speak, but a babyish voice interrupted him. The voice came from one of the blobs of slime that were splashed across the roof. "I hate you, Xian Li-lin!" it said.

My eyes widened. The scream spirit was still alive. It was in pieces, but alive. And drifting along the rooftop there were faces, dozens of ghost-faces. They floated, looking lonely and confused.

"The screaming faces," I said to Mr. Yanqiu. "They're the ghosts that were trapped inside the scream spirit." I turned to the blob of slime that had spoken. "You. You did this to them."

"I hate you so much! I hate you!" it blubbered.

"Good," I said. The eyes of dozens of ghosts were upon me. I strode across the rooftop and picked up my peachwood sword.

A fire was raging in my mind. It had begun when Liu Qiang betrayed me, trapping me in the spirit world and carving my flesh like I was no more than food. The fire started when that man opened my body so an assassin could ride me. But the wood had been dry for a long time; years, decades of rage came together in a pure white heat. Enough heat to cleanse the wounds of the world.

My anger was calm and deep. The White-Haired Demoness slaughtered my village. Men killed my husband. Liu Qiang cut me like paper. And this infantile, cruel spirit caught me in its body and tried to strip me of my memories. Tried to reduce me to an ache and a scream.

It made me think I was reunited with the only man I ever loved.

"Hate you, hate you so much, I hate you, hate you, hate you," it was whimpering. It had lost its power and with its power went its courage. Four eyes and a vicious mouth formed in the glob of spirit-slime, spitting childish insults at me.

I held my peachwood sword in a reverse grip, and with a calm fire of certainty I executed the scream spirit.

The ghost faces made no sound. After years or centuries of screaming, their throats must have been raw. But they looked to me, and their eyes showed me awe and gratitude.

I nodded to them, to acknowledge their suffering. It had ended now.

I glanced over Chinatown, surveying the chaos. The Kulou-Yuanling strode through Sacramento Street. That was Bok Choy's part of town. Tom Wong's message would be made clear. It would be writ in the crushed edifices and broken bodies of the Xie Liang tong. And anyone who happened to be nearby.

I wasn't going to let that happen. Father told me that Liu Qiang was a weakling and a coward. It burned me that a man like that had undone my robes, seen my skin, and touched me. He signed his name in my flesh with a knife. And now he'd made something of himself. By raising the Kulou-Yuanling, he made himself the most powerful man in Chinatown. Maybe even the most powerful man in the world.

The fire in me burned so hot I could no longer control it. But I didn't want to control it. I wanted to dance with it. I addressed the ghost faces and let the fire fill my voice. "Souls," I said. "Men. Women. You were trapped inside a monster, and that monster is dead. You are free now, and you will never be bound again. You were captured. Used. A monster burned you as its fuel. Tonight another monster walks the earth," I gestured at the Kulou-Yuanling, towering over Chinatown. "It is made from the corpses and rage and sorrow of a hundred men who died badly. I want to bring the monster down, bring justice to the men responsible, and bring peace to the dead men."

There was motion among the ghosts, and mumbling.

"I will make a compact with you," I continued. "Follow me into battle tonight and tonight alone, and I will protect you and burn paper offerings for you, for all my years."

The ghosts stirred on the rooftop. They shimmered like smoke in the moonlight. At last one spoke. "We are only little things now, and we have no memory of ourselves," he said. "We are so vulnerable. You offer us protection, but how can you protect us? You are just a girl."

I drew myself up and filled my words with flame. "I am Xian Li-lin, Daoshi of the Second Ordination, bearer of the Maoshan lineage, protector of the Haiou Shen, slayer of the scream spirit. I am Xian Li-lin, the girl with yin eyes, and I will protect you from harm. Follow me and have a purpose, or stay and be nothing," I said. I turned my back and strode across the rooftop, wielding my peachwood sword.

The dome of the Kulou-Yuanling's skull canceled the moon. Beneath the gigantic monster, in its long shadow, men were fleeing. It stepped on a vegetable cart and the cart crushed to pulp and splinters under the bones of its foot.

The monster was huge. Looking up at it made me feel tiny, like a mouse. Even Shuai Hu, the three-tailed tiger, would be no threat to it. The thought of Shuai Hu facing this was like the thought of a kitten fighting a man. And the Kulou-Yuanling was on its way southwest, to kill Bok Choy and the men of the Xie Liang tong. Anyone caught nearby would die as well.

It smashed its right arm into a balcony. The boards splintered upward, and bits of wood scattered all along Sacramento Street.

Perhaps it was the cry of gulls that made the monster turn its head.

Dark green fires roared in the sockets of its eyes. It stopped in its tracks and looked at us. All it knew was rage, but never, I would wager, never in the lives of the men whose corpses made the Kulou-Yuanling, never had any of them seen a young woman dangling in midair, carried aloft by a cloud of gulls. The Kulou-Yuanling stood still.

Then ghosts flew at it. They soared up the Kulou-Yuanling's leg bones. Dozens of them, pale faces trailing vapors, surged up through the giant skeleton's ribs. It took its eyes off the crowd of gulls that held me aloft, and looked down into its own ribcage. The ghost faces flitted through its body like fireflies in a hollow tree.

Liu Qiang rose to his feet on the Kulou-Yuanling's fleshless hand. He stared at the infestation of ghosts, then turned and looked at me. He looked shocked to see me alive. And maybe a little afraid.

The snakelike arm faced me, its three red eyes alert. Its malice and its strange intelligence stood in sharp contrast to the bewildered expression on Liu Qiang's face. Whatever nightmare spawned that creature, the arm was clearly Liu Qiang's master.

The shock and fear on the soulstealer's face gave way to anger. "Kill her, Kulou-Yuanling!" he shouted. "I command it!"

At his command the giant monster reached out a huge, skeletal hand and swatted at the seagulls that held me up. Each of its bony fingers was the size of my whole body. Where it struck, birds lost their grip on the rope. One swat knocked dozens of the gulls away, and I felt my weight begin to drag them down.

"Bring me on to it!" I shouted to the seagulls.

Liu Qiang heard me. The gulls brought me close to alight on the monster, and the soulstealer gave a command I could not hear. But the Kulou-Yuanling heard it, and understood.

I was ten feet from its collarbone and the monster skeleton opened its jaws. It looked like it was going to shout, but the voice that came from its mouth was like no human sound. It was the clanging of enormous cymbals by my ears, a noise so thunderous and awful that I thought my head would burst if the sound continued for another second.

The Kulou-Yuanling's gong was the mournful cry of a hundred dead men, amplified by death and awful power. Hearing that cry, I felt a touch of what the men felt as they died. There was hunger so great I wanted to gnaw at the flesh of my own arm. There was darkness all around me. Alone, isolated, unloved, and empty, I felt like I lived through each man's private sorrow, each man's brutal death.

The seagulls collapsed as one. They fell in a hush of crushed air and I fell with them.

The sound stopped. Dropping in silence, my ears ringing, I felt anger come over me. The Kulou-Yuanling wasn't the hundred men who died. It was a violation of those men.

By some insanity, some surge of willpower, some snarling rage, I lunged forward just in time to grab hold of the Kulou-Yuanling's lowest rib.

TWENTY-SEVEN

L iu Qiang's eyes were wide as he watched me cling to the giant skeleton's rib. The three-eyed snake spirit that had replaced his arm looked at me with the excited curiosity of boys who torture animals, and Liu Qiang began to chant an incantation.

I yanked myself up to a crouching position on the Kulou-Yuanling's lowest rib. The ghosts I had freed were flying in and around the monster's bones, confusing it. Liu Qiang shaped his fingers into magic shoujue. It was the single-handed seal of the Left Thunder Block, aggressive magic. He uttered a few words and launched his spell at me.

Whatever spell he cast, it didn't matter. Fast as lightning I drew my peachwood sword and cut the spell in half. I smiled as the spell's energies began to dissipate around me.

Liu Qiang looked frustrated. He began to chant. It would take him at least few more seconds. Holding my peachwood sword in my teeth, I jumped up and grabbed onto the next rib up. I pulled myself to crouching and made an obscene gesture in Liu Qiang's direction. At the top of the Kulou-Yuanling's ribs I would climb its spine into its skull, and inside there, I would try to find a way to extinguish the spirit fires behind its eyes.

Liu Qiang unleashed his next spell and I cut it down. "You're making this too easy for me, pisspot," I shouted. I placed my peachwood sword between my teeth and waited for him to start chanting another spell.

"Bring me over to her!" Liu Qiang shouted, and my eyes went wide. I wasn't ready to confront him yet. His monstrous arm frightened me. It had killed Hong Xiao-hao, and it seemed to hate me in a deep and ugly manner I couldn't comprehend.

The giant skeleton brought its hand in close to me and I took the opportunity to climb another rib.

I started to take a grip on my peachwood sword but the three-eyed snake spirit whipped out and bit my wrist with its needle-teeth. The sword slipped from my fingers and fell. Rows of punctures opened on my forearm, bleeding. My peachwood sword landed on the street with a clattering sound.

The snake spirit could have killed me in that moment. Without my peachwood sword I had no way to defend myself, no way to fight back. Liu Qiang's arm drew itself up to face me and made a sound in its throat like scraping iron. It was laughing at me, and the expression in its three eyes was grotesque.

It was somehow personal. The demonic arm wanted me to break down at my moment of defeat. It wanted to make me beg for my life.

I twisted away from it as fast as I could and jumped off the giant's rib.

Qinggong, lightness. I started to plummet and threw my weight to the side. There was a balcony. Was it within reach? Kind of. I grabbed at the balcony, scrambling for a grip, but the blood from my wrist made my fingers slick and slippery. I couldn't grab hold, could do no more than slow my fall a little.

I crashed into an awning and slowed some more. Then I landed rolling on the cobblestone street.

The impact left me stunned. I heard the clink of broken glass and knew my bagua mirror had shattered. One more weapon was lost to me. The combat was stripping me of my defenses, weapon by weapon, wound by wound, and now I couldn't even gather the wherewithal to do something so simple as get up.

Thirty feet up Liu Qiang stood like an emperor in the bone giant's hand. He was yelling at me, probably mocking. I didn't need to hear him to feel shamed. The Kulou-Yuanling smashed another balcony and punched a brick wall, cracking it. I could smell smoke. A streetlamp had been crushed, and its remnants burned slowly. A tangle of wires lay on the street, where a telegraph pole had been knocked down.

I lay stunned on my back and knew I could have stopped this. Should have stopped this. Every bit of destruction mocked my failure louder than anything Liu Qiang could say to me.

An orange blur streaked down from a rooftop to the Kulou-Yuanling's hand. The cat spirit tore at Liu Qiang's face. The soulstealer screamed. Mao'er gave a caterwauling cry and slashed Liu Qiang again. "Knifed me!" the two-tailed cat screeched. "Threw a knife in my neck!"

Liu Qiang cried out in pain and surprise, while his spirit arm coiled back to attack the cat spirit. Mao'er clung to Liu Qiang's head with all his claws and bit the man's face.

The snake spirit dug its needle-teeth into Mao'er's back, but Mao'er had done his damage. Liu Qiang staggered backward, and the three of them—soulstealer, cat spirit, and monster arm—toppled together from the bone giant's hand.

Liu Qiang's snake arm snapped out, reaching its jaws to catch onto something, anything. It dug sharp teeth against the giant's bottom rib but it couldn't find purchase, barely slowing their plummet. The three of them landed hard, across the street from me.

They landed on the boardwalk. I scowled. Could good fortune visit me for once? The wood boards absorbed a good deal of the impact when they fell. When I fell, the cobblestones absorbed nothing.

I needed to push myself up. It took effort, but I managed to force myself up to my hands and knees.

Mao'er was up already. Wobbling on four legs, with spirit blood flowing freely from his wounds, he looked at me. His fur was in hackles, and the blood around his mouth was sticking to his fur. For a moment he glanced at Liu Qiang and the white snake monster that substituted for an arm, as though the cat was appraising his choices—but then the moment passed, and the cat spirit slinked away.

Liu Qiang was struggling to push himself up, but his arm was alert. Its three red eyes studied me, looking for weaknesses to exploit.

I crawled toward my peachwood sword. Blood was trickling from my wounded wrist. I tried to taunt the spirit arm but the words came out between difficult breaths. "Can't . . . reach . . . me . . . you stupid . . . snake."

Liu Qiang had given up on standing for now. He reached into a pocket and withdrew a small yellow paper. I was five feet from my sword and he flicked his wrist, snapping the paper in the air.

It was shaped like a little man, and it flew at me. It came in low and fast, and it bit my neck. "Ow," I said. The bite stung. The paper man kept flying. It veered in midair to attack me again.

My father had mocked these little monsters. Flimsy, he said.

I grabbed it out of the air and crumpled it in my hand.

But there were already more of them, dozens more. They swooped around me, obscuring my vision. They bit me and it hurt. There were so many of them, biting at me, and the sharp little stabs of pain kept me from thinking clearly. The pain itself wasn't overwhelming. The bites were aches, nuisances, and they threatened to cost me my focus. But I could hear the sound of destruction. The Kulou-Yuanling finished demolishing a second wall. Broken bricks thudded to the ground.

Along with the thudding, I heard another sound. *Ding-ding-ding. Ding-ding. Ding.*

I heard the sound and I knew a way I could stop the Kulou-Yuanling. At least a way to hurt it, slow it down.

I could hit it with a cable car.

The plan gave me determination. Crawling, I fought across the swarm of paper men. They swooped at me, stinging me with their bites. Grabbing my peachwood sword, I struggled to my feet amid the swirling paper figures.

But my father had told me what he'd done. He hadn't used peachwood to kill the paper men. He had used steel. I placed the sword back at my belt, forced myself to stand up straight in the middle of the swarm, and withdrew my rope dart.

Getting it to start spinning wasn't simple. At each rotation it struck against little paper men. Each impact slowed it down. But each impact also reduced the number of attackers. After ten or twelve rotations, my rope dart began to pick up speed. It cut through Liu Qiang's paper men as if they were pollen.

Liu Qiang watched me with a grim look. He'd recovered from the fall and he pushed himself to his feet. His arm hissed and the sound was like a dagger scraping at bone.

I faced them. I could fight Liu Qiang with my rope dart. I could fight his spirit arm with my peachwood sword. But behind them the bone giant had caused one Xie Liang building to collapse, and it started to smash the walls of a second building.

Given time, it would reduce the southwest side of Chinatown to rubble and splinters.

I kept my rope dart spinning and ran toward the cable car line.

TWENTY-EIGHT

"**G**et out," I said to the men in the cable car. "Now."

They turned and looked at me for a few moments, and then the whisper caught and spread like flame through dry grass: "That's the exorcist's daughter."

In moments the compartment was empty, save for the gripman. He was a burly white man in his shirtsleeves. Only the strongest of men get to be gripmen. "Oi! Whatcha think yer doin?" he asked in English.

"Look over there," I said in English, and pointed.

"Wha?" he said. "Wha chew say?"

"Look over there," I said again, shaping the English words as carefully as I could.

The gripman squinted at me. "Can't unnerstandja," he said.

I sighed, extending my arm once more, pointing at the Kulou-Yuanling.

The man's gaze followed my extended finger out into Chinatown. His face went slack. In the moonlight he saw the monster. Ten feet taller than the tallest of Chinatown's buildings. The tremendous skeleton gleamed yellow and white under the moon.

"Egad," he breathed. "Wha?"

"Listen to me and pay attention," I said in my clearest English. "That thing will destroy Chinatown and then it will destroy the rest of San Francisco. It will kill everyone you love. I can only think of one way to stop it. We need to ram it with this cable car."

I don't know how many of my words the grip-man understood, but he understood some. He gave me a blank look, and then understanding showed on his face. A moment later, determination overtook his eyes. He bit his lip and nodded, then turned to the cable car's grip. The grip looked like a huge pair of pliers. His muscles strained as he closed the clamp back onto the moving cable.

With a lurching start, the cable car began to move forward. *Ding*, it went, picking up speed. *Ding-ding. Ding-ding-ding.*

I breathed a sigh of relief. This man was going to help me, and he knew what he was doing.

When a gripman wants to stop a cable car, he opens the grip and triggers the brakes. But tonight, there would be no brakes. The cable car moved along the line, heavy as boulders and moving as fast as a man can run. He was going to wait until the line was as close to the monster as it was going to get. Then he would release the cable car without engaging its brakes. If he did it correctly, the cable car would jump the slot and drive into the Kulou-Yuanling. It needed to be done with perfect timing.

Even if it was perfectly timed, it could kill us both. The gripman knew it too, and yet he continued driving toward the monster. His courage, his willingness to risk his life, impressed me. I'd grown used to thinking of these as Chinese qualities.

The cable car picked up speed while we waited in a tense silence. We were a block away, half a block away. We sped toward the monster. I caught sight of Liu Qiang standing on the street. He stared at the cable car, his mouth open in astonishment. He said something. The monster turned toward us. The fires in its empty eyesockets blazed green. The gripman started to pull the grip off the cable. His muscles strained.

The Kulou-Yuanling opened its mouth. Its jaws spread, distending in a way no human face could imitate. And then it gonged.

The voices, the screams and pain and loss of a hundred dead men rose up through its fleshless throat, amplified a thousandfold, and blasted from its mouth.

The sound was devastating. Deafening. The cable car rattled around us. My bones rattled inside me, and again the world flooded with despair. Hate and aggression and loneliness resonated through the bone giant's clanging voice, so much loneliness, and there was hunger, a madness of hunger. The mad dead giant skeleton's voice boomed through my brain, emptying me of thought. I wanted to weep. I wanted to bleed, to suffer, to feel something, anything, other than the horror of a hundred dead men filling my mind with their death cries.

The noise pounded inside my head, and I saw the gripman's face. His hands were tight on the clamp. The muscles in his arms were rigid, but his eyes had gone bloodshot. His face looked somehow even paler. His hair seemed to be standing on end, and his head looked like it was ready to burst apart.

"Now!" I shouted. Over the clamor of the Kulou-Yuanling's thunderous voices, I could barely hear the sound of my own voice. "Unhitch the cable now!"

There was no sign the gripman heard me. "Now!" I shouted. "Now!" The gripman stared blankly ahead, and his expression was one of exhaustion and misery. Then he pitched forward, with his head between his knees. Clutching his hands over his ears, he began to scream.

The Kulou-Yuanling's death gong must have lasted seconds at most, but it felt like hours. It shredded my awareness with its agony, until I could no longer think or act.

And then the sound was done.

Somehow I found myself curled up on the floor of the cable car, my hands over my ears, with tears streaming down my face.

And the trolley was still hitched to the cable.

"Aiya," I said, and pounded a fist against the cable car's wall in my frustration. I had failed again.

I pulled myself to my feet. My head swam, still ringing with the Kulou-Yuanling's mad cry of misery.

"Thank you anyway," I said to the gripman in English, and I hopped down from the cable car to the street.

Chinatown had gone mad. There was a sound like waves on the beach, rising and falling, and I knew it for the panicked screams of men. Men were fleeing in all directions, screaming as they fled. Every few seconds there was a drumbeat, loud and hollow and slow and steady, as the Kulou-Yuanling pounded a gigantic bone fist against the brick walls of the Xie Liang building.

My body ached all over. Once again my plans had failed, and Liu Qiang's had succeeded. My plan to ram the monster with a cable car had gone nowhere. The boom of enormous bone fists punching brick resounded down the block and across Chinatown. I looked up at the Kulou-Yuanling. It was obscenely large and shining in the moonlight, the raging skeleton of an impossible giant, orbited by a sparkling flow of qi energy along its meridians, driven insane by a hundred men's starvation and abandonment. It was a rampage five stories tall.

The seagulls had regrouped. Hundreds of them soared between the cracked yellow bones of the Kulou-Yuanling. A swirl of ghost faces twisted in and through its skeletal form, their once-screaming voices silent now except for the hiss of their passage. This had been my army, the most capable opposition I could raise to confront Liu Qiang's pet destroyer, and even in their multitude, they could do no more than slow the Kulou-Yuanling. I could think of no way to stop it.

I sighed. The Kulou-Yuanling had both hands free. It tore a chunk out of the brick wall, seven or eight feet of brickface, and threw it hurtling down the street. The wall crashed down at the streetcorner with a loud thud, taking down another telegraph pole as it fell.

A trickle of blood continued to dribble out of the wounds on my wrist where the spirit-arm bit me. I was so weary. I'd fought so hard, for days, to get to this point, and it was all for nothing. There was nothing I could do to change the outcome. A fifty-foot-tall human skeleton taught me just how little I could do. I saw the destruction it was bringing to the Xie Liang buildings, and I felt tiny and afraid.

Fear had been a part of my life as long as I could remember. When I was a little girl, I crouched all night in the bottom of a well, hoping the monster wouldn't find me. I heard a village die while I was hiding. And I was never going to hide again.

A smarter person would have given up. Would have turned away. But no one had ever praised my intelligence. No one except for my husband, and he was gone.

I knew Rocket wouldn't stand back and watch a giant monster tear down Chinatown. He would fight and die to protect people. But Rocket was a hero. And maybe it was heroism that killed my husband. Maybe Tom Wong was right; maybe there was no place for a hero in this world.

And besides, I was no nuxia, no heroic swordswoman out of the old stories.

Without even understanding why, I took a step forward. I took a step toward Liu Qiang and the evil creature that had replaced his arm. A step toward the Kulou-Yuanling.

Step by weary step I made my way down the street. My enemies stood at the corner, watching their monster demolish the Xie Liang buildings. They turned to face me as I approached.

Liu Qiang's face was bleeding from multiple cat scratches, but his reinforcements had arrived. Tom Wong stood amid the chaos, amid the gutter fires, the disarray of splintered wood from balconies, the shards of broken brick, and heaps of downed telegraph wire, and he was beaming. Where I saw devastation, he saw rapture.

The man with short hair stood near Tom, flicking nervous glances in his direction. I almost felt sorry for him. He'd gotten out of prison and wanted to gain face, make a name for himself among the Ansheng tong. I doubt he ever thought his path was leading him here, to filthy magic and overwhelming destruction. To the Kulou-Yuanling tearing down buildings.

A police constable ran toward the giant monster. He had a desperate look on his face and a pistol in his hand. He aimed the pistol at the skeleton's tremendous kneecap and I heard a gunshot boom through the night, then another. He fired again and again. The Kulou-Yuanling was not harmed.

"What do you think, Li-lin?" Tom asked. Behind him the Kulou-Yuanling noticed the policeman. It reached down a skeletal hand and caught him in its bone fingers. The constable fired his pistol again, and then he died in the monster's grip, with an awful sound of bones snapped and pulped.

"It's horrible," I said.

Tom grinned. "Tonight the Ansheng tong is reborn. Tonight the world will learn the true meaning of power."

"Do you really think you're the one who has the power here, Tom?" I said. "Are you the one who controls that creature?"

Tom's pretty face flushed. "Mr. Liu will tell it to do what I want it to do."

I shook my head sadly. "You're just a tool he's using, Tom. He needed you to bring the corpses here for the ritual, and now he'll use you to provide him with protection. But in a few weeks you'll be doing what he tells you, not the other way around. And you don't even know who tells him what to do, do you?"

Tom's face was still. "Who?"

"His arm."

He gave me a blank look.

"He's replaced his arm with some kind of monster, Tom, and it tells him what to do."

The spirit arm rasped, "Want to eat the baby's hands, and eat the baby's feet!" It snapped out at me. Its mouth opened and its sharp teeth gleamed like little knives. I stabbed at it with my peachwood sword and then the short-haired man came toward me holding a butcher's knife. Liu Qiang shaped the fingers of his hand into Immortal Sword and started chanting. Tom Wong took a fighting stance.

I stepped back. I couldn't fight them all at once. I needed the peachwood sword to fight the spirit arm and to break Liu Qiang's spells, but it wasn't all that useful against a steel butcher's knife. And Tom Wong was a superb martial artist. I wasn't sure I could take him in single combat, let alone when he was flanked by a sorcerer, a monstrous arm, and a gangster with a knife.

Tom launched a flying kick at my chest. He was too fast. I stepped back just far enough to lessen the impact but his foot still struck hard against my ribs and knocked me off my feet. Knocked the breath out of me. I landed hard on my back, my eyes wide. He was good. Maybe faster than me. Definitely stronger. He flashed a pretty smile.

I sprawled in a kind of daze, unable to move, and watched my assailants come at me.

Behind Tom, Liu Qiang was chanting. I saw his fingers twist from Immortal Sword to Purple Star to Demanding Knife. A spell shot out from his poised fingers and I knew I wouldn't be able to bring my peachwood sword around in time to stop it.

The spell came for me, thorny and bleak. Cold fingers of shadow reached for me across the dark street, and I knew I was going to die.

The spell rushed toward me, faster than I could scramble away. I felt the spell more than I saw it, a cluster of dark thorns closing in on me. Terror rose inside me and I wanted to scream as the spell closed in, its path jagged like broken glass. It stabbed at my face, at my eyes, and I couldn't help it, couldn't help watching in my final moments, and then the spell broke apart in the air.

"What?" I said. I turned to look at Liu Qiang, but his bewildered posture told me he didn't understand what happened to his spell any more than I did.

All of us, at once, turned our heads in the same direction. A man was walking down the street. Walking toward us. The man was slender. His footsteps dragged, but he still carried himself with an arrogant bearing I would recognize anywhere.

My father was wearing his most formal robe. It was sleeveless silk the color of the evening sun, covered with elaborate embroidery of cranes and dragons, and held together by three straps. Tied at his waist was a horsehair whisk and a sheaf of paper talismans. On another strap he was carrying his goosewood staff.

I stared. My father wasn't leaving anything to chance. He came armed with his heaviest investitures of power.

I felt my pulses slow down to normal, and a kind of elation rushed through me. My father came armed with so much magical power, as though he was intending to fight deities—and win.

"Liu Qiang," my father said, speaking the name with contempt.

Liu Qiang gave a nervous smile, and gestured to the Kulou-Yuanling, towering above us. "You see that, Xian Zhengying?"

"I see it, you little worm," my father said.

"You don't understand, Xian Zhengying," Liu Qiang said. "I made it. Right here in Chinatown, inside a building it was your duty to protect, I called forth a Kulou-Yuanling, and you couldn't stop me. No Daoshi has accomplished such a feat in eighty generations."

"Because we've all been better than that," my father said, and spoke a syllable. There was power in the syllable, magic. Father must have spent forty-nine nights stomping the earth to cultivate so much power in a single syllable. Power came roaring from the sound and rushed into my father's fingers. He began to shape shoujue gestures. Magical Cannon, Binding Collar, Two Dragons Pierce the

Mountain. He performed the motions with a devastating flawlessness of execution, but I realized something that stunned me.

My father's arrogance had always been his weakness. He had a tendency to underestimate his opposition, and sometimes that worked against him. But tonight there was none of that. He was not merely relying on the staggeringly great power of the Seventh Ordination, nor was he counting on his superior skill as a master of the craft, but he was also—and this astonished me—using only double-handed gestural spells.

Spells a one-armed man would be hard-pressed to defend against.

Even if Liu Qiang had been ordained to the Seventh, even if he waged a tactically brilliant magical battle, even then, with only one hand, he would stand no chance against someone of the same strength using a string of double-handed magical gestures to attack.

My father's strategy was cruel and nasty. It was completely unfair and it filled me with glee. Liu Qiang wouldn't stand a chance.

It took a Daoshi of profound accomplishment to execute so many double-handed gestures in sequence, but my father never let up, never relented. If I had ever doubted his mastery, he proved those doubts wrong as he rapidly executed a continuous sequence of flawless, increasingly difficult shoujue.

And yet there was fatigue in my father's posture. A labor in his breathing. A weariness on his face. The last two days had nearly killed him, over and over. My father's magic was potent beyond belief, his skill was legendary, and his strategy was invincible, but I doubted he could hold his own in a fistfight right now, especially against three men. A few solid punches might be enough to take him down.

It was up to me to prevent any of those solid punches from landing.

I glanced over at the Kulou-Yuanling. Seagulls—my seagulls—stormed the giant skeleton. Diving through its ribcage, the gull spirits picked at its bones, scraping it with their claws as they soared through and around the monster. Again and again, the Kulou-Yuanling grabbed at the birds, but its huge bone fingers were too slow. For now, the gulls were keeping the monster occupied.

Gritting my teeth, I got back to my feet. Trying not to wobble, I put on a wry smile and faced the men. "The odds are even now, Tom," I said to him. "I'll bet you a dollar that my father kills Liu Qiang."

Tom Wong looked at me, with a baffled expression. "Li-lin, what has happened that you're making bets? You sound like that prancing fool Bok Choy."

"Bok Choy is a bigger man than you are, Tom," I said. "At least *he* has never been forced to his knees by a girl, with the whole town watching."

Tom's pretty lips shrank to a pout and he came at me, which was just what I wanted. Come at me and not my father.

Tom took the initiative, launching an array of attacks. They were swift yet subtle. I blocked his strikes, stepped out of their way, or pushed them aside. He was trying to draw me into his rhythm, train me to respond when and as he chose, and leave me no opening to strike back. Then he would change his rhythm, expecting to take me off guard. But when he changed his rhythm, I'd make my move.

His left hand jabbed at me, jabbed again, his right foot swung a low kick, his right hand swung a full blow, and it was all I could do to keep from getting clobbered. I ducked, dodged, sidestepped, and blocked. Tom wanted to make me stick to him. It was a classic taiji strategy, drawing the opponent after you, into the void. I made no attacks. I blocked and sidestepped.

I didn't need to see Father and Liu Qiang fighting. I could feel it, as one feels a thunderstorm from indoors. It felt like wind, my father's magic. It was clear and certain. I heard him chanting. He invoked the Nine Heavens, summoned the Yellow Emperor's qi to strengthen his own body, finished a spell with "Quickly quickly for it is the

Law!" and launched into another without stopping for a breath. Liu Qiang withered under my father's onslaught. The one-armed man cried out, and his monstrous arm shrieked with pain, but Father's assault was unrelenting. Liu Qiang and his arm wouldn't last much longer.

Tom Wong curled his fingers into Tiger Claw and jabbed at my collarbone. I bobbed to the side but he was faster than me, and his hand knocked hard against my shoulder, staggering me a few steps backward. Tom advanced on me fast and punched for my face. Too fast for me. I raised my forearm in a desperate block but he was too strong; I only managed to shove the blow a few inches off target. His punch landed on my cheek instead of my nose.

Pain was sudden and absolute. Pain was everything, for a moment. In that instant all my training vanished, all my will to fight. I stood on the street, stunned, but Tom wasn't finished with me. He grabbed me by my arm and spun me around like a cloth doll.

He turned me about, twisting me off my centerline, so I could not recover my balance. I knew what his maneuvers were. He was using qin na, a martial art focused on grappling. And I'd never learned any qin na.

Tom was stronger, faster, and more skilled than me. And I didn't know how to grapple.

He curled his free arm around my neck and began to choke me with the crook of his elbow. He was going to choke me into unconsciousness. I couldn't let that happen. Finding my resolve, I planted my feet. I reached my free hand up, grabbed his wrist, and yanked with all my strength.

Nothing happened.

I yanked again but his arm didn't budge. I hadn't been trained in grappling. I didn't understand the workings of leverage. If there was a way to escape this chokehold, I didn't know it. I pinched and scratched at his arm, but it was useless.

Darkness blurred the edges of my vision. I tried to stay alert, to stay awake, but I felt unconsciousness begin to take hold. With my muscles starting to go limp, I saw a flicker of motion that caught my interest.

It was the man with short hair. He was stalking slowly behind my father. He was five or six strides away, approaching with stealth. He inched forward, taking the small and careful steps of a burglar. His butcher knife glinted in his hand. I wanted to call out, to warn my father, but Tom Wong was choking me. I could make no sound, and weariness was overwhelming me. Everything started to grow dark. Everything around me felt hazy, insubstantial, like figures within a dream. I felt my free arm go slack. My hand dropped to my side.

It felt something.

I was barely aware of it, but my fingers brushed against something, and it was no dream. My fingers were touching something solid.

I withdrew the rope dart from my pocket and stabbed its point into Tom Wong's thigh.

He cried out, and all at once the pressure on my throat released. I felt blood rush back into my head. For a moment everything seemed too bright. I felt as if I were waking up, and the street battle around me took shape in my eyes.

It felt good to recover my alertness and equilibrium, but I should have acted. Should have been quicker. Tom Wong grabbed the wrist of my hand that was holding the rope dart.

He held both my wrists, from behind, twisting my arms in different directions to keep me off balance. He certainly knew how to grapple. A grip like that would have immobilized someone much stronger than me.

But my wrist was still bleeding where Liu Qiang's arm bit me. And blood is slippery.

With a quick jerk, I pulled my hand free from Tom's grip. I spun to face him and stabbed the point of the rope dart into Tom's other forearm. Blood spurted from the wound. Tom shouted "Aiya!" I stabbed the rope dart at his chin, but he stepped back and dropped my wrist.

His eyes strayed to his injuries, the stab wounds on his thigh and arm. I took a step back, and then another, and started my rope dart spinning.

Tom looked back to me, with a scowl on his pretty face. "Seriously, Li-lin?" he said. "You know you can't hit me with that. All I have to do is catch the rope."

I launched it over my head, not three or five feet, but to its full fifteen-foot length. I brought it down in a devastating arc onto the head of the man who'd been sneaking up behind my father. He didn't even cry out, just toppled face-first to the street. His butcher knife clattered along the stones.

I snapped the weighted dart back toward me. It flew gracefully toward my hand, but Tom caught the dart. Our eyes met for a moment and then he yanked on it, tearing the other end out of my hand. The rope burned my fingers a little, and I winced.

Tom threw my rope dart to the side. I watched it sail far down the street. It hit the cobblestones with a metallic clap.

Tom's eyes went to his fallen friend and back to me. He shrugged. "So you knocked him out. You're still no match for me, Li-lin."

He punctuated his statement with a kick. He was too fast for me again. His heel hit the side of my head like a cannonball and I staggered to the side, dizzy. I struggled to maintain my balance. Do not fall, Li-lin, I told myself. If I fall, I won't be able to get back up.

Do not fall.

Do not fall.

Do not fall.

I fell.

On my back, dazed, I waited for Tom Wong to come over and finish me. It had been too much. I'd taken a punch in the face and a kick in the head. I was barely awake, caught in a half-dream. I heard a pounding, and I knew it was the sound of the Kulou-Yuanling beating its bony fists against a brick wall, but the sound of the blows melded somehow with the throbbing of my head, until it felt like my head was the building and the monster was pounding its enormous fists against my head, again and again, again and again.

Tom hadn't come for me. Instead, he was walking down the street, in the other direction. What was he up to?

Sprawled out on my back, I tried to get up, but my head was spinning. Nearby, the spiritual battle roared. "Nine-starred King of Birds, drive away filth," my father intoned, his words rhythmic, his syllables clipped and precise. He held his fingers in shoujue, elaborate gestures shaping the power behind his incantation. "Golden Men, draw me forward! Jade Maidens, defend me! I salute the Gate of Gold. I call upon the Jade Emperor. Filthy, strange, and foreign things, be banished. Quickly, quickly, for it is the Law!"

Magnified by the Seventh Ordination, bolstered by eighty generations of Daoshi, focused by his goosewood staff, and executed with perfect ritual, Father's spell felt strong enough to shake the world. Against my father's force, Liu Qiang's magical defenses snapped like twigs. The sorcerer cringed. The three-eyed white snake monster hissed at the end of his arm. It was a warbling hiss, a demented sound, not pain but fury. The fight would be over in a matter of minutes.

But where had Tom gone?

He came walking back down the street. Limping. There was a huge bloodstain along his pants leg. I did a better job of gouging his thigh than I thought.

Tom was holding something in one of his hands, heading straight toward my father. Where had he gone? What was in his hand? A knife or a hatchet could still change the outcome of the battle.

I needed to stop Tom, but I was no match for him in a fight. Yet as long as he was fighting me, he couldn't stab my father in the back. And that's all that was needed. My father could save the day, but not if I stayed down. I needed to stand up and fight, even if fighting Tom Wong meant I would get beaten. Sometimes it felt like that was my purpose in life.

I looked at my father. His face was intense with righteousness and glory, and I recalled all the times he had been ashamed of me. The expressions, harsh or sour, that crossed his face each time he was reminded that he had failed to father a son, or failed to cure my spirit sight.

He needed me, I knew that. My father didn't acknowledge it, but he needed me.

Right now what he needed me to do was stand up.

My skull was still pounding from Tom's kick. Above me the moon seemed to be moving, loosened somehow from the sky. I never, ever wanted to get kicked like that again.

Tom's gait was limping but steady. He strode toward my father. Father glanced at the younger man. My father's expression grew concerned. He pursed his lips. His face seemed sallow, almost the color of the bandages covering his left eye.

He gave his eye for me. He claimed it was just to save face. That might have been true on some level, but I didn't think it was completely true. I looked at the bandages covering his ruined eye. He gave his eye to protect me. My father raised me, devoted countless hours to teaching me, training me, trying to cure me. He refused to leave China without me. I meant more to him than he ever expressed.

I dreaded the pain. Dreaded the beating I was sure to take. But Tom Wong was walking toward my father with a weapon in his hands, and I needed to stop him. I rolled to my knees, and began to get my feet beneath me.

Father's magic gestures became more brisk. He abandoned his strategy of double-handed shoujue spells, fighting instead with an attack from each hand. The thought of casting two spells at the same time was mind-boggling. His attacks now felt like a hurricane. Liu Qiang cringed on his knees. His arm screeched. The soulstealer and his arm were about to be crumpled up and thrown away like blotted paper.

Then thunder shook the street. Thunder? I heard it echo off the buildings and was astonished. When did my father learn to speak words of thunder? Deities and Immortals spoke thunder. Men did not.

Father staggered, his hand to his side. I realized what the sound was.

Father didn't speak thunder. The sound wasn't thunder at all.

Tom Wong had shot my father.

TWENTY-NINE

"Tom!" I shouted.

He turned to face me. His expression was almost idle, but the gun was still smoking in his hand. Something ached in my chest. I could not believe that a man whose dearest friend was killed by gunfire would turn a pistol against a sworn brother.

My father's incantations stopped. There was a stricken look on his face. He clutched his side where the bullet landed, but still he stood.

My father still stood. He began walking forward. Walking toward Liu Qiang. His steps were pained but determined.

The one-armed man scrambled up to his knees and then to his feet. The two men faced each other. Blood marked both of their faces. Long ago my father cut off Liu Qiang's arm. Liu Qiang cost my father his eye. They were old enemies, and I knew my father wasn't motivated by righteousness any more than Liu Qiang was motivated by a plan. The force that drove them to this, walking across the cobblestones at the intersection of Sacramento and Dupont, was hatred.

Tom Wong turned back toward my father and aimed the pistol again. Pain clouded my head but I started to run. I ran toward Tom and my father, ran hard and fast to do something, to protect my father. Whatever it would take. Whatever the cost. I ran.

Time seemed to slow down. Tom's finger tightened on the trigger and I leaped. Not at Tom, since I knew he could swat me aside like a bug. I leaped in between Tom and my father, so the bullet would hit me instead of him.

The trigger clicked.

There was no clap of thunder, no burst of pain, no bullet. There was only a click. I stared at the pistol in Tom's hand.

He and I faced each other. My exhausted bearing was a stark contrast to his calm demeanor. He almost seemed bored. He pulled the trigger again, as if curious to see what would happen. It clicked again.

"That pistol," I said. "It's the one the constable used, to shoot at the Kulou-Yuanling."

Tom Wong shrugged, and tossed the empty gun aside. "Come on, Li-lin," he said, facing me. "Even if your father kills Mr. Liu, he's still going to die tonight. It's too late for him. But not for you."

I dragged myself toward the man who shot my father. Step after step. My head was ringing, whether from his last kick or the sound of the gunshot.

"Look at you," he said, as I continued to close the distance between us. "You're unarmed. You're a mess. You can't face me, and you know it. My kung fu is almost as good as Rocket's was."

I stepped forward and shot a powerful kick at his shin. He saw it coming, but he was experienced enough to know a fake when he saw it. He saw me faking the hard kick and lifted his other leg to kick at my head again.

Except I didn't fake my kick.

I only made it look like I was faking it. I kicked his shin, hard, and he'd placed all his weight and the force of a swift high kick on that leg. The sound from his ankle was sickening—tendon tearing from bone. His kicking leg flopped in midair and in that instant I made my decision. Tom had shot my father. There was no going back, not for him.

I grabbed his foot in the air and yanked it toward me, hard as I could. His entire body weight twisted against the ankle that supported it. The noise it made was enough to make me want to vomit.

Then I drove my elbow into his eye and dropped him on the ground.

I looked at him. His foot was facing backward. His ankle was ruined. He would need crutches to walk, as long as he lived.

In instants I'd reduced Tom Wong. He splayed out moaning on the street where I beat him. "No, Tom," I said, "your kung fu wasn't even close to Rocket's."

I turned from him and saw my father and Liu Qiang. The two men were standing face to face. Father was barely able to stand. A large bloodstain was spreading across the side of his sunset-yellow silk robe, and blood was trickling from many small wounds on his arms. I snarled. I knew what the small wounds were. They were bite-marks, the needle-sharp teeth of Liu Qiang's serpent arm.

Liu Qiang's face was torn where Mao'er had bitten and scratched him, but the eyes in his shredded face gleamed with triumph.

Father stood in a daze and Liu Qiang struck him in the chest with his human arm.

I recognized the strike.

Liu Qiang drove his fingers into Father's chest again and the strike disrupted the flow of my father's qi at a second point, then he drove them into another point of my father's chest and disrupted the qi at that point as well.

Liu Qiang was performing dian-si-shuei on my father. It was called the death touch for a reason. A sequence of five precise strikes to break a body's energy, followed by instant death. I'd never seen dian-si-shuei performed past the first strike. Father considered it yao shu, filthy magic. And Liu Qiang had just completed the first three of five strikes.

I sprinted at a breakneck pace. Liu Qiang struck my father again. One more strike in the proper sequence and my father would die.

I kicked my father in the back, as hard as I could. His head snapped backward and he toppled forward, colliding with Liu Qiang. The soulstealer's fifth strike landed in the wrong spot, brushing my father on the shoulder. Still running hard, I drove the heel of my palm into Liu Qiang's chin.

He staggered a few steps back, and I pulled my father away from him. There was no time to let my father fall gently. He dropped onto the street with a thud.

Liu Qiang's face was torn, his mouth bleeding from my hand. He laughed, sending bubbles of blood down his lips.

"You think you saved him, Li-lin?" the soulstealer crowed. "Four strikes, girl! What kind of power do you think he has left now?"

I took a calm step toward him. In one smooth motion I drew the peachwood sword from my belt and sliced it down at Liu Qiang's spirit arm.

It was a clean cut. Liu Qiang and his snake arm screamed, their voices human and monstrous. The sword severed their bond.

The snake arm dropped to the ground. It writhed, then reared back like a cobra. It looked at me with hatred in its three alien eyes. It opened its mouth and bared three rows of needle teeth. An unnatural stench rose from the thing, burning where it had been connected to Liu Qiang. It snapped at me, a surge of jaws and sharp teeth.

My peachwood sword split it down the middle of its head.

For a moment its innards were visible, pink and organic, like a living thing, but just for a moment. Then the creature withered like old leaves crumbling into dust, and its pale flesh turned to brown smoke.

The snake-arm-monster was gone, and in its place was some kind of thread. I squinted at it. It wasn't a thread.

It was a hair.

A single strand of long white hair.

My mind bent out of shape, staring at that strand of long hair. I remembered. I remembered *her*, and all the death she brought. I remembered her long white hair. "How—?" I said out loud, and then a spell hit me.

I moaned and clutched at my thigh. A spirit arrow. Foolish, Li-lin, distracted by memories while a Daoshi of the Fifth Ordination was trying to kill me.

Liu Qiang launched another spirit arrow. I staggered to the side and the arrow flew past. I could hardly use my left leg with the spirit arrow embedded in it. I could hardly think with the pain in my thigh.

"I will kill you, girl," Liu Qiang said, his voice shaking with rage. "And I will kill your father. And everyone will know that Liu Qiang was the strongest Daoshi of his generation."

I tried to take a step back but my left leg didn't cooperate. It stayed inert and I tumbled to the street. I held up my peachwood sword. It was my only remaining defense.

Liu Qiang smiled. It was a hideous thing to see, from behind the gouges and bruises and all the blood caked around his mouth. "I was saving this spell for your father," he said, "but you've earned it." Shaping magic gestures with the fingers of his remaining hand, he began to chant. The incantation and the shoujue gestures coalesced into a single magic, giving shape to the sorcerer's will. It hung in the air, a red miasma, and I understood.

I heard his words and understood. He was calling disease into my body. And peachwood offers no defense against disease.

THIRTY

I chanted a recitation from the Jade Text of the Primordial One, which only made Liu Qiang's gory smile grow wider and more hideous. "Quickly, quickly, for it is the Law," I finished, and a small magic swept out from my fingers and my words. My recitation of the Jade Text wouldn't be able to stop his spell. He knew it and I knew it. But the counterspell could hold off red miasma for a few minutes.

The disease spell pressed against me and my recitation slowed it down. Liu Qiang's red miasma would climb into me through my nose and mouth. Then tumors would multiply inside me. In an hour I was going to be infested with a dozen different kinds of cancer. In two hours I would be dead, a corpse resembling no human shape.

And all of that would start to happen once I breathed the contaminated air. So I needed to keep the red miasma out of my lungs as long as possible.

I began my turtle breathing. My counterspell bought me a little time to inhale pure air. I started to slow down my breathing, to sharpen my mind.

I took a long slow turtle breath. Liu Qiang circled me, lurching and strutting. He wanted to watch his enemy's daughter die.

Two minutes passed and my counterspell broke. The disease spell was all around me, a red and oppressive murk in the air. I had two-and-a-half minutes. I could exhale for two-and-a-half minutes.

And then what? Throw my wooden sword at the soulstealer? I was nowhere near my rope dart. No one was going to save me. Mr. Yanqiu was useless in a fight. Jiujiu and the spirit-gulls were busy distracting the Kulou-Yuanling. My father was unconscious.

No, actually, he wasn't, I realized. He was sprawled on his back in the street but his lips were moving. What was he doing? Liu Qiang had disrupted his qi. It would take him days to regain enough vital energy to perform any powerful spells.

And then I felt it. A tingle at the soles of my feet. It rose up through me like a shining.

Powerful spells are draining. After four strikes of dian-si-shuei, Father would barely have any qi energy remaining. But not every spell demands an investiture of energy.

The Third Ordination flowed through me like a sacred river. My body and spirit felt renewed. My nerves awoke in a kind of joy, as if all the mornings in the world took place at once, inside me, after a month of darkness.

I yanked the spirit arrow out of my thigh. It hurt, and the pain didn't matter.

I still had no defense against the disease spell around me. In about a minute I would need to breathe again. But at least I would die with the Third Ordination. It was something to be proud of.

And then waves of power came over me. All around me the world took shape in crystalline geometries, and they were beautiful. I could almost touch the perfected choreography of the stars, guiding our moments, and feel in my hands the pattern of all things shifting, from wood to water to metal to earth to fire, and back again to wood, in the unending transformations of the phases.

I received the Fourth Ordination and I couldn't believe it.

I watched my father. He began to chant the ritual of Fifth Ordination. When he was finished, I would be strong enough to match Liu Qiang.

Then Liu Qiang kicked my father in the face.

Father's chanting stopped. Liu Qiang kicked him again. And again. Blood sprayed from my father's mouth, spattering the soulstealer's shoes.

Father had ordained me to the Fourth. It wouldn't be enough to stand against Liu Qiang. And I really didn't care.

I stood and faced the soulstealer.

My turtle breathing was almost complete. There were moments of air remaining in my lungs. I gave up delaying the inevitable.

I looked at Liu Qiang, the man who cut me. His shoes were wet with my father's blood. With the dregs of my breath I spoke the Jade Text recitation again.

He was a Daoshi of the Fifth Ordination, and I of the Fourth. But it didn't matter. Ordination focuses the will, amplifies it. Neither Liu Qiang nor I could draw upon the eighty generations that came before us. There was his will, focused and amplified by the Fifth Ordination, and there was my will, focused and amplified by the Fourth.

I looked at Liu Qiang and my spell snuffed his red miasma.

He gaped. "What?" he said. "How?"

I smiled like a demoness and began walking toward him. Stepping back, he chanted and formed his hand into a shoujue. I snapped his spell with a syllable and a flick of two fingers.

His eyes flashed with terror and he began stumbling away. I locked both my hands together in the Heaven and Earth Net, shifting to the Copper Fence: double-handed seals, like those my father had used, shaped the magic of my willpower and my chanted spells. Liu Qiang held up his hand in the Five Darkness single-hand seal, but my father's strategy held, and the soulstealer began to scream.

I took another step toward him. It was time to take Liu Qiang down, once and for all. The Fifth Ordination made him more powerful than me, but using double-handed seals made it a more even battle.

But an even battle means that no victory is decisive. And this needed decisiveness.

I placed my left hand on my hip.

With my right hand I fought his magic with my own, single-handed spell to single-handed spell, Fourth Ordination to Fifth. I launched a strike from a Thunder Block hand seal, which he severed with an Immortal Sword gesture, but I was already performing a Mount Tai hand gesture—lifting a weight of spirit equivalent to Mount Tai, and bringing it down to crush him. He held up Immortal Sword again in response. Our magic clashed like armies. His spell was stronger, but I gritted my teeth and didn't release my Mount Tai gesture. Our eyes met there, on the street. He looked bewildered. We both knew his spell should be strong enough to slice through mine.

In one rapid motion I released Mount Tai and slashed out with my own Immortal Sword, while his gesture was still fighting against a weight of spirit that was no longer there. He cried out, and it was the frightened little sound of a frightened little man. He turned his sword fingers against me.

I smiled. He was fighting from strength. I was not. I had been fighting from weakness for fifteen years. I was used to fighting opponents who were much stronger than me. Sometimes I could even beat them. And Liu Qiang wasn't even that much stronger than me anymore.

He turned his sword fingers to strike at me, expecting to hit my own Immortal Sword gesture and crush it with pure power. But I released my sword fingers and dropped to the ground, letting his spell swing past over me. Then I brought the spiritual weight of Mount Tai down upon him once more. It hit him like an avalanche.

Liu Qiang fell to the ground, and dragged himself back to his feet. I advanced toward the soulstealer, one hand still on my hip, and I was smiling.

"You can't do this!" he cried, backing away. "You're only of the Fourth Ordination. You can't do this. You can't beat me. I heard him. He didn't ordain you past the Fourth!"

"You always were a weakling, Liu Qiang," I said, advancing on him.

He cringed at my approach. "Don't kill me," he said, raising his arm to protect his face. "Please don't kill me."

I looked at the soulstealer. I wanted this man dead. I wanted to strike him down and leave his corpse to rot on the street, unburied and forgotten. Just looking at his face brought a hundred years of anger into me, and I remembered how it had felt in Bok Choy's gambling hall, when I lost control of my anger. It took a room filled with gangsters to stop me from killing a man then.

I looked in the face of the little man. He had tricked me, pushed back my clothing and cut my stomach, cost my father an eye, and killed Hong Xiaohao. He had trapped me inside a spirit that convinced me my husband was still alive. He had unleashed devastation upon Chinatown. There was nothing I would rather do than kill him. And there was no one who could stop me.

But I remembered Shuai Hu, the Buddhist monk with a tiger's shadow. I made a promise to the monk, but did it really matter? Shuai Hu was a monster. He had no place in the social order. I was under no obligation to respect a promise that had been made to a monster.

But Shuai Hu treated me with respect.

I reached out and and took Liu Qiang's remaining thumb in my hand.

"No!" he shouted. "Don't! Please don't. I need it. I need a thumb!"

"If I break your thumb, you'll be helpless, Liu Qiang," I said. "Imagine being a man with one arm, and your only thumb broken. Someone like that would barely be able to feed himself."

Liu Qiang fell to his knees. "Daonu Xian!" he begged. "Please don't break my thumb, please, Daonu Xian!"

I looked over at the bone giant. It was demolishing another Xie Liang building. Three or four men were dead.

"How do I stop the Kulou-Yuanling?" I asked.

"I don't know!" he cried.

"What do you mean?"

The coward whined and said, "It's never going to stop destroying. That's what it does."

I twisted his thumb and made the soulstealer wince. "You commanded it before. I heard you giving it commands."

"Yes, but I commanded it to kill or shout or destroy. There's no command that will make it stop," he said. "It will never stop."

I released his finger with a sigh. I came so close. I defeated Liu Qiang, killed his spirit arm, and beat Tom Wong and his hatchetmen. And still there was no way to fight the Kulou-Yuanling. Over the skyline of wood and brick I saw the monster's skull shining in the moonlight, and I could see the qi circulating along its meridians.

I turned to Liu Qiang. "I'll let you keep your thumb," I said, "if you teach me something."

THIRTY-ONE

This is how I always imagined a higher Ordination: I thought my hands would crackle with power. I thought my body's energies would be rooted in the earth and branch up to the Seven Stars. I thought the sacred words would touch my lips reverently as I spoke them. I thought peachwood would feel like an extension of my skin. I thought ghosts would surrender at the sight of me.

I didn't think the Fourth Ordination would turn me into an idiot.

And yet there I was, on the roof of one of the tallest buildings in Chinatown, getting ready to jump.

I took a running start and leaped into the air.

In mid-leap I brought my peachwood sword down at an angle against the Kulou-Yuanling's collarbone, then scrambled for a handhold with my left hand. I only fell a few feet before I found a grip.

The bone giant turned the green fires of its eyes to look at me where I dangled. It hadn't realized yet that one of its meridians had been severed. I needed to act before it noticed.

I swung and spun, striking at the Kulou-Yuanling's Sun and Moon point with my peachwood sword. It was a clean cut. The channel of meridian energy sundered under the strike, giving off a stream of red and yellow sparks.

The Kulou-Yuanling felt it now.

Two out of five.

Learning dian-si-shuei takes years of training, patience, and practice. One has to memorize the six hundred forty-nine position points along the body's meridians and know how they work. The complex geometry of the energy body has to become as familiar as adding up pennies and nickels. One needs a precision far beyond the surgical to follow the pattern of strikes, planting each in its exact location without being able to see the flows of energy.

That was where this was different.

I could see the pattern of the Kulou-Yuanling's energy. Qi rose and fell around its bone frame, parallel streams of yin qi and yang qi, moving in opposite directions. The latticework of the monster's energy body was exposed to me, and exaggerated to fifty feet high. Little precision was required.

I jumped up and lunged at its Central Treasury point, where the energy from the back cascades into the energy moving along the front. It broke apart under the tip of my sword. The blue-green flames that roared behind the Kulou-Yuanling's eye sockets flickered and grew a little dimmer.

The Kulou-Yuanling opened its mouth and gonged.

"Gong," I echoed with a smile. With so much of its qi severed, the Kulou-Yuanling's voice was not as loud as a churchbell. "Gong," I said again, and clambered sidewise across its ribs.

It lifted a hand to pull me off its chest but I clung long enough to drive my sword against its Tranquil Sea point. A geyser of sparks shot out from the severed yin meridian. It was the fourth strike.

It wrapped its bone fingers around my waist and plucked me off its chest. It raised me up to face it. In the cool night air we looked in each other's faces. The flames of its eyes were flickering like dying candles. Behind the thin cracks of its bone-yellow face plates, I saw so much pain. A hundred men. The rage and pain and hunger of a hundred men who died here, far from the gravesites of their ancestors. Some were killed when gold mines collapsed around them. Others were massacred by mobs of bigots. There was no good reason for any of it. Each of these hundred men came here with aspirations and dreams. Each of their lives ended in tragedy.

Liu Qiang and Tom Wong had exploited their tragedies.

"I'm sorry," I said, and threw my sword into its Elegant Mansion point.

I had fallen earlier from about thirty feet. At that time I slowed my fall by grabbing at a balcony and smacking down on an awning, and still the impact left me battered.

I was fifty feet in the air over a cobblestone street when the Kulou-Yuanling came apart.

All the magic that held it together vanished at once. The light of its eyes snuffed out, and its skull and its jawbone, the teeth in its mouth and the vertebrae in its back, all the ribs in its ribcage, its arms and legs, all collapsed into ash and sand at the same moment, straight down on Sacramento Street.

I fell with it. I experienced a moment of odd curiosity as I watched the street rush up to break me.

Then there was a sound of wings, a feeling like my clothes had been snagged in thorns, and I stopped falling.

The spirit gulls had caught me. I turned my head. The flapping of a thousand wings sounded like a choppy sea. Jiujiu was leading them, a look of satisfaction in all her eyes. And riding on her back—

"You saved me again," I said to the spirit of my father's eye.

Jiujiu took the lead. I floated behind them, with Mr. Yanqiu on my shoulder. Held aloft by a cloud of three-eyed gulls, we drifted over the streets of Chinatown, surveying the damage as we passed. Two buildings had been reduced to rubble. We saw the corpses of four dead men.

"He ate them," I said to Mr. Yanqiu. "He was so hungry. So many of the corpses that made up the Kulou-Yuanling were men who starved to death in the mines, hoping for rescue that never came."

"That was all the mind it had," he said, with a brisk nod of his eye. "The Kulou-Yuanling had to obey Liu Qiang, but all it could remember was hunger."

"But it had no stomach to fill. It ate the men and remained hungry. It would have stayed hungry if it ate all the men in Chinatown."

Mr. Yanqiu shook his eye and sighed.

We arrived at the intersection of Dupont and Sacramento, where I had last seen my father. I had left him propped up to prevent him from choking on his blood, and then I had dashed off to destroy the Kulou-Yuanling. He was sitting up now. His eye was open wide and he stared at me with a slack look.

"Bring me down," I said to the gull spirits.

"Li-lin, what are you . . ." said my father, his voice hoarse and uncertain. "What is . . ."

"Let her down," Mr. Yanqiu told the gulls, and they lowered me to my feet.

"Can you stand?" I asked my father. "Let's get you to the infirmary."

"You are . . ." he said. "The seagulls . . . How could . . ."

"They are the Haiou Shen, Father, and I am their protector. But you need to see Dr. Wei. You've been shot."

"It's just a broken rib," he said. "Where is the Kulou-Yuanling?"

"It's dead. Its bones crumbled to ash on Sacramento Street."

"Dead? How?"

"I killed it, Father."

"Lil-lin, what did you . . ." he said, "how did you . . ."

"I used dian-si-shuei on it."

My father rose unsteadily to his feet. He stood facing me as one would face a stranger. A stranger holding a very large knife. "You know dian-si-shuei?"

"Not really. I made Liu Qiang teach me the basics. The five meridian strikes and their order. Enough to kill a very big target that's moving slowly and has its energy meridians right out there in the open. Father, you're bleeding."

"Liu Qiang." My father spat on the ground. "Where is he?"

"He's beaten. His demonic arm is dead. I'll tell you all about it at the infirmary, Father."

"I'll go when I'm ready," he said. "Do not tell me how I should act."

I sighed. He needed to get to the infirmary, but if I insisted on it, he'd only refuse more strenuously.

"Father," I began, "when I killed Liu Qiang's arm . . ." I was having a hard time saying the words. "Something strange happened."

"What happened?" he asked me.

"It changed into a strand of long white hair."

A significant look passed between us. "No," he said, looking away. "It isn't her."

"Father," I asked slowly, "is the Bai Fa Monu alive?"

"No," he said, blinking too fast. "The White-Haired Demoness is dead."

"Why did we come to America?"

He looked down. "Our village was gone," he said.

"Is that all there was to it?"

He would not meet my eyes. "Our village was gone," he said, "so we came to America."

"Mr. Wong said you refused to leave me behind."

"What of it?"

"Why did you insist on bringing me with you?"

He raised his gaze to mine. "You're really asking me that?"

"All my life, I was a disappointment to you. You wanted a son."

"Of course I wanted a son, Li-lin."

"Instead, you had me."

"I wish I had my pipe right now," he said, "or a cup of tea."

"And I would be happy to bring your pipe or prepare your tea, Father. But why did you bring me to Gold Mountain? You could have left me behind."

"Could I?" he said. "Yes, I suppose I could. But I had lost so much . . ." His voice trailed off.

"Your wife was dead."

His gaze searched my face. The silence that fell between us was deep and painful. "You don't remember," he said.

I stared at him for a long time. "What don't I remember?"

"You don't remember any of it," he said. "I should be glad of that. No one alive can remember my shame."

We stood quietly, facing each other. A breeze blew down the street, carrying brick dust and ashes, the smell of burning, destroyed things.

"Please tell me why you brought me to America, Father."

"You want to know why?" he said. "Your mother was dead. And so many others. My apprentices, my mother, my cousins and friends, they were all dead. My temple, my home, everything was gone. Not a stone remained of the village it was my duty to protect. Do you understand, Ah Li?"

"I was the only one you had left."

He looked at me for what felt like a long time. Eventually he looked away with a laugh, a raw, bitter laugh. "Is that what you think? You think I saw you as some kind of trinket, a souvenir?"

"I . . . I . . ."

"I brought you with me because you were the only one I managed to save. I failed everyone else. Out of everyone I was sworn to protect, you were the only one who made it out of the massacre with me.

"You were the only reason I did not loathe myself utterly, Li-lin. The one life I managed to save, other than my own. Our village was a charnel-house when I found you in the well. I found you alive. No one but you. My daughter. My redeemer."

There were tears in my eyes. I waited for him to continue.

"You clung to me, Li-lin, do you remember that? I carried you out of the ruins of our village. You clung to me."

"You called me Little Monkey," I said.

He gave a short laugh. "You wouldn't let go."

I wasn't used to seeing the expression on his face. It took me a moment to recognize it. It was affection.

Father's eyebrows made him look severe, but he also looked pale and sallow. He'd taken such a beating in the last few days. He could barely stand. His beautiful silk robe was now stiff with drying blood. He wiped sweat from his face and said, "What did you do with Liu Qiang?"

I took a breath before I answered. "I broke his index finger and let him go, Father. With the broken finger he won't be able to write any talismans or shape any shoujue gestures. He won't be performing any more harmful magic. And besides," I began, "I told him—"

"Why did you let him live?"

I sighed. "Because I made a promise to someone."

"Who?"

"Shuai Hu," I said. His look was blank, so I said, "He follows the Buddhist path. He's a tiger with three tails."

Father's eye went wide. He took a step back. "What are you saying? You have been consorting with monsters?"

"I needed his help, Father," I said. "He follows the Buddhist path."

My father held his hands out in front of him. It was a defensive gesture, as though he was certain I was going to attack him at any moment. "What has happened to you, Li-lin? You are a Daoshi. You have no business among the dirty spirits of gulls, let alone tigers. You have performed forbidden magic. And you let Liu Qiang go free."

"I promised Shuai Hu that I would kill no one tonight," I repeated. "And before I let Liu Qiang go, I told him if he ever causes trouble again, I would hunt him down. Wherever he hid I would find him and I would beat him down, break his thumb, and piss in his face."

I smiled. My father looked shocked, and then he looked bewildered. He stood staring at me, uncomprehending. And there were more questions I needed to ask.

"What happened to the Plague Box, Father?"

He stiffened. "What do you mean?"

"Li Zhenren, the founder of our lineage, had a Plague Box full of evil spells. The box would have been passed down through the generations of the Maoshan lineage, from senior student to senior student. It would have been passed into Shifu Li's hands. Shifu Li would have passed it to you, Father."

He glowered at me, saying nothing.

"The spell to create the Quanshen, the spell to create the Kulou-Yuanling . . . They would have been quarantined in the Plague Box. What happened to it, Father?"

He lifted his face to me. His eye burned with anger. "Enough," he said. "You ask too much. You have chosen a left-hand path so many times tonight, Li-lin. You tell me you are a protector of monsters, that you made a promise to a monster, that you performed dian-si-shuei and let Liu Qiang leave with his life. I do not know you anymore. You are erguizi."

I looked down. Erguizi. A child with two ghosts. A Chinese ghost and an American ghost.

He continued looking at me with a harshness only my father could manage. "Is there more?"

I swallowed and made myself face him. "Yes, Father," I said. "Tomorrow I go to work for Bok Choy and the Xie Liang tong. And I've decided that I'm not going to destroy the spirit of your eye."

He paled. I saw a look on his face I had not seen since I was a small child. On that day long ago, we walked in silence. We went from house to house, looking for survivors. There were none. I had never forgotten his expression. He looked like a man who had lost everything, who had lost any reason to live, a man whose every hope had been ruined.

My heart broke for him in that moment.

He cleared his throat. "I have failed you too," he said. "From this moment forward, I have no daughter." He turned and walked away.

It had only been a matter of days, but it felt like years had gone by. Just days ago Mao'er had shown me a niche between two walls off of Fat Boy Alley. I made my way back there, in the human world this time. It was a cold night to sleep outside. I curled up and slept.

I woke in the morning, sore and tired, feeling chilled to the bone. I sat up, rubbing my head where I'd been kicked. The events of last night played out in my mind. I had defeated Tom Wong in a fight, bested Liu Qiang's magic, killed his evil arm, and demolished the Kulou-Yuanling. It had been a victory, of the sort that legends tell of. I grinned a bitter grin, knowing that life goes on when the legends end. The hero triumphs, but then his story continues. He grows old, suffers, and dies.

After the heroine triumphs, her father disowns her, her social order rejects her, and she must spend years sweating in a dim, dank room, a plaything for men.

The injustice of it all made me want to howl, to weep, to tear at my hair and face. I had saved Chinatown, using my wits, my courage, and my power, and now I was going to become a whore.

It was for the best that my father had disowned me. If he no longer had a daughter, then my whoring would cause him no loss of face.

I stood to stretch my sore muscles. Every movement reminded me that I had taken a beating. It hurt to stand. It hurt to move. The sky above was cloudless for once, an unending expanse of blue that ranged from a crystalline, frost-blue to an inky cobalt I just wanted to dissolve into.

Moments earlier, I had felt like weeping for sorrow, but I did not shed a tear. Now, looking into the gorgeous depths of California sky, the beauty humbled me. I would not weep for Xian Li-lin, but I wept for beauty.

I came out to walk around Chinatown. There were hardly any men out this morning. No fish sellers, no vendors. Most were afraid, I guessed. It would take a day or two before people calmed down after last night's events.

I began walking. Everywhere there was rubble. Red brick dust and wood chips mingled with the yellow-white ashes of the Kulou-Yuanling.

Two buildings had been demolished. Two of the Xie Liang's gambling halls. Bok Choy would probably tell the constables there had been a fire. If I knew how the tongs worked, Bok Choy and Mr. Wong would send letters back and forth until an agreement was reached. Tom Wong would be blamed for the fire. The constables would take him to prison.

I wanted to remember Tom as he'd been before hatred twisted him. The pretty young man who had been my husband's friend. Rocket's death had struck us all, a devastating blow, but Tom had allowed resentment and bitterness to rule his days and actions. He sought a kind of power no one should pursue. Now he was going to go to prison. He was never going to be able to walk unassisted again.

My future looked bleak. No one would choose to become a fatherless widow working as a whore. But I knew I had what it would take to survive. I knew how to roll with the punches.

I should know. I've been punched a lot.

I walked to Xie Liang headquarters and knocked on the door. A young man answered. His hair was cut American-style. He gave me a quizzical look. "I'm here about a job," I told him.

The youth nodded, looking cross. "Does that upset you?" I asked.

He gave a huff. "I bet ten cents that you'd run away," he said. He opened the door for me. Shaking my head, I entered.

There was no gambling going on in the room. Instead, a few dozen men gathered in groups, speaking in quiet

voices. Each man in his own way appeared cowed, intimi-
dated. Those who had seen the Kulou-Yuanling had told
those who had not. An undercurrent of fear and tension
flowed among the men.

Whispers have their own kind of motion. From
mouth to ear, they spread through men like a ripple
through a pond. A hush spread now, overtaking the tense
room. I heard an insistent whisper. "It's her," the whispers
said. "It's her."

In moments, every face in the room was turned in my
direction. The silence in the room was absolute. I stood in
the entryway facing the men. The men sat facing me.

Then there was a sound from somewhere in the room.
It was the sound of flesh slapping flesh. I turned my eyes
toward the source of the sound. It was a man in his fifties,
balding at the top of his head. The edges of his mouth turned
down in what I was guessing was a perpetual grimace.

We locked eyes and he clapped his hands again. And
again.

At the fourth clap other men joined in. By two or
three at first, the clapping spread, and then it caught the
whole room in a single surge. There were thirty or forty
men in the room. All of them were applauding.

They were applauding for me.

I felt tears begin, but I fought them back. My feet
wobbled a bit. I didn't know what to do with my hands.
Nothing in my life had prepared me to be applauded. I
placed one hand on my hair and the other on my hip, awk-
wardly, as the applause continued. The posture made me
feel foolish so I raised my hands and started clapping too.

Then the cheering began. Now I was truly embarrassed. I looked down. I wanted to run away, to avoid the
embarrassment of this attention, and yet I could not help
myself. I smiled. I smiled so wide my cheeks hurt. Clapping
for myself felt dumb, so I placed my hands on my hips.

A skinny man came out from the back room, dressed
as a woman. He wore heavy American makeup. He reeked
of perfume. The whore of the day, I realized. The man who

had lost the most bets yesterday walked toward me. He smirked. I saw a flash of gold among his teeth.

I blinked. It was Bok Choy.

The leader of the Xie Liang tong, one of the most powerful men in Chinatown, was dressed up as a whore. I couldn't comprehend a man so powerful being willing to lose so much face. It boggled the mind.

At least I knew what to do with my hands now. I brought them together and bowed.

"Come with me," Bok Choy said with his habitual smirk. He turned and led me down a hall.

The applause continued until after I left the room. I was glad to be free of such embarrassment, but also delighted. Never before had I experienced such a feeling. I would treasure the memory through the years of my contract. There was a day when men had cheered for me.

I followed Bok Choy in silence. He led me up a flight of wooden stairs, to a small, dark room where two men were waiting.

With a giggle, he swept his arm around the room in an expansive gesture. "How do you like it?"

Looking around the dark, bare room, I felt tension return to my body. Despair took me in a wave. It was a soggy, nauseating feeling, facing my future. This was to be my place, my new home.

"There's no bed," I told him.

"You need a bed?" He seemed surprised. "I'll get you one."

I looked at him with such disgust. Pretending it had been an act of generosity to bring a bed so his customers could make use of me.

"What else do you need?" he asked me. "Candles? An altar?"

I couldn't handle this. It was bad enough that I had lost, lost so much, but now he was mocking the Dao, my path and the source of my power. I thought about attacking him. His men would probably kill me if I tried.

Butsowhatiftheydid?Itwasn'tlikeIhadanythingleftto
live for.

With a spinning kick I pinned Bok Choy against the
wall of the dim room. "Enough," I told him, "I lost, and I'll
work for you, but do not mock those things that are sacred
to me."

The gangster held back a snarl. I saw it, saw the muscles twitch around his mouth, saw him force a different
reaction. Self-control. His erratic behavior kept everyone
off-balance, but he never lost self-control. No wonder he'd
grown so powerful.

Bok Choy giggled, loud and hard. I felt the muzzle of
his gun press up against my chin. The cold metal sent chills
through me.

"Why shouldn't I mock you, Li-lin? Looks to me like
you deserve some mockery." He pressed his gun up higher.
I rose on tiptoes. "You signed a goddamn contract without
reading it." He shoved me back by the barrel of his gun,
then pulled out a second one and aimed it at me.

"Put your palms on the floor," he said. "Now."

The guns kept me cowed and compliant. I squatted
and put my hands down, feeling the dust on the floorboards. He took a step toward me, pointing the guns at my
forehead.

"Bang," he said. He dropped his arms to his sides. In
a casual tone, he said, "I have work to do. Look around the
room for a while, then come downstairs and tell me what
you need."

"What I need?"

"I figure you'll need some things," he said. "A bed.
Equipment. Books. A chuqitong."

"A punching bag?" I looked up at Bok Choy, the gangster dressed as a whore, the pistols in each of his hands.
"Why would I need a punching bag?"

Bok Choy giggled, waving a pistol in the air, and then,
by accident, he fired it. Up so close, the sound was a shock.
I felt it in my chest as much as I heard it like thunder in my

ears. His men jumped at the sound, too. They looked terrified. Something inside me wanted to curl up into a ball for safety.

"You really should let us handle the guns, Boss," one of his men said.

"Piffle," he replied, shrugging. The gun smoked in his hand.

The bullet had punched a hole the size of a fist through the corner where the wall met the roof. That gun had been pointed at my head, moments earlier. His accidental shot could have splattered my brains along the floorboards. Squatting, my palms on the floor, I began to shake.

Bok Choy turned back toward me. The smell of his perfume blended with gunsmoke and dust, to make the walls feel close, the room narrow. "You'll need a punching bag," he said, "because if you don't practice your kung fu, you'll be useless to me as a bodyguard."

"As a whatdidyousay?"

Bok Choy smirked. Gold glinted through his lip-sticked mouth. "Really should have read the contract, dunce. You'll be working for the Xie Liang tong for the next three years. You'll put that bagua stepping of yours to good use as my bodyguard."

"As *what?*"

"Bodyguard, moron. Keep me safe. You'll have other duties, too. You'll teach my daughter English. If she learns her lessons well, you'll reward her by giving her a kung fu lesson."

The words bent in my mind, melting into strange, waxen shapes. It couldn't be true.

"Uh?" I said, cleverly.

"If paying members of Xie Liang tong need an exorcism, you'll do it free. You work for the Xie Liang tong, so you don't collect red envelopes. You'll be paid fifteen dollars a week."

My eyes bulged. Fifteen dollars a week was a lot of money. It was almost double what most workers earned.

Mr. Wong paid my father twenty. My sewing never brought in more than three or four.

"Can I . . ." I asked. "Can I stand?"

With a gun in one hand, he gestured that I should stand. His men watched the gun, exchanging nervous glances. "No more attacking me, hear?"

"I hear," I said. I stood up, feeling dizzy. So much was changing. Fifteen dollars a week. Teaching English. Being a bodyguard. Teaching kung fu.

It sounded too good. I couldn't help myself. "Why?"

"What do you mean, Li-lin?"

"Why do you want me as your bodyguard? You have dozens of men. There are men in Chinatown with far more training than I have."

"You're forgetting something, Li-lin."

"What's that?"

"I've seen you in action."

I gave a short laugh and rolled my eyes. "You saw me lose my temper and hurt people I didn't mean to."

"Yes. That's it exactly. I saw you fight from anger. You know what else I saw?"

I waited.

"You were raging, Li-lin. Out of control. You fought for pride. You fought for a fool's reason," he said, "but you didn't fight like a fool."

"I don't see how my foolishness would be an advantage to you."

He shook his head, managing to fill the gesture with mockery. "Fools are the only people I trust. Someone who values loyalty over money is a fool. And fools make the best bodyguards. Only fools are willing to sacrifice their lives to protect someone."

"I wouldn't give my life to protect you," I said.

He threw back his head and laughed. His laughter came out in quick, nasal sounds. It went on long enough that it made me nervous. When his laughter died down, he looked at me, his eyes gleaming to match his golden tooth. "Would you risk your life to protect my daughter?"

I said nothing. I thought of Hua, so cheerful and innocent. If that girl was in danger, I'd protect her. To keep the child safe, I'd fight recklessly, against absurd odds, or jump in the path of a bullet. He was right.

Bok Choy understood me well enough to manipulate me. I didn't like that at all.

But the life he was offering me . . . The job, the place to live, the pay. It was very appealing. I loved the idea of teaching English to a child. I didn't mind the idea of working as a bodyguard, even though I wasn't sure how I felt about being *a gangster's* bodyguard.

There was something else, though.

"You want me to perform exorcisms," I said. "But you don't believe in magic."

"Did I say that?" he said. His grin was wider and less sane than ever. "Maybe I was lying."

"So what do you believe?"

"I believe that the gods I worship and the books I read are no concern of yours," he said. "I also believe that you now have a better job than most women in Chinatown."

I met his gaze. He was daring me to contradict him. After a few moments, I said, "Better than most men, too."

His laughter had a triumphant spark to it. One of his men shook his head and handed him a dollar.

"Say it," he said. "You work for Bok Choy now."

I looked at him, the unpredictable, violent, dangerous gangster—who had just given me a decent job. Looking him in the eyes, I said, "I work for Bok Choy now."

THIRTY-TWO

L ater that day I walked to the Flower Lane. I found the front door of the Buddhist monastery open and climbed the steps up to the second floor.

There were eight men in robes, performing prostrations in front of a statue of Guanyin, the Buddhist goddess of compassion. Shuai Hu was one of them. He looked up and saw me standing at the door. He continued to prostrate himself before the goddess. I sighed. Holy men would be the death of me. I waited for what felt like hours while he completed his ritual.

Eventually he stood, bowed, and came over to talk to me. "Daonu Xian," he said, with his silly smile. "I am pleased you are not among the dead."

"As am I," I said. "I kept my promise, Shuai Hu."

He smiled. His big cheeks looked cheerful and accepting. "What will you do now?" he asked.

"I signed a contract with Bok Choy," I said. "Three years. I will be his bodyguard, and I'll teach his daughter English and kung fu."

"Your kung fu is excellent," the monk said.

"Great men trained me. My kung fu is no more than should be expected," I acknowledged, "but it could be better. Shuai Hu, would you like to spar with me? Sometime?"

I was surprised at how awkward it felt to ask him that. My voice came out in a nervous squeak.

"No," he said.

"No?"

"No, Daonu Xian. I would not like to spar with you."

I stared, surprised and feeling rejected somehow. Unworthy.

"I would prefer it if you do not come here again," he said.

"But why?" I asked.

He held me with his gaze. "For over a hundred years I have observed the Dharma, Daonu. I strive to be better than the animal I was born to be. You make that more difficult," he said. He looked away. "I desire you. Do not come to me again."

I blinked. There were so many things I wanted to say to him—arguments I wanted to make, longings I wanted to express, questions I wanted to ask. But instead I bowed to the statue of the goddess, turned, and walked down the stairs and out the door.

Early the next morning, before sunrise, I filled a flask with warm water. I found a nice ceramic cup, climbed to the roof of the Xie Liang's headquarters, and called the ghost of my father's eye to join me.

The stars and streetlamps spread a pale light over the early morning mists that hung in midair over Sacramento Street. I poured steaming water into the teacup. Mr. Yanqiu climbed into the cup and made happy noises.

I didn't know what my future held. Sitting on the roof of the Xie Liang headquarters, I told Mr. Yanqiu about the day's events. It had been a long time since someone had really been interested in hearing what I had to say.

Fog was gathering over the flat roof of the building which was my home for the next three years. Later today my supplies would start to arrive. I would start a Hall of Ancestors for the Xie Liang tong. There I would commemorate the names of the men who had been killed in the Kulou-Yuanling's rampage. I would burn offerings for Hong Xiaohao, who gave his life for me. I would send letters to China to arrange a wedding between him and some young woman who had died without a husband. It made me feel good, knowing I could do that for him.

This was Chinatown, and it was my world. I thought of my father, and the Ansheng tong, where Mr. Wong would watch the constables clap Darby cuffs on his son's wrists. I thought of Dr. Wei trying so hard to belong to two worlds at once. I thought of his wife, all alone because the world of her childhood had been destroyed. So much had changed in the last few days. There was a murmur in the air behind me. I sighed. Four or five ghostly faces hovered nearby, spreading a blue glow. They were the last of the ghosts I had liberated from the scream spirit. Most had dispersed, but a few of them still followed me.

Light began rising from the east. I reached out and scooped Mr. Yanqiu out of the teacup. "Hey!" he said. "Careful!"

I lifted him to my shoulder. There was a moment of quiet.

"Li-lin," he said, "what is this?"

"It's a pocket, Mr. Yanqiu."

"And what's it for?"

"It's for you. I sewed pockets into the shoulders of all my robes, so you can come with me."

"Come with you?" he said. "Are you going somewhere?"

"I'm always going somewhere. But right now," I said, "we're going to watch the sun rise."

AUTHOR'S NOTE

The Girl with Ghost Eyes explores the lives of working-class Chinese American immigrants at the end of the nineteenth century. These were people whose values, aspirations, and systems of belief differed from the society outside Chinatown. Like any work of historical fantasy, some elements are factual and some are not. There are areas where cultural details have been compressed or skewed for the sake of telling a good story.

Culture is not monolithic, and these thousands of people were individuals. For storytelling purposes, *The Girl with Ghost Eyes* has condensed some of the extraordinary diversity of these people who came to America driven by dreams of a better life.

Language:
Most of the people in Chinatown were from the Sze Yup region of Canton, now known as Guangdong. But some immigrants came to Chinatown from other parts of China and other parts of Asia. They came from different regions and different ethnic backgrounds, bringing numerous distinct languages and dialects with them. For the sake of simplicity, all Chinese words in *The Girl with Ghost Eyes* appear in Mandarin rather than Cantonese and other dialects. Most of these words are written in the modern mode called Pinyin. But Pinyin contains many diacritical marks—imagine accents, umlauts, and other markings. These diacritical markings have been stripped off. If you wish to learn more

about the terms, please visit thegirlwithghosteyes.blogspot. com, where I'll present both the Pinyin and the Chinese characters, as well as their pronunciation.

Other terms have entered the English language to such a degree that I chose to use the familiar spellings rather than the Pinyin. These include terms such as tong, Buddhism, and kung fu.

Measurements:
It's likely that immigrants would think in Chinese measurements, such as chi, bu, and li, but the Qing Dynasty fell a hundred years ago, and these measurements have changed a number of times in this turbulent century. In order for the details to make sense to readers, characters in *The Girl with Ghost Eyes* measure space in inches, feet, and miles; they measure weight in ounces, pounds, and tons.

Religion:
The Girl with Ghost Eyes focuses primarily on Daoists. In the immigrant community, there were also Christians, Buddhists, and Confucians, as well as people who came from ethnic minorities, bringing their own forms of reverence.

The Maoshan traditions of Daoism were real. Eight thousand monasteries once dotted the area around Mt. Mao, and the systems of belief that spread in this area are famous for their focus on exorcism, mediumship, and occult practices.

But the origin of the Maoshan tradition, as described in *The Girl with Ghost Eyes*, is purely fictional. There was no such historical figure as Li Zhenren. Maoshan was not founded to compensate for any supernatural transgression. Instead, intellectual curiosity drove Maoshan's founders to formulate theories regarding the underlying logic behind life and death.

Li-lin and her father perform Daoist spells and make use of talismans, incantations, deities, magical hand gestures, ritual dances, peachwood, burnt paper offerings, and astrological almanacs. Without exception, every single detail of their ritual magic is closely based on reality, but these details come from a variety of sects, schools, and lineages. I described them as accurately as possible, but by drawing from more than one tradition, I represented a tradition that has never existed—a fictional tradition.

Etiquette:
In this place and time, a number of conventions would have guided the conversations of Chinese and Chinese American people. I decided to write the dialogue without many of these rules. After all, conventions of etiquette guide conversations in today's America: we begin with Hello or Hi, we shake hands or hug, we cover our mouths when we cough, we say "bless you" when somebody sneezes, we end with a Goodbye or See ya later. To an outsider, this etiquette seems artificial, but to someone within the culture, it feels natural. Everyone has a culture; it's just that our own culture is often invisible to us.

Folklore:
Within the folk tales of any single nation, there are regional traditions that should be considered distinct. The tales of ethnic and cultural minorities may intersect with the mainstream, but they also deserve to be understood as their own traditions, and preserved as such. Some tales were popular during a certain era but not before or after. In *The Girl with Ghost Eyes*, I aimed to represent these cultural specificities with depth and insight, but there are still some areas where, for the sake of telling a story with contemporary resonance, elements of traditions have been folded together.

One example is The Night Parade of a Hundred Demons. Many, many sources of Chinese folklore describe nocturnal hordes, crowds, armies, and processions of ghosts and goblins, devils and ogres. I could not find any specific term in Chinese for these armies or processions. The story needed a term, so I found a Japanese term, hyakki yakko, which translates as "night parade of a hundred demons." Japanese folklore and Chinese folklore are distinct from each other, and should not be considered interchangeable.

It's my hope that you take *The Girl with Ghost Eyes* and these notes as a starting point in an exploration of cultures and historical events, not a definitive source of knowledge. I hope you feel inspired to learn a new language, take a class, go on a trip, or read some non-fiction.

Even better, I hope you'll politely ask your friends, neighbors, or relatives to tell you stories they heard when they were young—and preserve this lore for future generations.

ACKNOWLEDGMENTS

Research for *The Girl with Ghost Eyes* took years of constant focus. First and foremost, I would like to thank Sally Elizabeth Wright for her support during that time.

Literary agent Sandy Lu plucked the manuscript out of the slush pile and championed it through the rigors of the publishing industry, and for this I will always be grateful. Bringing her own experience and staggering intellect to bear on the material, Sandy held the book to the highest standards, and deserves so much praise.

My editor at Skyhorse Publishing's Talos Press, Cory Allyn, took a chance on this unusual book. He came to the story with fresh eyes, clear observations, and profound understandings. His contributions were amazing, and I am endebted to him.

Many Chinese and Chinese diasporic families welcomed me into their homes, telling me stories and answering questions, suggesting what should be included and how certain people and events should be represented. I hope this book lives up to their acts of generosity.

Peijun Gao and her family fed me, challenged me, and filled me with stories. Shuling Yi's accounts of life as a Daoshi's daughter and Shifu Li Shu-Hong's detailed recollections of exorcistic rites were tremendously valuable resources. I want to acknowledge their contributions.

I finished writing the book before Stephen Kuo and I met, but he has been a friend and a brother through this experience. I never tire of talking all night about Mr. Vampire.

For twenty years, I have been lucky enough to have a brilliant friend in Thomas W. Potter. Both monk and tiger, Thomas's tremendous insight into storytelling has helped me develop as a novelist.

I also want to thank my parents, Warren and Rebecca Boroson, who raised me, taught me language, instilled a love of stories in me, and supported me through everything. My brother Bram Boroson, who is both a professor of astrophysics and a swashbuckling pirate on the high seas, has always guided me toward good books and fresh ways of seeing.

BOOK CLUB DISCUSSION QUESTIONS

1. Li-lin is torn between tradition and change, between her native land of China and her new country. How does that shape her as a person? How does it affect her decisions?

2. Li-lin's father left China as an adult, but Li-lin came here as a child. How does this generational difference affect their relationship?

3. How does Li-lin's understanding of monsters change throughout the book? What is the nature of the monstrous? How do you know something is monstrous, rather than simply different? How does the notion of monstrosity fit into the conflict between tradition and change?

4. We're familiar with tales of people fighting monsters with wooden stakes, garlic, holy water, and silver bullets. Li-lin uses a peachwood sword, yellow paper talismans, a bagua mirror, incantations, and finger gestures. How did the different toolbox change the nature of the story?

5. How is *The Girl with Ghost Eyes* an American story? What would be different if it were set in China?

6. Li-lin's husband died two years ago. How has this affected her as a human being? How do the events of this story alter Li-lin's approach to grief?

7. How does meeting Shuai Hu (the tiger-man) impact Li-lin's development as a person?

8. Li-lin struggles with what is expected of women in her time and place. She wants to face her challenges while

living up to her roles as a dutiful daughter, a chaste widow, and a good woman. How does she balance these needs? How does she use weakness, perceived and otherwise, as a source of power?

9. In Li-lin's lineage, a person's power isn't determined by skill, knowledge, or hard work, but by Ordination—a credential that can be given or withheld, by decision of the senior Daoshi. Li-lin is only as powerful as her father allows her to be. When the dog-monster attacks Li-lin's father, how does she manage to defeat it?

10. There are nonfiction books about Daoist magic and Chinese notions of ghosts and ancestors. What do you think is different between nonfiction and a story that immerses you in the folklores?

11. Mrs. Wei is the last of her tribe, the only one who remembers the rituals of a culture that has been eradicated. How is she like Li-lin, and how is she different?

12. What do you think comes next for Li-lin and Mr. Yanqiu? What do you think will happen with the tongs? How do you think Li-lin and her father will interact in the future? What do you expect to happen in the second book in the series?

13. There are millions of people in the world today who follow beliefs and spiritual practices similar to Li-lin's. How do you think this story might have affected your understanding?

Recommended Reading

Daoism
Taoism: An Essential Guide, by Eva Wong
Daoism: An Overview, by Stephen Bokenkamp
Daoism in China: An Introduction, by Wang Yi'er
Taoism: The Enduring Tradition, by Russell Kirkland
Daoism Handbook, by Livia Kohn
The Teachings of Daoist Master Zhuang, by Michael R. Saso
The Daoist Tradition, by Louis Komjathy

Chinese Folklore
Strange Tales from a Chinese Studio, by Pu Songling, trans. by John Minford or Sidney Sondergard
Censored by Confucius: Ghost Stories by Yuan Mei, trans. by Kam Louie
Fantastic Tales by Ji Xiaolan, trans. by Sun Haichen
A Chinese Bestiary, by Richard Strassberg
Monkey, by Wu Cheng-en, trans. by Arthur Waley

Chinese American History
The Chinese in America, by Iris Chang
The Making of Asian America: A History, by Erika Lee
Chinese Laundries: Tickets to Survival on Gold Mountain, by John Jung
Sweet and Sour: Life in Chinese Family Restaurants, by John Jung
San Francisco's Chinatown, by Judy Yung

Unbound Feet: A Social History of Chinese Women in America, by Judy Yung

Unbound Voices: A Documentary History of Chinese Women in America, by Judy Yung

RECOMMENDED MOVIES

The Linghuan (Spirit Magic) genre:
    Mr. Vampire (Hong Kong, 1985)
    A Chinese Ghost Story (Hong Kong, 1987)
    Mr. Vampire 3 (Hong Kong, 1987)
    Magic Cop (Hong Kong, 1990)
    A Chinese Ghost Story: The Tsui Hark Animation (Hong Kong, 1996) (This movie was one of the inspirations behind Hayao Miyazaki's *Spirited Away*.)
    Grandma and her Ghosts (Taiwan, 1998)
    Journey to the West: Conquering the Demons (China, 2013)

The Triads genre:
    Election (Hong Kong, 2005)
    Election 2 (Hong Kong, 2006)
    Monga (Taiwan, 2010)

Classic kung fu cinema:
    The Bride with White Hair (Hong Kong, 1993)
    The Legend of Drunken Master (Hong Kong, 1994)
    Once Upon a Time in China (Hong Kong, 1991)

ABOUT THE AUTHOR

When M.H. Boroson was nine years old, a Chinese American friend invited him to dinner with his family. Over a big, raucous meal, his friend's uncle told a story about a beautiful fox woman. She had a magic pearl and she stole men's energy.

Boroson wanted to learn more about this fox woman, so he went to the school library. They had Greek, Norse, and Arthurian mythology. They had vampires, witches, werewolves, and fairies, but they didn't have anything like the story his friend's uncle told—not even an encyclopedia entry.

This baffled him. A number of his friends were Asian American; why weren't *their* families's stories in the books? He asked his friend's uncle to tell him more stories. He started asking other kids if he could interview their families. If they said yes, he'd go to their houses, bringing a notebook.

In college, he studied Mandarin and Religion (with a focus on Chinese Buddhism). Years later, he decided he wanted to return to his study of Chinese ghost lore and write stories full of magic and monsters, using these incredible cultural details as metaphors to dramatize the experiences of immigrants in America.

The stories would be told from inside the culture, centered on people whose lives had been treated as marginal—inverting the margins, subverting stereotypes. Chinese American characters portrayed as three-dimensional, diverse human beings—facing challenges, earning a living, supporting families, struggling to hold on to traditional values in a new country. Exciting, action-packed stories that base their fantasy imagery in Chinese folklore, but tackle issues of vital importance in today's world, like race, class, gender, culture, and power.

He started taking notes. He bought hand-written Daoist manuscripts. He interviewed over two hundred Chinese and Chinese American people, asking about their family histories, ghost stories, and folk beliefs. He took detailed notes from Chinese stories, like Pu Songling's *Tales from the Liaozhai* and ancient texts like the *Shan Hai Jing (Classic of Mountains and Seas)* and *Journey to the West*. He watched movies like *Mr. Vampire* and *A Chinese Ghost Story*. He took sixty thousand pages of notes.

As he performed the interviews and the stories began to take shape, he realized these historical conflicts remain relevant to this day. The struggles of immigrants are timeless and universal. Xenophobia still shapes our discourse around "illegals." The Exclusion Era and the Geary Act echo in the controversy over California's Prop 187. The Tong Wars provide insight into both small-scale gang violence and large-scale organized crime, which are still part of our society. The events of this time and place have been re-enacted in today's headlines, again and again. The events of this period provide us with a lens to understand more of our world as it is today.